Diary of a Prison Officer

By

Josie Channer

Published by New Generation Publishing in 2020

Copyright © Josie Channer 2020

First Edition

The author asserts the moral right under the Copyright, Designs and Patents Act 1988 to be identified as the author of this work.

All Rights reserved. No part of this publication may be reproduced, stored in a retrieval system or transmitted, in any form or by any means without the prior consent of the author, nor be otherwise circulated in any form of binding or cover other than that which it is published and without a similar condition being imposed on the subsequent purchaser.

www.newgeneration-publishing.com

New Generation Publishing

This book was shortlisted in the Pen to Print Book Challenge Competition and has been produced by The London Borough of Barking and Dagenham Library Service - Pen to Print Creative Writing Programme. This is supported with National Portfolio Organisation funding from Arts Council, England.

Connect with Pen to Print
Email: pentoprint@lbbd.gov.uk
Web: pentoprint.org

Dedicated to Deloise Channer

Chapter 1

Day Forty-Seven (Kenya)

19th October 2018 6.00 p.m. - Nairobi (Kenya)

I awoke to the sound of birds on this, the last day of my backpacking trip through East Africa. I've been able to use this time to clear my head, write my blog and just think about me for once. Today, I went into town to get my hair done. It would cost £70 to get my waist-length single braids re-plaited in London. I hoped that my cockney accent would not give me away too soon so I could be mistaken for a local and at least be given the African price. The staff at the campsite advised me to take the mini-van into town, a private bus service that the locals use. There was a man waving one down on the dirt road outside the campsite, so I tagged along with him. There was a man acting as a conductor and taking money.

"Are you going into town?" I asked.

"Yes, yes," he replied, as he signalled at me to hurry and get in.

I was quite chuffed with myself as it looked like I had bagged the last seat. However, we kept on stopping for passengers. I thought, "Surely not, there's no way *another* person can fit in this van" but they could, and they did. There were about fourteen people squeezed into our seven-seater mini-van. I sat jammed between a six-foot- two-inch tall Maasai man and an old man with a goat. Out of the window I watched Maasai men walk tall in their red cloaks against the orange earth. The Maasai man, sitting on my right, started to argue with the conductor, with me and the old man trapped in the middle. The conductor had short-changed the Maasai man—who had a machete strapped to his side. The old man looked as worried as I was. As voices became raised and other people put in their two pence worth, I closed my eyes and took a deep breath in. I prayed, "God, *please, please* don't let me die here". The conductor finally conceded. After an hour, the mini-van ground to a halt in a field in the middle of nowhere. The van emptied.

"Where are we? I thought you were going into town?" I asked the conductor standing in the field alone.

"Yes, yes," he replied as the van drove off.

It started to rain hard. The dirt road turned into mud that stuck to the bottom of my trainers and splashed up my trousers. Another van came in. I ran over to it.

"I want to go to town," I said

"You need that van over there," a man said.

As I ran to the other van, I knew I had no phone signal. Slightly panicked, I asked, "Are you going into town?"

I was squeezed in again, only this time we were all soaking wet. I finally got into town about 10.00 a.m.

It sounds pretty cool to backpack through seven African countries in forty-seven days. But although I had gained over seven stamps in my passport, all the notions I had of Africa were turned upside down. I was unprepared for the journey ahead, both physically and mentally. This journey turned into a search for information and truth; a journey in which I discovered a deeper understanding of my identity. The continent now means so much more to me than war and famine.

Instead of packing books to read, I packed a few of my old diaries. I hoped to find in those pages, the reason I once loved going to work and how I fell in love with my husband. On long truck rides through the African wilderness, my diaries have taken me back to a time before I started writing my criminal justice blog, before I became a political activist and before I found true love. I can't put it off any longer. I have to decide before I go back to London. Should I quit my job? Should I divorce my husband? Those are the questions I've come to Africa to answer. But somewhere along the way, I lost the questions I came with. In this paradise, I found different questions that needed an answer. Questions about me and who I am.

'Don't Treat Me Like an OSG'

First Day

16th January 2003 7.30 a.m.

"So, Amber, tell me about yourself," Maria said as a prison gate slammed shut. She was unfazed by the unnatural, 'dungeon-like' environment we were walking deeper and deeper into. Then another gate clanged shut and she started wittering on about herself, as we struggled to keep up with the training officer. It was our first day as prison officers at Her Majesty's Prison Holloway. We went through one door and onto a wing, which then led to another door that led to another wing, then through another and upstairs, which led to another wing. In the dimmed artificial light, the training officer occasionally glanced back. She all but charged forward yelling, "This is B unit. This is A unit. And this is Level 3", as she led us around the maze-like prison with corridors that snaked around corners and thick metal doors locked behind us at every turn.

"Europe's largest female prison and it's the UK's highest security prison for women" the training officer shouted back at us, as if we were on a guided tour. "It was rebuilt in 1971 and designed with a hospital layout with wide corridors and dormitories. The idea being that women were mad, not bad. I've been here a long time and I can tell you for a fact that some women are just plain old bad."

I hurried along in my new uniform with the creases from the packet still visible. The thunderous sound of prisoners banging on their cell doors shook the prison.

"This is Amber Campbell," the training officer said to the three officers sitting in the office.

They then abandoned me on D3 unit and told me to observe the three officers.

"So, tell us about yourself Ms Campbell," one officer, Ms Freeman, said as she stretched over to flick on the kettle.

A piercing alarm from our radios then shattered the calm

of the room. The deafening siren continued to ring as the three officers stood frozen as if they were at the starting line of a race.

"Urgent assistance required on healthcare. Urgent assistance required on healthcare."

They were off. The northern voice over the radio repeated its instructions, but the two officers standing nearby, Ms Hook and Ms Rot, did not need clarification, they knew where they were going. I stood with my heart pounding, overpowered by the screeching alarm from my radio. A lonely cigarette packet and lighter sat on the office desk.

"What are you waiting for? Go, go," Ms Freeman barked at me.

I scrambled to the stairwell, where I joined an army of officers charging down the stairs. Not knowing where I was going, my main concern was not to get left behind as the wave of officers swung around corners and opened and closed gates. I followed the wave onto the prison's mental health unit.

"Tornado, in the association room now," ordered an officer.

I stepped to one side as the tallest, fittest, strongest, male officers made their way through the rest of us to the association room. In the background, I could hear what sounded like a party and women making merry. To my left, officers were putting on overalls and riot helmets as Whitney Houston's "I Wanna Dance with Somebody" could be heard in the distance. I shuffled against the wall, trying not to get in anyone's way.

"Amber." An overexcited Maria made me jump. "You'll never guess what? Four prisoners have taken over the unit office and have taken one of the mental health nurses hostage. They're in there now having a party, I think they have smuggled in alcohol. Tornado will take back control!"

"Tornado?" I asked.

"They're specialist riot officers."

Tornado then emerged from the unit association room.

They wore the same overalls and riot helmets as the rest of the officers. Yet, they looked so different, powerful and unified. An officer that made me want to stand to attention and salute, led them out.

He had a square jaw and an old-fashioned look you only see in Disney films; respectable, like Prince Eric in the film *Little Mermaid*.

"That's Senior Officer King. He's a manager on Level 3, our Level, and I think he will be our manager."

Mr King then turned his head to look at Maria and I. A rush of blood went to my brain.

"Why are you both not ready to go in" I stood mute.

"Sorry sir, it's me and Amber's first day. So, we were told just to observe," Maria said.

Mr King stood tall at the end of the manic corridor that overflowed with officers that fell silent to listen to what he had to say. Most of what he said went over my head as I became entranced by his deep blue eyes and the energy of his voice. His feet rooted him to the floor like a strong oak tree, spread apart, but not too far apart. His fist clenched tight and punched forward as he spoke.

Like silent ninjas, a Tornado team led by Mr King approached the doors of the unit office that had been barricaded. The flash of light from the blowtorch went unnoticed by the prisoners as it cut through the wall of metal, office chairs and bedframes piled high. From the waist up, the safety glass exposed the scene of disorder in the office. Toilet paper decorated the large room. Cheers of joy went up as they destroyed HMP property. First, they ripped the unit Observation Book to shreds, then they cut up an HMP tracksuit. A prisoner, petite but well toned and with a gold tooth, called Ms Aziz led the 'conga' around a terrified nurse. She lay helpless in the office chair, tied down and gagged by strips of bed sheets, so tight I could see from a distance that her circulation was being restricted. A flash of white smoke that cut off all visibility and a large bang stunned the prisoners. The Tornado team was now in control. Through the mist, they appeared to pick off the prisoners one by one and bundle them out of the office. The mist cleared to reveal the freed nurse. It seemed too surreal, like a movie. But this was real life and I might one day, play the leading role.

"That was amazing," Maria whispered in my ear, struggling to contain herself. I pretended that I wasn't interested, as my heart rate settled down. We headed to the unit door when OSG Sherry's distinctive northern voice came over the radio again.

"All movement in the prison to cease. I say again, all movement in the prison to cease."

As we waited by the door, I thought back on how my day started. I got to the prison thirty minutes early this morning. I stood outside the prison gates and chain-smoked in the dark. My cheap knee-length coat hid my uniform but left my nerves on full display. Prison officers walked past me. They seemed unfriendly, hostile even. 'Was this the job for me?' I wondered. But 'beggars can't be choosers' my mum always says.

"You all right, chuck?"

I'm terrible at guessing where people with northern accents are from. I'm a Londoner and anything outside of London is alien. But here was a friendly face and not from London.

"I'm looking for the training department." I knew where it was, but why would I be standing outside the prison at 7 a.m. in the morning unless I was lost? She pointed me in the right direction and introduced herself as OSG Sherry.

Maria and I huffed and puffed at the inconvenience of not being allowed to move out of the unit as we walked to the officer's smoking room. I sat at the desk and looked out the narrow window at the prison vans coming in to the prison courtyard. What sounded like an earthquake hit the prison. I grabbed the desk with both arms and sat up in my chair wondering what the hell was going on.

The thunderous noise of prisoners banging their windows with whatever objects they could find shook the prison. Maria walked over to the window. A van was bringing in the notorious Maxine Carr, who provided a false alibi to the police for her boyfriend Ian Huntley, claiming to have been with him at the time of the murders of two young girls in Soham. Prison cells surrounded the van in the prison yard. Through the cracks of their windows, the women screamed obscenities and looked down on the object of their outrage. Prison officers quickly moved her to the Vulnerable Prisoner Unit.

"So, tell me about yourself?" Maria continued.

I wasn't sure what to say, but there wasn't much to tell. I found a full-time position at GAP as a sales assistant in Oxford Street when I left college at 18. My full-time earnings were just £698.25 a month, of which £400 was swallowed up by my council rent. That left around £100 for my travel expenses, and £150 pounds for bills, which left me around £50 a month for food.

It's said, "work pays". Well, I calculated that while I was working at GAP, I was only £20 per week better off than I would have been on Job Seeker's Allowance. When I was travelling to work with holes in my shoes, I felt that the extra £20 was worth it to keep some dignity.

Ten Months Later

20th November 2003

I wish I started this diary when I first began working at Holloway. It's now difficult to fill in for the last ten months, but today was typical of my days as a new officer. I got into work at 7.15 this morning to find my D3 colleagues Ms Rot and Ms Hook, in the office eating breakfast. As I walked in, they walked out to the smoking room—but not before telling me to put on the kettle. I balanced the three cups of tea on a rickety, old tin tray to the smoking room. Relieved that I didn't spill the whole thing, I collapsed in the chair.

"What are you doing?" said Ms Rot. "You'd better unload the breakfast trolley." I felt nervous, and all I could say was "okay".

As I walked to the kitchen, Ms Hook yelled after me, "You make a crap cup of tea," followed by collective laughter. I said nothing, and as I unloaded the breakfast trolley, I knew how the rest of the day would pan out, making tea, being the gofer and just feeling uncomfortable.

"D3 is a difficult unit. I'll try and teach you what I can, but not everyone's got what it takes to work on here," Ms Freeman explained over tea. "It's the largest and the most challenging unit in the prison. D3 is the gateway to the prison; all must pass through to be assessed and then be allocated to the appropriate unit—which could be up to Level 5 lifers, Level 4 convicted, or the rest of Level 3 (units A, B, C) remanded prisoners. All new prisoners spend at least four days on D3, all mixed, lifers next to prisoners on remand, and prisoners with mental health needs.

They all stay on D3 before officers move them to a unit where they can settle."

There's Ms Rot who makes a point of wearing the male uniform, which isn't that different from the female one. Her short back and sides jet-black hair against her pale skin gives her a cold look of death. There's also Ms Hook, her Goldilocks-blonde hair and cute button nose gives her a deceiving first impression of sweetness.

"Ms Parker, I was wondering—" Ms Hook interrupted Ms Hall.

"My name is Ms Hook! Not Parker. Are you deliberately trying to insult me? Didn't you read the email that went out to everyone in the entire prison? Are you the only idiot that didn't read it?"

"I'm so sorry, I've just got back for maternity leave. Before I went off you had just got married. I read the email that said you didn't want to be called by your maiden name anymore," Ms Hall said.

"You must be the only person in Holloway that doesn't know that I'm getting a divorce after only being married for seven months?" Ms Hook said.

Ms Rot and Ms Hook walk around the prison looking down and mocking other officers. When I tell other officers what unit I'm working on, they sympathise with me. Mr Adie told me yesterday, "Black officers don't last long on D3".

Some days are good, and some days are bad. Overall, I spend most of the time doing the jobs that my colleagues don't want to do (getting the post, taking out the rubbish, and picking up prisoners from around the prison). The only time they talk to me is when they want me to make tea. I always make it whilst thinking they might be nice to me after I've handed them the cups.

And then there's our senior officers who are in charge of the whole level. Mr King spent today trying to organise a new dressmaking workshop for prisoners.

Throughout the day, his peer and colleague Mr Smith teased him for being a "bit of a pussy".

"I think some of those girls that took the nurse hostage on healthcare may have taken your sewing class yesterday," Mr Smith laughed. "Mate, a word of advice, give these girls an inch and they'll take a mile."

"Isn't your fitness test next week?" "What?"

"Oh mate, you're in trouble. You're in real trouble." Mr King said.

"Give over. I've got ages before my name gets called up," Mr Smith sat up in his chair and put his magazine to one side.

"No, I saw your name on the board at the gate. You want my advice, you need to lose a few inches around the middle and run a few miles by next Monday or you're in trouble. I'm going on a 5-mile run tomorrow morning with some of the men from Tornado, you're welcome to join us," Mr King mocked.

"Piss off." Mr Smith said.

Senior Officer Smith transferred to Holloway from a male prison a few months ago. I overheard him barking at Mr Jamu yesterday "Move that prisoner now – that's a direct order!" Someone needs to tell him we are not in the army. Both our senior officers spend most of their time with the D3 officers.

D3 unit is also the location of the senior officers' (SO) office, based at the other end of the unit is the unit office. Next to the unit office, you'll find the prisoners' association room. Some evenings when all the prisoners are locked in their cells, I sit on the soft blue chairs in the association room to do the next day's food order with the unit office door open so I can hear a cell bell or the phone if it rings. Half way down the landing is the staff smoking room and the unit kitchen and dining room on the corner. All units in the prison are laid out the same.

I'm at home now and as awful as work is at the moment I can't wait to get back to the warm prison. I've just finished watching a *Sex and the City* episode where it's Carrie's 36th Birthday and she's unhappy that she hasn't got a soulmate. Sitting in this flat of mine on my own with a Pot Noodle, I wish I had a soulmate. I've never had the type of friends that Carrie has, until now.

Maria

I spend my lunchtimes in the C3 association room with the other Level 3 officers Maria, Ms Hall, Mr Adie, Mr Jones and Mr Jamu. Maria's a five-foot nine ex-model. She makes even our standard black and white uniform look glamorous as she strides down Holloway's long corridors. Half White German and Black Nigerian, she commands the attention of prisoners. She holds a Master's degree in Finance and has become a master of reinventing herself. She's lived in London for a while now and her German accent has faded. Born and raised in Germany, she never felt like Germany was home. When all is quiet on dark, rainy evenings, Maria often tells me about her experiences of constant harassment by the police, the racist abuse, the attacks and threats she suffered whilst growing up in Germany. Although beautiful, a hard exterior now warns off anyone thinking of messing with her.

Ms Hall

Paulette Hall works part-time, a prison officer for five years. She's devoted to her job, her three young children and Jesus. She's one of the few prison officers that wear the skirt. Overweight and on the short side, "My bum just doesn't look right in HMP trousers" she told me. This morning, I walked past Ms Hall in the corridor humming joyful gospel songs, which she does when she is upset, in a vain attempt to lift her mood.
　"You okay, Ms Hall?"
　"They have moved me to work on level 5 this morning to cover an officer that's gone home sick."
　"Well it's only for the morning." I replied.
　"They always move me, it's not fair—"
　"Morning, Ms Campbell," Mr Smith interrupted. "Morning, part-timer," he said to Ms Hall as he walked past in an undermining tone that Ms Hall was meant to dismiss

as banter.

Determined to keep a lid on her feelings, Ms Hall hummed the hymn 'How Great Thou Art', as she walked towards the exit.

Mr Adie

A PhD graduate that has been an officer for ten years, Mr Adie tells me every now and again 'I've seen it all'. On his first day, other officers shortened his full Nigerian surname to "Adie".

"I don't mind what they call me," he declared looking at me through tortoiseshell spectacles that mirror his round face.

This afternoon, he marched onto D3 heading towards the senior officers' office, eyes fixed and full of rage. I could overhear a distressed Mr Adie arguing with Mr King. I called Maria who was working on A3, and we agreed that she would phone Mr Jones on B3 and I would call Ms Hall and Mr Jamu on C3 to find out what had happened.

At tea break, the six of us gathered in the C3 Association room, and Mr Adie still shaking with rage, told us what happened on B3. Over lunch, he informed a prisoner that because she was now a convicted prisoner, she would move today to another unit.

"She spat in my face," he said, his voice breaking in complete disbelief.

His anger now turned to Mr King who said all he could do was place her on report and Governor Rose would see her in the morning for the assault. Until then, she would remain on the unit. We gasped and shook our heads.

"She needs to be taken to the Block now, or I'm not working on the unit," he demanded.

"That's right," we chanted in solidarity and anger as he raged on about how prison management didn't protect its staff.

After tea break, he went back to work on B3 and the prisoner enjoyed her evening association with the other prisoners like nothing had happened.

Mr Jones

Mr Jones is a dashing former RAF pilot. A single fifty-five-year-old man that doesn't look a day over thirty-five and who enjoys the attention he receives from female officers. He's been in the job for two years and said he was considering joining the police before accepting the post in the prison service.

"They offered me the job by the Met police to become a PC but I found out that my application was priority because I'm Black. So, I turned it down. I don't want to be offered a job just because I'm Black. I want to get it on merit," he told Maria, Adie, Mr Jamu, Ms Hall and I one lunchtime in the C3 association room.

Personally, I would have just taken the job. His comment sparked a debate about "merit" versus "positive action", a debate that the C3 association room would hear on many occasions over lunch.

To his horror and to my amusement, Mr Jones' playboy antics caught up with him at work today.

"Why haven't you called?" demanded Ms Hudson, a divorced fifty-four-year-old from Level 5.

"Not in front of the prisoners," whispered Mr Jones shoeing her into the office where Mr Adie and I sat up to listen.

"I called you five times, left messages, if you're not interested, then at least, have the guts to tell me," she went on.

"Sorry, but we can't talk about this here. We're at work," he begged.

"You bastard!" she shouted.

Mortified, Mr Jones headed for the office door. "I'll call you tonight. We can't talk here."

As he walked down the landing leaving her in the office with Mr Adie and I, she yelled after him "I won't let you treat me like this." A round of laughter from the prisoners followed her statement.

Before stomping off the landing herself, she turned and insisted "I will not let him treat me like this."

Mr Adie told everyone about the confrontation and it gave him plenty to tease Mr Jones about for the rest of the day.

Mr Jamu

Ms Hall and Mr Jamu are the most undervalued officers on Level 3. Mr Jamu joined the Service four months after me. We are both new to the job and struggling to fit in. In the office the other day, Ms Hook called Mr Jamu a 'stupid Paki' when Mr Jamu fumbled over the office desk, knocking Ms Hook's cup of coffee.

"I'm only joking, you're not offended are you, Mr Jamu?" Ms Hook asked when she saw my reaction to what she had said.

"Oh no, Ms Hook," Mr Jamu replied, as he frantically wiped up the spilt coffee with blue roll.

"I'm sorry, but I'm offended." My reaction was followed by a few seconds of awkward silence.

"Oh no, Ms Campbell, I'm fine," Mr Jamu tried to reassure me.

"It's just a bit of banter," Ms Hook said as she confidently sat back in her chair and sipped her coffee.

I would report the matter to the SOs, but to be honest, I didn't want to get involved as I had my own problems to deal with, without fighting Mr Jamu's battles.

"If he won't stand up for himself, why should I get involved? Why should I stick my neck out? He told Ms Hook that he didn't mind being called the 'P' word, so what can I do?" I complained to Maria and Ms Hall hoping that they would justify my decision to do nothing.

"You will only get accused of using the race card if you say anything," said Ms Hall.

The Move

The senior officers have moved me from D3 to B3. I can't believe they're doing this. The reason they gave was all rubbish. They say it's because they want me to learn the basics first (I know the basics) and they don't think I fit in as part of the team on D3. In other words, I don't fit in the D3 clique. Okay, I can't stand the officers, but I've come to like the unit. I've taken ownership of that and now they want to move me to some dead unit. Great! I'm so not valued on D3, maybe it's better I move. Well, I don't think it's worth making up a fuss as they've already made up their minds. Mr Smith said; "We *thought* you could handle D3."

This morning, I checked the cells of the East Side of the unit before they told me to do the cells that no one wanted to check.

"What are you doing? You need to do the checks on the South Side," Ms Rot demanded.

I walked past her with a smile on my face.

"Well I've already done the East, so looks like you or Hook are going have to do the South," I chuckled.

It was a small victory, but I didn't need them to tell me which cells to check. I didn't care anymore. If they wanted tea from now on, they knew where the kettle was. "Miss, can my mum come and visit me next week?" a prisoner asked me.

My victory was not only small it was short-lived. The situation forced me to admit my lack of knowledge in front of Ms Hook and Ms Rot.

"I'm not sure, I will try and find out -"

Cutting me off, Ms Hook turned to the prisoner.

"Ms Campbell is a new officer and I'm afraid she doesn't know anything. Give me twenty minutes and I'll come back to you with what you need to do."

"Ms Campbell, why don't you do something useful and put the kettle on?" Ms Rot said.

Christmas Party

2.30 a.m.

I've just got back from the staff Christmas party. It seemed strange that even in a pub a mile away from the prison and not a black and white uniform in sight, officers still called each other by their surnames. I don't know any officer's first names anyway, apart from Maria. It would almost feel like a mark of disrespect to call an officer by their first name inside or outside the prison.

A new officer joined D3 unit seven days ago and has fit in like he's been there for seven years. Mr Potter is an over confident former army sergeant. I overheard that he left the army straight after coming back from six months in Iraq. His short army-style buzz haircut was still sharp. He can't dance at all. He moved on the dance floor like a tattooed, wooden plank. Ms Hook was crying into her beer about her marital problems.

"Everyone on D3 is so messed up," a drunk Ms Hook blurted out.

"What do you mean?" I asked.

"What do you mean? What do I mean? Obviously, we're all screwed up. Ms Freeman's a pensioner and having to"-

"Well, I'm not quite a pensioner yet"- Ms Freeman interrupted.

"You're old. No offence, but you're too old to be a prison officer. Mr Potter got kicked out of the Army."-

"They discharged me because of injuries," Mr Potter interrupted Ms Hook.

"Oh come on, no one believes your story about getting shot in Iraq. We all know something went down over there. And Ms Rot only falls for straight women," Ms Hook said, as she flicked back a yellow locket that had strayed onto her face.

"That's right, I can't help myself. It's like I'm addicted to the pain of it all," Ms Rot said.

"And as for you," Ms Hook looked at me with contempt, "you're the most screwed up of us all."

"I'm doing just fine." I said.

"Well you are dyslexic, aren't you?" Ms Freeman said. I don't remember telling Ms Freeman or anyone else that I was dyslexic. I looked back at her blank. "I have noticed a few things that makes me think you might be dyslexic. We all have. Don't worry, I'm a little dyslexic myself, not anywhere near as severe as you, but I understand."

The thought of them all discussing whether I might be dyslexic, or just stupid, filled me with dread. At that moment, I wanted to stick my head in a pile of sand. There's nothing anyone can do about it. There's nothing I can do about it either.-It requires so much effort to get what's in my head down on paper that it's draining. Sometimes, it feels like I spend hours on one simple word worrying if it's spelt right only then to go on to the next word.

"Dyslexia?" Ms Hook said.

Ms Freeman tried to settle her down. "Yes, dyslexics often get their letters muddled around."

"Well let me help you out Campbell, the word 'said' is spelt S.A.I.D, think you can remember that?" Ms Hook said.

"Thanks," I said. As I stood up, I slammed my coke on the table and headed to the bar for something stronger.

"She's not dyslexic, she's just stupid," Ms Rot shouted out after me.

I lit a cigarette in the crowded bar and my eyes searched around desperately. I was so relieved to see a friendly face walk through the door and head in my direction, Mr Jones.

"Evening, Ms Campbell, how's it going?" he said with a spring in his step.

"Where's Maria, Ms Hall, Mr Adie and Mr Jamu?" I asked desperately.

"I'm not sure..." he said, but stopped and looked like he had seen a ghost. "Bloody hell, what's she doing here?" he said, ducking behind me.

Knocking back another whisky I said, "Mr Jones, haven't you sorted things out with her yet? Oh no! She's seen you."

Ms Hudson marched over in our direction pushing past everyone in the crowded bar. I turned to Mr Jones and said "I don't know why you messed with a Level 5 officer, we all know they're mad. If she attacks you, I'm not getting involved."

It's a well-known fact that the officers that work on Level 5 ('The Bronx' as the prisoners like to call it) are a bit mad and don't have a clue about what they are doing. They would most probably say their officers are full of character. It's also a fact that Level 3 officers are a bit 'stuck up' and think they know everything. We would say we like to run a tight ship. However, there is one fact accepted throughout the prison and that is that officers are superior to OSGs (Operational Support Grades). Prison officers treat OSGs like second-class officers, who wanted to become prison officers but were rejected. They have no contact with prisoners only doing work such as bringing up the prisoner food trolleys, working the control centre and giving prison officers their keys. Hence the phrase "Don't treat me like an OSG".

On the other side of the bar, the D3 lot was getting drunk, as was I. Funny thing drink, for a few minutes it made me forget all the horrible things that my work colleagues had said only a short time ago. For maybe fifteen minutes, I thought I washaving a good time and I was amongst friends. The drink made me brave. I watched Mr Potter trying his best on the edge of the dance floor.

"Mr Potter, you need to take dancing lessons."

"What do you mean, I'm on fire baby," he replied, waving his hands in the air. I couldn't help, but double over with laughter.

"Come, let me show you my moves." He grabbed my arm, pulling me in the direction of the dance floor.

"No way, I don't want to be seen dancing with you, or anyone in this place. There's only one officer that's on fire and he isn't here."

"Who's that then?"

"Mr King. Mr King is hot, everyone knows that."

Ms Rot and Ms Hook laughed. I sobered up and realised that I was not amongst friends and I wasn't really having a good time at all.

"Who the hell invited an OSG?" yelled Mr Potter pointing at OSG Sherry who was sat with two B4 officers on a neighbouring table.

"Leave it out, Mr Potter," said an annoyed Ms Rot.

"No, no this is an 'officer only' do. If I had known that *anyone* was welcome, I would have invited the night staff and the—"

"Shut up, dick head!" Ms Rot yelled.

Sherry got up and headed for the door. No one said anything, but Ms Rot went after her.

"Hey!" Ms Rot called out.

Putting on her coat in a fluster Sherry said, "It's okay, I only came because Ms Hendrick invited me."

"I'm sorry about that, Mr Potter's drunk and bit of a prick. Let me buy you a drink. I'm Ms Rot. I work on D3. So, do you work on reception or? Sorry, what's your name?" Ms Rot asked.

"I know who you are, I've given you your keys every morning for five years. I'm going to go home, maybe another time," Sherry said, as she walked out.

11/12/03

This morning after the night before, I wanted to die of embarrassment over what I had blurted out about Mr King, but maybe everyone was too drunk to remember what I had said anyway. Standing in line to collect my keys, Ms Hall joined the line and chuckled in my ear "I'm feeling HOT". So everyone knew.

Ms Rot was holding up the key line.

"Hi, I didn't get your name last night. Can I have a quick word?" she tried to whisper to OSG Sherry, who was standing behind the thick glass.

"What? Sorry? I can't hear you."

"Ms Rot you're holding up the line," yelled an officer standing in line.

"Give us a minute," Ms Rot yelled back and tried again to get the OSG's name and failed. It was 7.25 a.m. and the line behind her grew by the second and more impatient. Ms Rot yelled, "What's your name?"

The line went silent as everyone wondered why an officer wanted to know or even cared what an OSG's name was?

"I'm Sherry."

The appearance of Mr Jones broke the silence. Word had got out about his run in with Ms Hudson.

I was on A3 for Dinner Patrol. Mr King said he wanted to see me in the SO's office after I'd finished overseeing dinner. It was only about twenty minutes, but it felt like twenty hours wondering what he wanted to see me about. It turned out something that Ms Hook had said about me concerned him. I denied that there was a problem between us.

"She's not my best friend or anything," I said.

"I'll pull her up on what she said about you anyway. I'm also going to share the concerns I have with Mr Smith so he can keep an eye out for anything," Mr King said. "Mr Smith! He'll just tell everyone and the whole thing will be blown out of proportion. There's not a problem between me and Ms Hook, so you don't need to say anything to anybody."

Mr King continued to tell me a load of BS about why I had to move to B3.

"You seemed more alive when you first started. I've watched you become more and more withdrawn. Are you sure there's not a problem?" but before I could answer, he carried on, "It's obvious you can't handle D3 and you'll be better off on a quieter unit."

I felt like crying, but I couldn't get the tears out. All day, I had to put up with Ms Hook crying and telling everybody (apart from me) about her marriage breaking up.

Later, I felt I should have told Mr King something, even if it's just how I feel.

"Don't trust him, don't tell him anything. He's not their boss, if he's their friend," Mr Adie warned me.

20/12/03

This morning, Ms Freeman taught me how to do the Transfer List, which is a big thing. It's the SO's job to do the Transfer List. Whoever does the list is in charge of the unit.

Whoever gets into work first, starts it. But the pecking order of D3 dictates who finishes it. Ms Freeman, the big mama of D3 or the SOs do the list.

I was thinking about what Mr King said.

"You can trust me. I know this is difficult for you, but you can trust me. And this will all stop, I promise you," he said.

"I'm sorry but, I don't trust you," I said. Mr King sat back in his chair. "How can I trust you when they're your friends?"

"It upsets me that you feel that way. Just because I have lunch with them every day it doesn't mean I'm their friend. I like to have a laugh with the D3 lot, we sometimes go to the pub after work, but I'm not their friend. I'm their manager. I'm your managertoo and I want to protect you."

What he said didn't seem to make sense, but he lent forward and rested his hands on mine on the table.

"You can trust me."

With that the truth flooded out of me. His face darkened. At first, I thought it was disbelief, but now I knew it was anger. If only he could have even a little glimpse of what I've had to put up with over the past twelve months, he would hate Miss Hook too. I'm definitely going to B3 now.

This afternoon, I sat in the C3 association room with Mr Adie, Maria, Mr Jones. "Mr King's going to do nothing. If anything, I bet things get worse," Mr Adie said.

Mental Health

This morning, Ms Hook, Ms Rot, Ms Freeman and I unlocked the unit for breakfast and the green corridors became alive with women. The women busied themselves with getting mops and buckets to clean their cells and queued patiently for the bathrooms. The smell of perfumed shower gels and creams drifted down the unit.

Sitting back in her chair with a cup of tea in hand, Ms Freeman crossed her legs and said "So, Ms Campbell, tell us some more about yourself."

The bell literally saved me.

"Bloody hell, who's that now?" Ms Rot slammed down her mug on the desk.

There was a brief pause, as they looked at the board to see whose emergency bell had sounded.

"Don't worry, I'll go." Ms Hook got up with little enthusiasm.

Ms Freeman and I left the office and strolled down to the officers' smoking room looking for chocolate biscuits.

"So, tell me some more about yourself." She looked at me with high expectations.

I'm twenty-three years old and I live in a rat-infested council estate on my own in Hackney. I'll tell people the reason I joined the prison service was because I wanted to help people, but the plain fact was that I simply needed a job.

"But I've got plans. I'm not going to live there and just be a prison officer forever. I know I've got a lot to offer the prison service." I hoped I'd convinced Ms Freeman that I was going places.

"I'm sure you've got lots to offer. Good luck."

She was not convinced.

The sound of fast-paced footsteps approaching the smoking room interrupted the conversation.

"We've got a problem here. Get Mr King round here now," Ms Hook said.

I sat alone not knowing whether to go or stay put and

finish my tea. At first, I strained my ears to listen to the commotion in the distance, I stood up as screams of terror engulfed the unit.

A prisoner called Ms John has been on D3 unit for a while as there were no spaces on the mental healthcare unit. Her matted afro hair and strong body odour deters the toughest officers and her silence makes her even more terrifying.

This morning, she emerged from her room with a full-to-the-brim bucket of excrement she had hidden under her bed for two weeks. The unit descended into chaos. Ms Rot was the first to be hit. Dark brown thick excrement dripped down Ms Rot's perfect white shirt. Ms Hook ran back to the office and locked herself in while screaming women banged on the door and begged to be let in. I ran in to the glass association room bringing with me as many prisoners as I could before I locked the door.

Other prisoners hid where they could, under their beds, in the bathrooms and in the smoking room, barricading the doors behind them.

I yelled into my radio "Immediate Assistance Required! Immediate Assistance Required!" The siren rang throughout the prison. Ms John stood by the unit door waiting for the officers that would answer the call. Mr Smith was the first officer through the door and he was met by a full bucket of excrement in his face. Ms John had covered herself in her own mess and stood licking out the bucket goading officers to dare take her down. I watched her from behind the glass with the other women defying about fifteen officers as they encircled her. They nervously moved forward and when she jumped forward, they jumped back. In that moment, she was the one in control. For the first time in her life she, a mad Black woman who had always been the least of the least, had power. I continued to watch as they then forced her down to the ground like a dangerous wild animal. Five male officers piled on top of her. From behind the glass windows, I heard the crack when they smashed the side of her face to the floor and I winced as the first punches and kicks were delivered to her body. Yet, she resisted. I felt her agony as they used all their strength to bend her wrist back to a deformed position. She complied with officers' demands, but her surrender meant nothing. They carried Ms John to the segregation unit. We evacuated D3 unit to the gym for several hours while an outside company came in to professionally clean the wing. Mr Smith and Ms Hook had to be taken to hospital after swallowing excrement.

The Pact

I caught up with Maria and Ms Hall for lunch after the incident and told her what had happened.

"Hopefully they'll train us how to deal with prisoners that have mental health problems," Maria said.

"We've been in the job for over a year, if they were going to give us training on mental health, they would have done it by now," I said.

"Do you think I'll ever make Governor?" Maria asked.

"Sure, if that's what God has planned for you," said Ms Hall "Why don't you put in for the graduate programme. You have a Master's degree, don't you? That's how Governor Rose got to be a governor so young. Straight out of university and within two years, she was a governor."

"Let's not get ahead of ourselves now," I said.

Ms Hall's excitement seemed in danger of spiralling out of control.

"Well why not? Maria is just as good as Governor Rose. Plus, Maria's got life experience."

Maria agreed, but the fact was that Holloway had no Black senior officers let alone Black governors.

"Maria will be the first! In the name of Jesus."

Ms Hall could visualize a Governor Maria strutting the corridors of Holloway. Ms Hall's excitement was infectious, after all she had said it 'in the name of Jesus', so it would happen.

"What about you, Ms Campbell?" a pumped-up Ms Hall asked.

Looking at my feet, I said in a timid voice, "I don't know."

My answer did not satisfy Maria or Ms Hall.

I continued, "I just want to make a difference." They were still not satisfied.

"I guess I wouldn't mind being a tornado officer. They can get called out to any prison in the country when there's a riot. But I'm no good at restraining prisoners."

"Not yet, Ms Campbell," a serious Ms Hall insisted. "Not yet, but you will become good at restraining prisoners and when you are, you'll be the best riot officer the prison service has ever seen, in Jesus name."

"In the name of Jesus!" yelled Maria raising one hand to the heavens.

"Okay, your turn, Ms Hall," I said firmly.

"Well you know I'm only part time," Ms Hall said.

"So what, you can't use that as an excuse," Maria replied.

"I would love to be a senior officer. I don't think they would let me do it part time."

"They will. In Jesus name, they will," Maria said.

We left the C3 association room with a vision and encouraged that we could be whatever we wanted to be. I had a feeling that becoming who we wanted to be in the prison service would be a long a difficult journey. We didn't say it out loud but over lunch, I think we made a pact with each other. The pact was to be more than just work colleagues. We had pledged to be each other's coach, mentor, chief defender and most vocal cheerleader.

Amber's Blog 2018

Posted – 8th September 2018

Written in the Backpack Hostel in Cape Town, South Africa

'Dirty Protest' is what we would call them, and I would deal with my fair share during my years at Holloway. Most of the prisoners that conducted dirty protest had mental health problems, as with Ms John. I often asked myself if women with mental health problems should be in prison? If we cannot rehabilitate those of sound mind, what can the prison system offer those with mental health needs? On the healthcare unit, there was just one on-call doctor plus a few nursing staff that would administer medication, and that was it. From my experience, the prison system could offer nothing.

Most healthcare prisoners never leave the unit. They might come out of their cells for only two hours a day, and always under close supervision by prison staff who receive no mental health training. And from that, we release them into society to live next door to you and me with the support of "care in the community". I believe that it is the failure of care in the community that leads to the breakdown in their treatment that gets them into prison in the first place. Many of the prisoners on the healthcare unit were re- offenders, yet the cycle for mental health and drug addiction has never been broken.

From my experience in the prison service, I believe that we need radical new legislation to address a failing system. If I had the opportunity, I would examine the way we deal with less serious crimes, and how we treat offenders with mental health and drug-misuse problems.

Chapter 2

Cape Town (South Africa)

8th September 2018

10.00 a.m.

I've just arrived at the Backpack Hostel in Cape Town, South Africa. I wrote a blog post and read the first part of my diary on the flight over here. Oh, how I have changed in fifteen years! It was my first job, and my first love. I have yet to read why I fell in love with it so. I also still can't remember why I fell so deeply in love with the man I've been married to for all these years. But I know it's in these diaries somewhere.

I'll be on the road for the next six weeks travelling up to Kenya. I'll meet the other people on my tour tonight. My flight landed at 7.00 a.m. this morning, so I'm tired. But I have to discover something of Cape Town before we leave tomorrow. I can see Table Mountain from the hostel window, and it's as breathtaking as I imagined.

It was about nine hours into the eleven-hour flight from London Heathrow when I looked up from my diary and noticed that I was the only Black person on the aircraft. The other passengers were mostly White South Africans returning home after their holidays. In Cape Town airport, it was much the same thing. Aside from the Black terminal workers, mine was the only other non-white face. I almost didn't notice, and when I did, it made me wonder about the socio-economic position of Black South Africans. I wondered if, since the end of apartheid, life really had changed for them. Being the only Black person in a foreign airport is something I've become accustomed to on my travels. However, I didn't feel like a guest this time. Even though I consider myself Jamaican, and English by birth, I'm in Africa, *my* homeland. It's a great feeling. As silly as it sounds, I couldn't wait to get out the airport and put my feet on African soil. I sometimes wonder who my ancestors were, maybe great Zulu warriors? But that's very unlikely as most of the slaves came from West Africa. I've travelled through South America, India and China, and I've put this trip off for way too long.

4.30 p.m.

I've just come back from a little exploration trip around Cape Town. I went to the harbor to see if I could visit Robin Island, but the tour was full. So, I had a look around the bay. It was so clean. The colonial style buildings sparkled as though it was all built yesterday against a perfect blue sky. I then went to District Six Museum. It tells the story of how 60,000 Black Africans were forced to move in the 1950s when the government declared the area "White". I then walked back to the Backpack Hostel using the map in my *Lonely Planet* book. I enjoyed getting a little lost today in this stunning city. Everywhere was buzzing with people. I went to Grand Parade and stood in front of City Hall, the place where, in 1990, Nelson Mandela gave his first speech after being freed from twenty-seven years of imprisonment. With Table Mountain as an impressive backdrop, this city for me rivals Rio as one of the most beautiful cities I've ever seen. There's a real multicultural feel, there's a sense of history and history in the making. However, I haven't seen the 'Cape Flats' where most of the Black community live, and have been living since their resettlement there in the 1950s. I sat down in a small restaurant to have lunch when I was approached by a guy with shoulder-length brown hair in his early twenties from Manchester.
"British?" "Yes."
Over a coffee and a sandwich, he told me he's over here for a year working. He's celebrating quitting his job today and is confident he'll get a new one tomorrow. Cape Town, from what he told me, seems to be the place to come for fun, happiness and opportunity.

11.00 p.m.

I've just had my first group meeting with the people I'm going to be spending the next six weeks with. There are twenty-two of us from all over the world. After the induction talk, at around 9.00 p.m., I went to the petrol station to get some cigarettes (which I'm supposed to be quitting). On the way, I saw someone get run over. I froze in amazement. I, who never sees anything worth seeing, was the sole witness to this incident. A woman had been crossing the road when a silver BMW appeared and sent her flying into the air. She tumbled down onto the bonnet of the vehicle, and was then tipped back onto the road where she landed with a thump. The car screeched to a halt. After the initial shock, I ran over to where an obviously wealthy White man had run over a not-so-well-off Black woman. She looked like a bag lady. The man was in his early fifties, tall, and going for the George Clooney look. He was shaking as he spoke into his mobile phone and gave his details to the emergency services. I knelt beside the woman. She was crying in pain, and I tried to comfort her.

"I'm pregnant! God save my baby!"

As other cars drove by, four Black men in dirty tracksuits, came out from nowhere like vultures and collected her plastic bags that littered the road, then ran off into the darkness. Another man appeared over the helpless woman and, right in front of me, calmly yanked off her red backpack. I looked on in shock, barely able to believe my eyes.

"What are you doing?" I screamed in an explosive rage that made him jump.

He replied, "Don't worry, I know this woman."

"Give me that." I snatched the bag out of his hand.

A swarm of private security men then arrived on the scene and took charge of the situation. The ambulance soon joined them. Then a light-skinned Black security officer arrived. His main concern was to reassure the driver, who was by this time close to a breakdown with his head in his hands.

"*These people* do it all the time," said the security officer. "Don't worry, she is not really pregnant."

He then commended me on my "bravery" and, knowing I was a tourist, said somewhat sarcastically, "Welcome to Africa."

Chapter 3

9th September 2018

About 6.00 p.m., (South Africa)

This morning, my tour group left the Backpack Hostel at 8.00 a.m. We went to the District Six Museum, then on to the Cape Flats township, where Black Africans were forced to move in the 1950s, and where they still live today. As we drove into the township, it reminded me of my childhood. Many children in the West are raised as I was, in rundown innercity housing developments among families that can barely make ends meet. As we drove past groups of children playing with skipping ropes and footballs amongst broken glass, boarded-up houses and graffiti, memories of my own happy childhood came flooding back. Walking through, I sensed the same community spirit, and as the other members of the group clutched their bags, I felt safe. However, as we ventured deeper into the township, I realised that it was much worse than anything I had experienced. Even the nice areas seemed rundown with three families in one room, and the bad parts were the shantytowns. On the beachfront, we passed some new buildings; beach side apartments to die for. Which I guess commands a high price. So, on one side of town you have these fancy apartments, and on the other you have families living in tin shacks. We then drove out of Cape Town to our first campsite. The countryside seems so green and fruitful.

The good thing about this trip is that I'll be able to read my prison diaries uninterrupted during our long drives. I'm reminded of the rush I used to get every time the alarm would sound on my radio. But I've been a prison officer for fifteen years now and I'm struggling to see what has kept me there all this time. I've received a job offer to work as a manager with a chain of coffee shops in east London. No prisoners, no stress, no shifts, just what I need.

Saving Lives

Night Shift

11th February 2004

I've been back at work after my leave and my first week of nights with Maria and Ms Freeman.

I'm still on D3 and there doesn't seem to be any signs to suggest that I'm moving to B3 anytime soon.

My night shift started at 7.30 p.m. on Monday and continued until 8.00 a.m. At the start of my shift, I walked past Mr Jones as he was clocking off.

"Be careful, Ms Campbell, it's a full moon. This place goes crazy when there's a full moon," he warned.

I felt a sudden burst of anxiety about what lay in wait for me in the week to come. I walked into the staff office to find a flustered Maria searching through the contents of her bag that she had spilled out over the desk.

"Amber, have you got any spare tampons?"

Her question was a welcome distraction. Rummaging through my bag, I thought how it was funny that Maria and I always started our period around the same time. In fact, all the female officers and prisoners seem to be on their period around this time.

"Ahrr! A full moon. This time of the month must be a nightmare for Mr Jones." I laughed out loud with great delight. No one knew what I was talking about and ignored my 'out of place' comment.

Overall, the week of nights was boring. We spent most of the time watching films and eating takeaways. Monday night was *Escape from Alcatraz* with a curry, Tuesday, we binged watched a box set of *Porridge* with a pizza, on Wednesday *The Green Mile* with a Chinese, and on Thursday, we watched another *Porridge* box set with pizza. There's a night patrol staff member on every landing, but they don't have keys to the cells. If there's a problem with a prisoner in the cell, all they can do is press the alarm and wait for us to arrive. On Friday night, at about 2.00 a.m., when the others were watching *The Shawshank*

Redemption, I was just about to doze off when the sound of the alarm bell ripped through the control room like an electric shock. The five of us jumped to our feet and ran down to the youth offending unit. Before we got to the unit, we could hear the thunderous noise of panic from the other young women banging on their cell doors. The night officer who was shaking like a child's rattle led us to the cell. Looking through the hatch, we saw a seventeen-year-old prisoner. Her name was Ms Locksmith, she stood on the windowsill holding a ripped sheet. She had jammed one end of it into the closed window at the top, and the other end of the sheet looped around her neck. Thank God Ms Freeman was there. She entered the room, but within two steps, Ms Locksmith jumped. Ms Freeman rushed forward followed by Maria and

I. Ms Freeman held Ms Locksmith's body, and Maria grabbed her left arm, and I her right. With the sheet still wrapped around her neck, and the other end in the window, she fought us as we held her in mid-air. I didn't know what to do with her arm until she tried to punch me in the face. While I was trying to remember the correct Control & Restraint technique of restraining the arm of an aggressive prisoner, Ms Freeman and Maria had freed the girl and were covering her with a sheet. Still kicking, screaming and biting, and with her right arm not yet under control, we moved over to the bed where she surrendered. An hour after talking to Ms Freeman, Ms Locksmith was okay to be left with the night officer checking on her every five minutes.

My role in the incident was small, and considering I never really managed to control her right arm, my presence was most probably more of a hindrance. But I left work in the morning thinking/knowing I had helped save somebody's life.

Council Flat

I'm desperate to move forward with my life and get out of this dirty council estate. People are leaving excrement outside my front door. Maria is convinced it must be some racist. I don't know what other reason it could be, as I don't play loud music and I'm always at work.

"Racists have the best reason – you're black. What are you going to do about that? The only thing you can do is move out. You need to move out before they throw bricks through your window," Maria said.

I spoke to the Asian family opposite, and they've had the same thing. Our block is mixed. It must be someone from outside targeting us.

I went along to a resident's meeting this evening, which seemed pointless. There was no one there from the council, and all they could say was "that's terrible". I have to be at work early tomorrow. It's hard to find the time to push the matter further with the police and the council. I want to move to Barking, it's not too far away and I already know the area well. In Barking, I might even get my dream house, a house with a garden. But first, I need to buy this place on the 'Right to Buy' scheme. It sounds mad but I know that I can turn this crumbling, dirty flat in to a nice home that someone might want to live in. I've got the paperwork; the council will give me 70% off the market price and Halifax said they could give me a mortgage without a deposit. When it all goes through the first thing I will do is paint my front door red, I've always wanted a red door. I wish I could get a message to the racist and ask them to hold off while I put the flat on sale.

Maria & Ike

After work today, I went over to Maria's place. She's renting a room in North London in a four-bedroom house. I also met Ike, a close friend of hers. Ike is a Master's degree student from Nigeria who's infatuated with Maria. She towers over him, making him look quite dweeby. Like a devoted pet, he sits in the corner for most of the evening with his eyes following her around the room. Over cups of tea and crisps, Maria showed me photos and wittered on about her one true love in Nigeria. Ike listened, envy draining the blood from his face when she showed me the photo of the tall and well-built son of an oil tycoon.

"His father is also a chief," she boasted, as she pushed another photo in my face.

"When was the last time you saw him?" Ike asked, a deceitful smirk on his face. He added "Friends in Nigeria tell me he's cheating on you."

At that, a vexed Maria put away the photos that were spread out on the floor and an uncomfortable silence entered the room. I got the feeling that status and acceptance by Nigerian high society meant a lot to Maria. But Ike wasn't finished.

"All is not lost. You're good looking, and you have a German passport, so you'll find another rich Nigerian man easily."

"What is your problem?" I said.

Offended, Maria stood up. "Ike, I think you'd better go."

He tried to back pedal on what he had said.

"I'm only joking," he added. But I wasn't convinced.

Friends with Benefits

I was only on an early shift (7.30 a.m. – 1.00 p.m.), it seemed as though it would be a bad day as soon as I walked onto the landing. Ms Hook was there to inform me that Mr King had asked her to do the list. But the tables soon turned. Ms Phipps, known as 'Crack Head' Ms Phipps, is a regular Holloway prisoner with a severe crack-induced psychosis. She often sits on her own scratching her ulcers and twitching from side to side, before exploding into a rage about invisible things. Ms Hook couldn't handle it when she flipped out this morning. From the smoking room, I could overhear the drama escalating out of control. Ms Hook was moving Ms Phipps to B4 (as she was now a convicted prisoner), but Ms Phipps wanted to go to A3. With every word Ms Hook said Ms Phipps just became more and more angry, although everyone knows that Ms Phipps is harmless. I eventually stepped in and calmed the situation. Ms Hook walked back to the office and closed the door behind her. After I had moved Ms Phipps to B4, I returned to the office and said to her, "That was close, good job, I was around."

At lunch today sitting with Ms Hall and Maria, it's clear that Maria and Ike are now in a relationship.

"Ike is just a very good friend," Maria said.

"Yes, a very, very good friend," I responded with a smile before Ms Hall, Maria and I laughed out loud as the three of us sat in the C3 association room.

New Car

Today, I went to church to thank God for my new car, a Peugeot 206 GTi sports with alloy wheels. Every morning, I look out my flat window (that's flaking brown rust), at my new sky blue car sparkling in the sun. I've never been very materialistic, but when everything else in life is broken, covered in rust, grey with dirt, and smells of shit, it's nice to have one thing that's nice.

Wing Cleaners

Serving dinner yesterday evening with the help of the three Jamaican unit wing cleaners, Ms Black, Ms Brown, and Ms White (it's not a joke, that's really their names), I tried to reach common ground.

"I'm Jamaican too," I announced out of the blue.

Ms Black looked at me blankly, Ms White's whole body cringed and Ms Brown laughed out loud.

"And when was the last time you went to Jamaica, Ms Campbell?" Ms Black asked.

"Well, I've never been to Jamaica," I said.

Ms Black kissed her teeth and said something fast in Jamaican patois, which she knew that I wouldn't understand. "You're not a real Jamaican, Ms Campbell," Ms Black said.

"Leave her alone," Ms Brown rushed to my defence and

Ms Black kissed her teeth again. "Don't you worry, Ms Campbell, when you go to Jamaica, look me up. I'll make sure I take you to all the nice parts."

Ms Brown's face always seems to glow with happiness. Her laugh could often be heard three units away.

"You should be Ms Black," Ms Black would mock, referring to Ms Brown's deep brown skin. Ms Brown had been teased about her skin tone all her life and she had ready prepared rebuttals.

"You should be Ms Red, yet your head is so nappy."

Ms Brown laughed with Ms Black and Ms White, but at night alone in her cell she wondered if her life would have turned out any different if she had been born with light skin and 'good' hair. I asked Ms Brown why in the world she would bring drugs into the country and risk leaving her children. I wondered if it was greed. It didn't take long to work out she had little choice. She could risk being caught with drugs at the airport, or risk starvation.

There is an overwhelming sense she and the women in here for drug smuggling are victims themselves or just pawns in a larger game. This evening, Ms Brown came back from court after being sentenced. She had fainted in the dock when the judge gave her twelve years.

It was just me and Mr Adie on duty. At dinner, Ms Brown asked if she could have any leftover chicken. Mr Adie said no because it's now prison policy that we don't serve seconds. But when everyone was locked up, Mr Adie went all over the prison looking for an extra chicken. Ms Brown, Ms White and Ms Black are the eyes and the ears of the unit. They know who's done what, who's bullying who, and who's got something they shouldn't. They are loyal to the officers, and they're rewarded for that loyalty with extra association time in the evenings. If you're ever caught in a corner without another officer in sight, you can always rely on a wing cleaner to raise the alarm. That evening, I sat with the three women to watch with them their favourite TV series, *EastEnders*. Ms Brown sat between Ms Black and Ms White. Ms Black shouted "Yes" and the cheers went up throughout the prison as we watched Little Mo stand up to her abusive husband Trevor on the TV.

Out Clubbing

At the weekend, I went out with Maria and Ike to a Nigerian wine bar in the West End. Maria let me borrow one of her designer handbags for the evening, one that cost £800. I spent most of the evening worried that I was going to spill my drink on it and wished that I had just taken my own £15 handbag I got from New Look. Maria has about thirty pairs of designer shoes and about twenty designer handbags.

"You only need three. A bag for work, a bag for when you're not at work and a bag for church. A pair of shoes for work, a pair of shoes for when you're not at work and a pair of shoes for church," I said.

Maria laughed.

Ike has now moved in with Maria because he couldn't afford the rent on his own. Maria insisted that they are still "just friends". As we walked through the lavish doors of the wine bar, Ike was eager to grab Maria's hand, which she pushed away. Leaving Ike behind, she wrapped her arms around me.

"Now, I'll show you how we Nigerians like to party," she said. We sat in a centre booth.

"Maria, you look stunning as always," said one man. "How's Okiemay (referring to her one true love in Nigeria). Can I buy you and your friends a round of drinks?"

They lined up to greet our table, and Maria leaned over and said, "She's or he's the daughter or son of such-and-such chief, or the prince of such-and-such."

Report

Maria came into work today with a black eye and a chunk of hair missing. I don't know what she told the senior officers. She spent most of the morning reapplying makeup to hide it. She's also got bruises all over her arms.

"I bruise easily," she said trying to trivialise the severity of the state she was in.

"What do you mean? What the hell is going on, Maria? Is Ike beating you up? You need to get out of that house."

"I'm fine," she insisted.

I can't believe that someone so strong, someone who's been through so much already can behave like this in this situation.

"I'm fine, Amber," she said again trying to reassure me.

Ms Carr, a twenty-eight-year-old prisoner on A4, barricaded herself in her cell and slit her throat with a razor. She's a known self-harmer, but not violent to others. Once we forced our way into the cell, the medical staff could take over. There was blood everywhere, but she missed an artery. Barely. There were too many officers on the scene, so I walked back down to D3 to find one of our own prisoners, Ms Phipps, smashing up her cell. A rattled Mr Jamu was trying to calm her down as she threw her chair at the cell door. Mr King was still on A4, but to Mr Jamu's relief, I was back.

I left Ms Phipps in her cell for half an hour to calm down, and just check up on her every few minutes. We later found out she had just had a bad family visit. I still had to nick her for smashing up her cell. Maria was busy all day, so I didn't get a chance to ask her to help me write the report. I needed to get the report in to Mr King by 8.00 p.m., so he could file it with the Block ready for Governor Rose to see first thing in the morning. By the evening, despite trying to write it all day, I still hadn't been able to write it. At 8.00 p.m., I felt a wave of panic. Every word was a struggle. Even words I know how to spell I doubted. The more I focused, the more the words danced on the page. 'How do I spell the word said, is it s-a-i-d or s-i-a-d' I asked myself over and over as the sweat from my hand dampened the paper. I stood up from the office chair and gasped for air. I then walked up and down the landing with a mix of anxiety, helplessness and frustration, all wrapped in a bundle of self-loathing.

It was 8.20 p.m. Mr King marched around up to the unit

office. "Ms Campbell, where's the report?"

I explained that I was struggling to write it. "You see, I'm a bit dyslexic, so it takes me longer," I said.

"Show me what you've done."

Reluctantly, I handed him the report I had been working on all day. All my effort, and anxiety had amounted to one sentence on the page.

'At about 9.30 today, I walked on to D3 unit and prison officer Mr Jamu said that a prisoner Ms Phipps had smashed up her cell.'

Standing in the office he stared at the paper and I waited for his response in silence. I'm not sure why he took so long to read the sentence. He might have been struggling to work out what I had written, as I'm sure it was covered in spelling mistakes. Or he could have been in shock that it had taken me all day to write that.

"Pass me a blank report form and a pen," he said, sitting down.

He started writing the report for me. It was a pragmatic solution, there was no time to discuss the issue there and then. I continued to wait in silence as he wrote. I replaced my anxiety with gut ranching embarrassment. I thought 'I can't do this anymore'.

"Okay," Mr King said, getting up from his chair in a hurry with the completed report in his hand. He didn't make any eye contact with me as he left the office.

I'm devastated. I've realised that even though I love my job, I can't do it. I can't have a breakdown every time I need to write something. It's not fair on my colleagues and I can't think of a solution. I have no choice, but to resign.

1/5/04

"I handed in my notice today," I said.

"What! Are you joking?" a shocked and confused Maria asked.

In the C3 association room I told Maria, Ms Hall, Adie, Mr Jones and Mr Jamu what had happened yesterday evening.

I continued to smoke my cigarette.

"They can't fire you, that would be against the law. We should take this to the union," said Mr Adie.

"Why didn't you call me, I was working on Level 5," said Ms Hall.

"How could you have helped if you were working on level 5? Anyway, I can't go on like this."

"You're good at your job, you just need a little extra support. We'll work it out," responded Ms Hall.

The office phone rung. It was Mr King asking me to come to his office to discuss what happened yesterday. That focused minds on a solution.

"They have to give you extra time to write reports," said Mr Jones.

"Mr King has to let us help you," said Maria.

They came up with a list of what I believed to be unworkable demands for me to take to Mr King.

"You should have someone with you as a witness. I can come with you," offered Mr Adie.

"I need to face this on my own, but thanks."

I remember when I got the letter from Hackney College. It started "unfortunately…" I didn't need to read the rest. They thought I was not ready, and I did not have the grades to do an advanced level course, anyway. They advised me to apply for the intermediate course.

I wasn't stupid, why couldn't they see that. There had to be a way to show them I was more than capable.

Almost illiterate, I bought half a dozen entry-level English reading and spelling books and would spend hours every evening going through them thinking if I could just learn the basics, I'll be okay. One evening, I watched a BBC documentary on dyslexia. Could I be dyslexic? The next day, I went through the Yellow Pages and found a specialist that could assess me. I took on an extra cleaning job with Hackney Council so I could pay for an assessment and some tutorial sessions.

Transfer List

On Friday morning, I decided that *I* would do the Transfer List. I woke up on a mission and got into work at 7.00 a.m., thirty minutes before the start of my shift. I sat in the List chair and resolved that nothing short of the number one governor would get me out of that seat. Ms Hook came in five minutes later.

"Actually, I was going to do the List today," Ms Hook said.

"It's all right, I'll do it."

In shock at my stubbornness, she replied, "Well, I know what I'm doing!"

Yet again, I replied "If you would like me to move anyone, I will, and if I need any help, I'll ask Mr King."

Ms Rot and Mr Potter walked in. "What you doing sitting there?" Ms Rot said.

Ms Freeman also came in to see what was going on.

"Mr King won't want you messing around with the Transfer List, you don't know what you're doing, so get up!" Ms Hook insisted in a raised voice.

I yelled back more determined than ever "You go and get Mr King, go and get who you like because I'm not moving."

She stomped out to the SO's office, where I know Mr King could overhear our argument. Mr Potter and Ms Rot followed Ms Hook to the SO's office and stood outside. Was he going to stand by me or was he going to back Ms Hook? I waited with Ms Freeman in the unit office preparing myself for a fight. I've got thirty days to work out my notice, I might as well go out with a bang. The SO office door opened and I could over hear Ms Hook muttering to Ms Rot and Mr Potter, they did not return to the unit office, but went into the smoking room. I was puzzled.

"Would you like a cup of tea, Ms Campbell? It looks like you're doing the Transfer List today," Ms Freeman said.

I refused to move out of the chair until I had completed the entire List. On Monday morning, Mr Smith knew all about that exchange and called me to find out what was going on. There were one or two mistakes, like I had moved a convicted prisoner onto A3 unit which is prisoners on remand only, but overall, the SOs were impressed that I had completed the Transfer List on my own.

Every year, the prison moves officers around the prison in an attempt to curb the endemic culture of bullying. Every year, officers hope they're not the ones who have to move. However, D3 officers never get moved.

"Don't you know, Ms Campbell, D3 officers are special and D3 officers have the ear and favour of their SOs who will go to great lengths to lobby on their behalf," Mr Adie informed me.

I expected my name to be on the List, but it wasn't.

Maria with Bruises

This morning, Maria came into work again with a bandage around her arm. She told the senior officers she fell down the stairs and needed to be put on light duties. At lunch, she told me she and Ike had had a fight in which "she gave as good as she got." He had twisted her arm up her back, leaving it sore and bruised. She assured me it was a fight that "just got out of hand" and she was making plans for her life that were more long-term. She applied to buy a flat under the Key Workers Scheme, which would give her some housing security.

Ms Hook seems to be working on B3 a lot, and I haven't seen Mr Potter for a while either. Ms Rot works the opposite shift pattern so when I'm on duty, she isn't. So, it's just me and a whole bunch of probationers left to run the most hectic unit in the prison.

4/11/04

The last couple of days I've kind of been in charge on D3. As the most experienced staff member, I'm rising to expectations. However, if anything goes wrong on the unit, it feels like it's my fault and something I have to take responsibility for. I've come a long way, and I feel that others are starting to see that.

I went around to Maria and Ike's place last night where Maria had cooked a special Nigerian meal for me to try. Cooking brought Maria a feeling of belonging, staring at the pot she remembered the hours in the kitchen listening to her grandmother who often visited her as a child in Germany from Nigeria. Her grandmother would have been proud of Maria. Amongst many other accomplishments Maria had also become a great cook. As the three of us sat down to eat, her phone rang. Looking at her mobile to see who was calling, she dashed out of the room in excitement answering her phone with, "Hello, my darling." When it was clear that she wasn't going to come back in a hurry, Ike and I carried on eating without her. We could hear her laughing and joking in the corridor with her one true love, and I could sense a deep resentment from Ike about the situation. Today, I asked Maria about it.

"Ike knows that my heart will always be with Okiemay."

12/11/04

The prison management allowed Ms Hook to become acting senior officer for the evening shift. It's only for a single evening shift, but then I think of the more experienced Level 3 staff they could have given the opportunity to, such as Mr Adie or Ms Hall.

"If you're Black at Holloway, your chances of getting such opportunities are slim," Mr Adie complained.

Maria and I haven't been out on the town for a while now, and she doesn't want me to come over to her place after work like I used to. She's started wearing long-sleeved shirts, and she doesn't seem her normal demanding self. If we go to the gym during our lunch break, I notice fresh bruises. But she always says, "It's nothing." I don't know what I can do.

Maria beaten by Ike

This morning while I was still in bed on my day off, I got a call from Maria. She said, "Can you come over to get me?"

She didn't need to say any more than that. "I'll be there in thirty minutes."

When I arrived, she was standing in the front garden with two suitcases and two boxes. It was only when I got out the car that I saw what damage he had done to my beautiful friend. Ike had caught her grieving over the news that her one true love had got engaged to another woman in Nigeria. He pounced on her, punching her repeatedly in the face.

"Don't worry, you can stay at mine for as long as you like. The council has put security doors at the entrance to my block, so you don't have to worry about bumping into any racist trying to put crap on the doorstep," I laughed. Maria responded with a blank face. "The sofa isn't that comfy, I think you might be better off on the floor…"

"Where are you going, Amber?" She had noticed that I was not going my normal route.

"To the police station."

"No," she insisted. "It's over now. You know I don't want to go to the police. I might get in to trouble at work."

We argued about it in the car, but she was adamant she did not want to go to the police. I looked over at what was once my glamorous German friend. Ike had broken her. Too ashamed to go to the police, too frightened to go home and now on the run with her possessions in boxes.

"Why have you stopped the car?"

"We need to get out off here, have some fun, forget about how crap everything is."

"I can't go out tonight. Look at my face."

"Why don't we go to New York?" I said.

New York

29th December 2004

I'm here in New York to see in the new year. Ms Hall, Maria and I have been bickering all the way here from London. As soon as we arrived, Maria flipped out because we were paying $600 each for the hotel suite I booked, when I said it would be about $500. It was lucky that I booked a hostel in Brooklyn that Ms Hall recommended just in case. So, we cancelled the reservation at the New Yorker Hotel and went to Brooklyn. Leading us down a narrow, mouldy hallway, the receptionist showed us to our room. A thin, plastic mattress lay bare on two rusting bunk beds, carpet decorated with stains and the paint peeling off the bars on the window. Ms Hall, Maria and I stood in the frozen room lost for words listening to the faint sound of police sirens and two local drug addicts arguing at the end of the hallway.

"Thanks, but I don't think we'll take the room after all."

Maria lost her $100 deposit out of the $300 we had to pay up front to reserve the room at the hostel, and she made sure I knew about it all the way back to the New Yorker Hotel. When we arrived at the hotel, we had lost the suite, so we ended up in a standard room at the New Yorker. I can't believe that I paid for Maria's flight to come out here for her 30th birthday only to have her complain the whole time.

"Anyway, tomorrow's New Year's Eve. We should decide now where we're going. I don't mind going to Times Square but I think we should go clubbing, that's what Carrie, Miranda, Samantha and Charlotte would do," I said.

Standing in front of the full-length mirror, Ms Hall frowned disapprovingly at herself, a wave of worry seemed to overcome her as she rubbed her forehead.

"Everyone over here is overweight," Maria told Ms Hall. "You'll be one of the skinniest women in New York."

Ms Hall seemed unconvinced.

Maria's visit to New York six years ago was the highlight of her short modelling career. Modelling was always just meant to tide her over while she was looking for something in finance. But the job in finance never came and then the modelling work dried up. The bruising on Maria's face has faded, but she applies an extra layer of makeup now, thanks to Ike, out of habit. Sat with her legs crossed on the bed staring into the small hand mirror for an hour she perfected her masterpiece, her face, a shimmer of gold eyeshadow to bring out her hazel eyes and bold American red lipstick to finish. I always wondered how Maria seemed to look stunning in any shade of lipstick when I struggled to find one shade to suit me. I pulled out my lip balm, which gave me a slight shine.

Unpacking the designer bags and shoes that Maria let me borrow, I wondered how the women in *Sex and the City* would spend New Year's Eve and whether we, three Black women from London, could outdo them.

1st January 2005

2.00 a.m.

This has been the worst New Year's Eve I've ever had and to think that I'm in New York. We left the hotel at about 8.00 p.m. It was too late to get into Times Square, Ms Hall didn't want to go there anyway because she's scared of big crowds.

"Sod it," I yelled, after an hour of walking around in circles in high heels trilling behind them with my arms folded. "I can't be bothered to argue with you guys anymore."

I cringed with a mix of embarrassment and annoyance as Maria tried to haggle with nightclub door staff over the price of entrance. Ms Hall stood to one side hoping that Maria's efforts would be in vain. All the bars were full, all the nightclubs were overpriced and the countdown to midnight loomed closer and closer. We ended up in some dreary restaurant watching the Times Square celebrations on a TV. My mood sunk to an unstoppable low watching the chunky small 1980s TV box that had been fixed to the wall. Squinting my eyes, I looked over at Maria and Ms Hall and knew whom to blame for this disastrous night. After the countdown, we went back to the hotel. I went to the reception desk to ask for a single room as I couldn't even bear to look at them anymore, but no rooms were available.

7.30 p.m.

I stormed out of the hotel room bright and early this morning to go to the Statue of Liberty on my own. Dominating the skyline, I could imagine how the early immigrants felt when they first came to America with all their hopes and dreams of starting a new life in a new world, and then being greeted by that breathtaking symbol of optimism. On the way back, I went to the History of Immigration at Ellis Museum. I was so impressed that they have something that not only acknowledges, but *celebrates* diversity. And I am envious that people can have dual ethnic identities. American and Irish. American and Italian, and on and on. They hold on to their origins with pride, and no one questions their right to be both.

"Where have you been all day? We've been worried sick about you," Maria said, switching off the hotel room TV.

"I've been out enjoying myself," I said.

That was a half-truth. Sitting alone at the foot of the Statue of Liberty the key ingredient was missing in this *Sex and the City* holiday, my friends.

When we get back to London, I'll only have a few days left to see out my notice. I've got six months of living expenses in my emergency savings account, which should keep me afloat until I get another job. Asda have offered me a job, which I'll take up if I get nothing else. I had a job interview for the post of a station ticket office worker last week and I've got three other job interviews lined up next week at the Post Office and the Council.

2nd January

Last night, I put my anger to one side to go out dancing. After dancing so hard, our feet were throbbing, and we left the nightclub in high spirits. A group of White guys outside the club smoking wolf whistled at Maria as she walked by. "Looking good, want to come home with me tonight?"

Maria turned and thrusted her middle finger in the man's face. "Screw you," she spat.

There was no time to digest the shock of Maria's reaction, as she then told him that she was going to punch him in the face. The men readied themselves as if they were in a smoke-filled pub after a game and an opposing side just walked in.

I turned to Ms Hall and yelled, "We have to leave now."

Ms Hall seemed oblivious to what was going on around her. "I've lost my travel card! I can't find it."

I couldn't take the madness any longer and had to do

something. I told Maria in front of everyone I thought she was rude and talking complete rubbish. The guys were like, "Ohooo!" then laughed. Relieved that I had deescalated the situation, I marched the pair to the subway with Maria trying to justify her behaviour by claiming that they called her a 'black bitch'.

"I was there, you liar! There's no way anyone said that to you," I said. On the train back, Maria sat opposite me.

"They think they're better than me."

I listened in silent disbelief as she continued.

She kept going on about how I don't understand how hard it is for her as a black woman. Her rant was met with grumbles of agreement from the seven or so people on the half empty train. She continued to tell me and everyone in the carriage that as a black woman, she needed to "defend" herself.

"Why can't I walk the streets without the fear of being harassed, assaulted or raped? Why do men think they have the right to treat me like their property? And why is it that when I defend myself as a black woman, I'm the one that's in the dock?"

"That's right, sister," yelled a lone black woman at the other end of the carriage.

"I won't stand there and be called a black bitch," said Maria.

Gasps of "Hell no" followed from passengers on the train.

"We're harassed, locked up and killed by the police, face ridiculous levels of unemployment, and have to bring our children up in ghettos."

"It's always somebody else's fault, isn't it? Life isn't fair. Black people just need to get over it and take responsibility and stop blaming everyone for our problems," I replied with my nose in the air.

"Oh my God." Maria brought her hand to her mouth in horror, her body recoiled in disgust. "You're a Conservative."

"No," I protested my innocence at her insulting charge.

However, I had to put Maria straight. "I don't know why you keep going on about racism, sexism and all the other isms that's keeping you down. Y*ou're* not the only woman that feels undervalued, underpaid and under threat. *You're* not the only black woman to be called a 'black bitch,'" I leant over to Maria unwavering. "and *no one* called you a 'black bitch' anyway," I said through gritted teeth.

During what seemed like a trial-by-jury of race on the New York subway at 1.00 in the morning, the only words a tearful Ms Hall could muster was, "I can't believe I lost my travel card." Was I the only sane person in New York?

3rd January

This morning in the New Yorker Hotel breakfast room, Ms Hall read out a list of suggested activities she had scribbled in her notebook. She did not notice Maria and I narrowing our eyes at each other over the breakfast table to see which one would draw pistols first.

"What have you got planned for us tonight?" I asked Ms Hall, cutting her off mid-sentence.

"Well, I thought we could have an early night. Our flight's at 11 tomorrow morning so…"

"Oh, come on." I threw my arms up and head back. "It's our last night in New York. This is a *Sex and the City* holiday. What would Charlotte do?"

Maria let out a pip of laughter, as though she had been trying to hold it in, but couldn't contain herself any longer. I glared at her.

"I'm sorry I don't mean to laugh," Maria said. "I just wanted to know if Ms Hall is Charlotte, who are you?"

"I'm Miranda."

"So, I must be Carrie, right?" she asked.

"Sorry, I don't remember any crazies in *Sex and the City*."

"I'm crazy? You think we're here on some *Sex and the City* pilgrimage. Do you really think we have anything in common with those fictional characters? The last time I looked, I'm in so much debt, this time next year I'll most probably be bankrupt. And you're living on the third floor of a tower block on a rundown council estate, soon to be working in Asda. That's a long way away from Miranda's plush Manhattan apartment. I think there're some crazies sitting at this table and it isn't me."

Maria returned to sipping her coffee. Her savage attack left me mute. I sat with my fist clenched on the table knowing that deep down she was right. No one had told Maria that the civil rights movement had prevailed, that everyone was now colour blind and racism was a thing of the past. Maria was still fighting for her rights. A gut-wrenching sense of injustice had Maria standing in the middle of the subway yelling at me. Maria and I are both black women, both of us were born and live in Western Europe, yet I thought, we were worlds apart. Maybe if I hadn't been so busy watching *Sex and the City*, I might be just as angry as Maria. The thing is I am angry that I'm having to leave a job I love and I can't seem to find a way to change my situation no matter how much I try.

"You know, I didn't find my travel card."

"You lost your travel card?" Maria replied with care.

Ms Hall's eyes filled up.

"Oh, for the love of God, Ms Hall, please, please can you stop going on about your stupid travel card," I said.

Their eyes turned to me with daggers.

"Maria's just escaped a violent relationship, she's homeless and has no money," Ms Hall barked back at me. "Don't you care?"

Before I could defend myself, Maria piped up.

"You know Ms Hall doesn't feel comfortable going out to nightclubs. Why can't we do something we all enjoy together, instead of insisting we go out clubbing," Maria said. "Okay, I understand why it's hard for you, Maria."

"How could you possibly understand what it's been like for me. I grew up in a country that didn't want me. I was told every day to go back to my own country, but that was my country and I had nowhere to go back to. Do you know what it's like to belong nowhere?" Maria said.

I hung my head in shame. What could I say when they were right? They stood up, united. I had to decide whether to pick a fight or stop my best friends walking away.

"You belong in London. You're a Londoner now, like me. I'm sorry you're both right." I stood up. "I've been an idiot. I didn't know you were in debt, Maria, I should have known, I want you to know that I'm here for you now. Ms Hall, I know you hate clubbing and would rather be in church. I love you just the way you are and I don't want to change you. Us being together will make this a perfect holiday."

I waited in hope as they considered my grovelling speech. I let out a sigh of relief as Maria let slip a smile.

"Come here." Maria threw her arms around me.

"Group hug," Ms Hall shouted as she threw her arms around us.

We went to the John Lennon memorial on the edge of Central Park, had lunch at the Hot Dog stall in the film *You've Got Mail*, and we completed the day back at the Statue of Liberty. And just like that, we outdid the women in *Sex and the City*.

Ms Locksmith

I was one of the first on the scene when the alarm sounded for immediate assistance on the Vulnerable Prisoner Unit. It was Ms Locksmith. The 17-year old that had tried to kill herself when I was on night duty. I saw her corpse hanging from the inside door handle by a ripped sheet, her face purple and eyes open and white froth dribbling from the corner of her mouth, we were too late. For a split-second, which seemed to freeze everything around me, I looked at her and thought "Oh my God, this is the first time I've seen a dead body." We cut her loose and took turns to do chest compression and mouth to mouth. We got a pulse, but it was faint. We continued until the paramedics arrived and rushed her out, but I overheard them tell Governor Rose that it didn't look good. I spent the rest of the afternoon in the SO's office with Mr Smith waiting for news. He's so easy to talk to even though I hate the way he's so reluctant to get involved in issues on our Level and is always thinking about when he's next on leave. Then the dreaded phone call came. It was close. Thankfully, Ms Locksmith has pulled through with no brain damage; they will keep her in hospital for a few days to recover.

Access to Work

Mr King called me to his office. I opened the door as I arrived and his bouncy demeanor seemed 'out of place'.

"Have you heard of 'Access to Work'?"

Mr King explained the government scheme that supports people with disabilities in the workplace. He rattled off the many ways the scheme could support me, including an adapted computer with dyslexia support software on it. He said that a workplace assessment has been arranged for next week.

"In the meantime, I've had it agreed that I can give you extra time to complete reports and if you would like help from any other officers, they can have time off duty to support you. But I want you to know I'm here for you too."

I didn't know how to take in all the information. I wasn't sure how I got from having no choice but to resign to having my own computer, extra time and support from other officers.

"So, I don't need to quit?" I wanted to clarify.

"Quit what?" he asked perplexed, forgetting I had handed in my notice and tomorrow would be my last day.

"My job. I don't need to quit my job?" I asked.

The emotion of the last thirty days finally hit me. My hand trembled as I put it to my mouth to cover my face but I could not hide my eyes that were filling up with tears of joy. Some people take finding a fulfilling job for granted, I never have. I knew when I left school with nothing that I would have to fight my way through life. But this time, I was planning on giving up, maybe too soon. Through my water-filled eyes, I could see the man that refused to give up on me.

"No. You don't need to quit."

Amber's Blog 2018

Posted – 11th September 2018
Written in Fish River Canyon campsite - Namibia

Dealing with self-harm prisoners and suicide attempts became a daily part of my job; so much so I rarely mentioned them in my diary. Those at risk of self-harm or suicide were required to be checked every five to fifteen minutes. Some were placed on constant watch. The support that was given was high, the goal being to keep them alive whilst in custody. After all, no governor, government, or prison officer wants dead prisoners on their watch. During my years at Holloway, five women died in custody. One of them was just seventeen years old.

One winter's evening, when white snow covered the prison exercise yard, a prisoner died in my arms. She had become overwhelmed by a sense of helplessness. She, like so many women, pressed the emergency buzzer before she jumped with a noose around her neck, hoping someone would hear her cry for help. But her desperate act ended in tragedy. Every time it snows, I'm reminded of how prison crushed the hopes of that prisoner. I think about everything I said to her and all the things I did for her. I then think about all the things I wish I had said and all the extra things I could have done for her.

I struggled to cope with the death of a prisoner on my watch. I felt powerless and guilty. It was around that time I started writing this blog on how prisons can be improved. Back then, the prison system was unable to work with people as individuals. Working with prisoners as individuals would require prisoners to be dealt with according to their needs and vulnerabilities. Rather, I found that prisoners were dealt with like cattle. A rigid prison regime that focused on control. Such a regime would work well in the army and in a boarding school. But I saw how the spirit of many prisoners would just crumple up. Prisoners had limited access to specialist support for their needs. At the same time, there were too many agencies involved that were not speaking to each other. Police, prisons and probation worked in silos. That was in 2002, has anything changed?

Chapter 4

Why Have I Come to Africa?

11th September 2018

9.00 a.m., Fish River Canyon (Namibia) (In the truck)

Yesterday, we crossed the border into Namibia. We left Cape Town at 7.00 a.m. for an expected eight-hour drive. We were all freezing cold this morning, but as we drew closer to the Namibian border, at about 3.00 p.m., it suddenly became sweltering hot.

We're on the road again. Our truck, a 4x4 version of a coach, has twenty-four seats. It's far from five-star travel, but it's spacious and we have access to our lockers at the back of the vehicle. Anyway, last night I spotted our strange truck driver, John, sitting on the grass with Jackie from London having a cigarette, so I joined them. The three of us lay on the ground looking up at the stars. Venus and the Southern Cross were like jewels in the sky's crown. For a few hours, our driver was talking about his family, life on the road and apartheid—which was a little heavy for a first conversation. But it seemed like something he was desperate to get out of the way. He's only twenty-three years old and walks *everywhere* barefoot. He went swimming last night in the dirty river that runs along the bottom of our campsite. A mass of wild blond hair hangs over his forehead, and facial hair masks the rest of his face. He has said little so far. He sits there staring at everyone like he's wondering whom to eat first. Jackie from London is the other smoker in the group. She's forty years old (she looks about twenrt) and is here with her older sister and brother-in-law, who is also called John. Last night, I spoke to Jackie for a while and I think we will really get along.

13th September

7.00 a.m., Naukluft National Park (Namibia)

We're having breakfast at the bottom of the sand dune after getting up early to watch the sun rise over them. I couldn't be bothered to go all the way to the top. Well, to be honest with myself, I couldn't make it to the top because I was so out of breath. I came back down and told John the Driver I had decided to give up smoking next week, at which he gave his full support and encouragement.

"You'll never do it," John laughed. "Why do you want to give up anyway? I love my fags. I've been smoking since I was fifteen."

Which explains why his fingers are yellow and why he also couldn't make it to the top of the sand dune. We were soon joined by Jackie who couldn't make it to the top either.

Last night, we stayed at Naukluft National Park in Namibia. It's a huge camp site with some posh guest rooms for those who don't want to rough it. Yesterday, we went on a walk through the desert. A local guide who came from a family of Bushmen told us how the Bushmen survived in the desert. They use ostrich eggs to store water, and then bury the eggs in the sand. It was amazing to learn how free these people were. The few remaining Bush people have now been moved to the government settlements. Our guide told us that when the White people came, they put up fences around what they claimed as their farms. This restricted the Bushmen's movements for hunting.

"When the White settlers found diamonds in the area, it was all over for the Bushmen," the guide explained.

The Bushmen talk really opened my eyes to the different cultures here. I thought all African tribes were the same. Our guide spoke about how the Bushmen would travel for days in the desert to find food, and how they used their knowledge of the environment to live successfully in the desert.

I've become painfully aware that my knowledge of African culture and history is impaired. For the first time, I can see a Black African culture as strong and free. Instead of feeling empowered about what I have learned, I feel uneasy, cheated and frustrated.

15th September

1.15 p.m. - Swakopmund (Namibia)

We're now in Swakopmund for a two-day visit. We arrived yesterday evening. It's an ex-colonial town that's cold. To be honest, I hate it here already. The only Black people in this town are the ones who are cleaning the streets or waiting on tables. I forgot about the history of this whole region. It isn't just South Africa that's screwed up. I didn't think I'd feel this way, but I'm stressed out by it. The Black people here seem so beaten down and so poor.

Yesterday afternoon, I was the only one from our group to go on the township tour. I was afraid that it would make me even more angry, but on the contrary, once in the township, I felt a sense of peace. I went to an eighty-year-old chief's home first. She was elected four years ago by her tribe, which was interesting as I didn't know that chiefs could be elected or that they could be women. I had a traditional African meal, which consisted of fried worms, ground powder (rice/oatmeal you rolled into a ball with your hand) and dipped into a spinach sauce. I say "traditional", which makes it sound like a meal they wouldn't usually have. But in fact, they eat that kind of meal 3–4 times a week. The worms were tasteless. As I chewed, I imagined it was chicken in my mouth. I wondered whether I should have just swallowed it whole and got it over and done with, like taking a pill. The ground powder looked and tasted like mashed potato. The mild and full nature of the ground powder went well with the rich spinach sauce. Amazingly, on our tour we have so far not had any traditional African food.

After the township tour, I joined the rest of the group in an Italian restaurant for dinner. So far, I'm disappointed with the tour. I feel sorry for the people that are only doing two weeks. Their experience of Africa seems only to be sky diving and visiting cold, ex-colonial towns. What is the impression they're left with? Everything that's clean, fun and modern is white European. Everyone who is Black African is sweeping floors and living in the shantytown. Is this the reality of Africa? Or the reality that the tour groups want us to see?

It was Scot's birthday; I think he's now thirty. His parents migrated to Scotland from Pakistan in the early 1970s where he was born and raised. Scot sung a Pakistani celebration song followed by an acapella version of 'I'm Gonna Be (500 Miles)'. A White Namibian man came over to our table and wanted to teach us all a song. In German, he sang at the top of his voice, which got the applause of a few people in the restaurant. It was the old Namibian National Anthem sung before independence from South Africa—which spelled the end of apartheid in the country. I asked him what the song meant, and he said something about how "*they* came to a barren land, but still stayed because *they* loved the land". With "Restricted Access" signs in shop windows and light-skinned black women waiting on tables while the dark-skinned black women are out the back-washing dishes, I'm not sure how much has changed for Black Namibians. I thought about going Quad biking this afternoon but decided not to as I remembered that our guide on the Bushman talk said driving on the sand harms the wildlife that lives just beneath the surface.

Last night, half of the group got drunk at the bar above our hostel. I stayed only until about 11.00 p.m. as this town has dampened my party mood. In our dorm, I spoke to one of the other Black women from London, Jackie. I had noticed that whenever people asked what country she was from, she would say "Britain", "London" or "I'm British". She would never say "England", or "I'm English". Unlike Scot who always yells back "I'm Scottish". Over dinner, she told me she didn't feel comfortable saying she was English. She preferred to use the broader term "British" to describe herself. I spoke to her bother-in-law, John (John from London), on the same subject the day before.

"We, as Black people, we're not accepted as being English," said John from London.

"Why should we need, or wait for acceptance? 'Ethic Minority', 'Coloured', 'Half Caste'; these are all names and labels we have been given. Isn't it time we took control of our own identities?" I said.

A black person in Scotland would say first they were Scottish, as Scot does, but this doesn't take away from his ethnic heritage. I think some Black people feel that by saying they're English, they may be disowning their African/Caribbean roots, which we as individuals and as a community are proud of.

"What is the big difference between saying you're British or English anyway?" Jackie asked.

Identity is a strange thing. It's not just one thing that makes up who you are, but several things. Nationality, city, age, gender, sexuality, religion, class; the list can go on and on, and all these make up "identity". I've found that many people of colour feel insecure about their identity. I've always been proud to have been born and raised in England, not Scotland, Wales, or Northern Ireland, but England. My England may differ greatly from another person's England. My England looks like the row of sari shops on Green Street; sounds like my evangelical church on Sunday morning; tastes like jerk chicken rice and peas; and smells like my favourite 'pie and mash' shop in Dagenham. That doesn't make it any less English, as culture is ever-changing and is made up of many fragments. Growing up in east London, I was at least eight years old before I realised that when they were talking about 'ethnic minorities', they weren't talking about white people. But for many, the experience of racism inhibits them from taking ownership of their own country.

16th September

1.00 p.m. - Cape Cross (Namibia)

We're now in the middle of nowhere underneath a mountain. There are no showers, no running water, no toilets, and no other campers. It's just us our tents and the truck. I'm so glad to get out of that town. The only thing good about it was a break from sleeping on the hard ground. We've just seen some Bushman paintings on the rocks here, which are 2000–5000 years old. John said little is known about the way the Bushman painted them, as the tribe is now mostly extinct and their history which was oral has been lost. The paintings are small, faint, and not at all detailed. You can just make out a rhino and some stick people.

17th September

7.30 p.m. - Etosha National Park (Namibia)

We're here at Etosha National Park for two nights. I've just started my period and thank God, we've got decent toilets here! We were on the truck by 8.00 a.m. and got here about 3.00 p.m., so I read a fair bit of my diary and wrote a blog post. So far, it's the only part of the trip I am enjoying. Those few hours on the truck every day is relaxing. It's the only time I feel like I'm on holiday.

18th September

About 7.00 p.m. - Etosha National Park (Namibia)

I feel terrible! I could have done with a nice easy day in bed. Instead, I was on the truck at 7.00 a.m., and have just got back. However, I got some good photos today, and I didn't get as frustrated as I did yesterday.

    This morning, I asked if I could sit up front with the driver as I didn't want to fight with the rest of the group to get to a window. I also wanted a little bit more than our tour leader Sarah offered. Her knowledge on animals is, "That's an elephant", and that's it. Sarah is a thirty-year-old White

Zimbabwean who seems icy. With the responsibility of making sure that the meals are cooked, that the accommodation is booked, and that everything runs on time, she is really the leader of a military operation. She therefore doesn't talk to us unless she's giving out orders. She's the opposite of our easy-going driver, John, who has no responsibility and knows a lot about animals. So this morning, I got to be up front with the driver. My luck today was the first (and only) day that Sarah was driving. We sat in uneasy silence for most of the morning, but towards the end I made an effort to strike up a conversation. I asked her about the rest of Africa as I wanted to travel along the west coast. She said I wouldn't like it as it was "still primitive". I would have been there all day trying to explain to her that just because people do things different, it doesn't mean they're "primitive". I've never been good at small talk, and I opted to sit in silence instead. Anyway, after lunch, to my relief, she suggested that someone else take a turn in sitting up front with her.

10.15 p.m.

Everyone's already gone to bed. I also need to turn in as we've got to get up at 6.00 a.m., but I've just had a moment of clarity. Karen (from London), Emma, Tanya and I were in the ladies' bathroom talking about the effects of racism and apartheid. Tanya asked if we felt angry. I said "Well not really." But I now recognise what I felt in Swakopmund, and that *awful* knot I've been feeling in my stomach ever since is anger; a kind of anger I don't think I've ever felt before. I'm angry, with myself, that I don't know my history or culture, and now that history and culture may be lost. I decided today that I was going to suppress whatever it was I was feeling, but now I think I need to let whatever I feel run its natural course.

When we drove into the park, everyone got excited when a group of elephants walked past. There was a sudden surge to the windows. I got so pissed off with twenty-two people crammed at the glass of our huge truck—which did a good enough job on its own to scare away the animals. The possibility of me getting a decent photo was next to nil. I always seemed to get to the window too late or at the wrong angle. It was so frustrating to see my photo opportunities walk by as I watch helplessly. John from London was buzzing from the ordeal.

"Well that's what we came for!"

I looked at him blankly.

"To see the animals!" he proclaimed.

In that moment, I realised that that wasn't what I've come here for. This last week, I've been feeling like such a party pooper. Everyone's having a good time, but I'm unsatisfied and disappointed with everything. I feel incomplete. Some people's eyes lit up when they saw the animals. For others, it was simply on the list of activities. For others still, it was merely a question of getting their passport stamped at each border crossing point. I could hear the sighs of fulfilment all around me. It was written on their faces "Yes, I got what I came here for."

So, I need to find what I've come here for. I know that at some point I need to make a decision about my future. But for now, I want to find culture and for me, culture is something you experience, something you feel, smell, see, hear and taste.

.

Chapter 5

20th September 2018 6.00 p.m. - Ghanzi (Botswana)

We're in Botswana and staying at a campsite just past the border. We left Windhoek at 8.00 a.m. this morning, and it's been another non-stop day, it's hard to get a moment to myself to write this.

Yesterday afternoon, the group left me in Windhoek city centre because I wanted to get the photos from my memory card transferred to a CD. Sarah gave me the address of the hostel and her mobile phone number. Sarah then waved me off the truck. When I needed a taxi back, no one knew where the hostel was. I must have stopped about twenty cabs and Sarah wasn't picking up her phone. I spotted a mini-van with a travel guide tour logo on the door, *Windhoek Tours*, sitting in front of the tourist office across the street. I asked the two guys standing by the van if they knew where the hostel was and they must have been the only two in Windhoek who did. I got in the front seat. While I was making polite conversation, I had my hand on the door handle ready to jump out if needed. Everyone said I was mad for getting in the van, but I had to get back before it got dark. I was so pissed off with Sarah.

"Oh, sorry I left my mobile in the truck," Sarah said with a slight smirk on her face. "You're so lucky. You could have been kidnapped, raped and murdered," Jackie said.

The group were a little surprised that I wasn't kidnapped, raped and murdered in the two hours I was on my own in the centre of town. Part of me thinks they're being ridiculous. While the other half of me knows that my naivety could have landed me into serious trouble. There was a time when I was young and naïve. The prison service has helped me to grow and face the realities of life sooner than I would have liked.

Then You Look at Me

Burning Cell

02 February 2005

Today a group of women who had barricaded themselves in a dorm on D3 overnight made weapons out of the cell wall sink that they smashed up.

Dear Governor Rose,
  We are fed up of being treated with disrespect and spoken to like animals by your racist prison officer Ms Hook. If Ms Hook isn't removed from Holloway Prison immediately we will burn down this place.

  Ms Hook had, not for the first time, suggested to the Black British prisoners in the dorm that they could "go back to Africa" if they didn't like the way they are treated in Holloway. As soon as I got in to work this morning, I was ordered to put on my riot helmet, overalls and protective vest and they evacuated the landing. There were four women ready in the dorm with sharpened weapons, one of them was Ms Aziz who I remember took a nurse hostage on the healthcare unit. She stood ready for a fight at the cell door. When she saw the officers approaching, her smile revealed her gold tooth. Twelve officers broke down the door and stormed inside. I was part of the reserve team. I sat in the association room listening to all the commotion taking place outside with Mr Adie and Governor Rose.

  "Mr Adie, you need to take over from Ms Rot on the left," yelled Mr King from the door way.

  "Mr King," Governor Rose said clutching a black leather, business folder, "If there's anything I can—"

  Mr King interrupted, "No, but thanks for asking, Ms Rose. If you can stay in here, I would appreciate it."

  "Of course. Oh, and please, just call me Mel," Governor Rose said.

  A former Cambridge postgraduate and Tesco executive,

the thirty-three-year-old joined the prison service three years ago. She is tipped to be the next Head of Prisons at the Home Office. It was obvious from her straight face she was not the type to tolerate any condescending jokes about her being a fiery, little red head. Although she was little, had red hair and was a dragon when she wanted to be.

Looking around the room, Mr King saw I was the only one left. "Where's Mr Jones?" he asked.

"He was called back onto the unit," I replied.

"And Mr Potter?"

"I don't know."

Somewhat hesitantly he said "Okay, you're up, Ms Campbell." He looked unsure. "I need you to take over Mr Peterson on the legs."

"Okay, right," I bounced to my feet, as if to say I was ready. "I can do arms if you—"

"No, I need you on the legs," Mr King cut me short.

"Yes, okay but if you need me on the arms, I can handle it, I know I can."

"No. I said I need you on the legs," he insisted.

As I walked in to the cell Ms Rot was walking out with blood running down from her face. I could hear the crazed screams and walked over debris as if I was walking into a war zone. Thank God all I had to do was sit on the prisoner's legs. Mr Peterson had been kicked in the stomach and limped out when I took over. Mr Adie was on the left arm, Ms James was on her right. Ms Freeman was in charge of the prisoner's head and was therefore in charge of our team. When she said move, we moved and when she said stop, we stopped. We carried the prisoner down the stairs to the segregation unit.

During the incident, Ms Aziz hit her head on the floor and had to be taken to hospital. She came back at around 5.00 p.m. I saw the prison van drive in taking her back to the Block. By 5.10p.m., the prison alarm went off again and we all knew it was her. I raced down the stairs and could see the black smoke creeping up the stairwell towards me.

She had set fire to her cell on the Block. I was one of the

first on the unit with Mr King not far behind me. As I entered the unit that was filing up with smoke there was confusion as to what cell was on fire or who was where. Ms Hall ran past me with a fire extinguisher.

"This way," she said.

A unit officer opened the cell door, smoke rushed out. Ms King, Ms Rot and Ms Hall with a fire extinguisher charged in to the small signal cell blind to what was waiting for them in there. Ms Aziz charged forward to attack. Struggling to even breathe, my eyes filled with water as I stumbled my way to the back of the cell. The noise of officers yelling and prisoners screaming overwhelmed me. In the fog of smoke, I had got hold of the prisoner.

"Down, down, down!" someone yelled.

On the floor, the smoke cleared. I looked up and I had taken hold of the prisoner's head, which meant that I was in charge. I was the number one. Mr King had the prisoner's right arm and Ms Hall had her left, both looked up at me. The black smoke threatened to engulf us and Ms Aziz was still fighting, there was no time to think 'I can't do this'. I said to myself I need to get us out of this burning cell.

"Are both arms under control?" I yelled.

"Yes!" they both yelled back.

"We're going to move the prisoner to the association room!" I yelled "Up!"

Other "fresh" officers took over and restrained Ms Aziz once we had moved her to the association room. We then collapsed in a fit of coughing caused by smoke fumes. The fire brigade came on to the unit. Mr King didn't have time to catch his breath, he needed to organize the evacuation.

"Mr King, we need to ensure that this is written up properly. All the officers that have been involved need to stay..."

"Ms Rose, this incident is not over, please can you stay out of the way," Mr King snapped at Governor Rose. He then turned to me like he did earlier, but this time he was sure of his decision.

"Ms Campbell, I need to sort out the evacuation. Can you

make sure that Ms Aziz is moved to D3 and sort out her transfer to another prison? I want her out of here by tea time."

The lights flickered and as the smoke cleared Mr King looked back at me. I stood, perhaps in a different light and for the first time he saw me. I was no longer a girl that needed protecting or rescuing, I was a confident prison officer he could depend on to manage a situation.

06/03/05

7.30 p.m.

Later, when it had all settled down, I sat alone in the unit office to write the report using my new computer.

"How's the computer?" Mr King said, making me jump.

"God, don't sneak up on me like that. It's great. Look, you just talk into it and it writes for you."

He leant over to have a look at the computer screen. His cheek touched mine slowly and deliberately.

"Sorry," he said with a smile.

"It's okay."

"You were really something this morning."

"What do you mean?"

"Nothing, just with all these new officers I needed a competent officer to help me manage the situation and I think you did good." There was a moment's silence and for the first time he really looked at me

"Anyway, now you have this new computer, I guess you don't need me anymore," Mr King added.

"Don't worry, Mr King, you're more to me than just a proof reader."

Mr Adie entered the office, putting an end to the conversation.

1/04/05

"You need to start with the smallest debt first, throw everything at it and pay the minimum on everything else. When you knock that off quickly, you can move to the next one, then the next one."

Going through Maria's credit report with Ms Hall, Maria hung her head down low in shame as I went through the list of county court judgments. Her taste for designer handbags and shoes had clocked up £20,000 worth of credit card debt. However, a personal loan she took out that had been used to support Ike and a failed joint business of theirs added an extra £21,000.

"Get rid of the car. There's no way you can afford to pay £500 a month. Listen, you can do this. Forty-one thousand is a lot of money, but you don't need to declare bankruptcy. I know you can pay it off in a few years, you just need to throw everything at it. You need to cut up those credit cards and cancel your overdraft." Maria looked terrified as that was the only safety net she had. "Don't worry, all you need to do is get maybe about £1,000 in your savings account as an emergency fund so you don't go into debt again.

"We can set up a Level 3 Perdner," said Ms Hall.

"What's that?" Maria asked.

"It's a savings club. Say we get ten officers and we each put in £100 a month, the pot of £1,000 rotates every month. My mum was part of one in Jamaica. We can start one this month and God will provide you with a safety net, so you don't have to turn to those credit cards ever again. You might think these loans and credit cards are a blessing but I'm telling you they're from the pit of hell," Ms Hall said.

"That's a great idea. Maria. You can do this, I know you can," I replied.

"I hear Mr Adie's a landlord on the side. Why don't you ask him if he can put you up in one of his flats? The Lord might touch his heart and he might give you a discounted rent."

"That's a long shot," I interrupted. "Landlords, all they care about is money. If anything, Maria would be lucky, if she doesn't get ripped off. Just because we know Mr Adie it means nothing, he's still a landlord."

"There's no harm in asking. After all, I've got nothing to lose."

"Okay," I said as my hand rested on her knee. "Maria, you can do this, I know you can."

She pulled out four credit cards from her bag and had a final look at them. They had in a way brought her so much joy and only an hour ago she could not imagine life without them. But I was right, they had to go and without emotion, she cut them in half.

Move to C3

On Friday afternoon, I went into the SO's office to find out what unit I would be covering over lunch. Mr King and Ms Hook were there, so I wanted to be in and out as fast as I could. But Mr King wanted to tell me about the move of 33 prisoners from D3 to C3 unit, as he was going off duty. D3 unit would be closed over the weekend for refurbishment and they will install television sets in all the cells.

He started off by saying, "Mr Potter and Ms Hook will coordinate the D3 move to C3…" After that, I wasn't interested in anything he had to say.

Mr Potter is such a nightmare to work with. Last weekend, I was working with him on what should have been an easy Sunday morning. The women were out of their cells on the unit and everyone seemed in good spirits.

"Lock them up! Lock them up, Ms Campbell!" he bellowed from the other end of the unit.

I jumped out of my chair and instructed the women to return immediately to their cells. I thought there was a fight or something. It turned out that two women were squabbling over the last mop and bucket. Fifty-five women, some of whom were on the phones to their families or in the bath went crazy because Mr Potter can't de-escalate a mop and bucket dispute between two women.

Today started at 7.30 a.m. in the D3 smoking room with Mr Potter boasting about what an amazing officer he is. Ms Hook was then eager to outdo Mr Potter.

"Mr King asked me to coordinate the move because I know what I'm doing. Most of the staff on Level 3 are illiterate," Ms Hook said.

Ms Hook had told the prisoners the night before to have their bags ready by 8.00 a.m. for the move. It was no surprise that most of the women were not ready at 8.00 a.m.

"Get your crap together and move now right now!" I heard Ms Hook yell.

"Who do you think you're talking to?" the prisoner yelled back.

"Down, down, down!" Mr Smith yelled as he pounced on her.

It was 8.05 and the alarm rung out around the prison. I watched in disgust as Mr Smith and several other officers restrained the prisoner. There was something about the white saliva that appeared at the corner of Mr Smith's mouth and the blue vein of adrenaline pulsating in his forehead that tells me he enjoys restraining prisoners. His demeaning tone and orders often provoke the women to respond in a way that would give him the excuse to jump them.

It was late morning before the first trickle of prisoners arrived on C3 from D3. Ms Hook had made a big deal out of the fact that she had re organized the C3 office and was now diligently writing up the prisoners' names on the whiteboard. I looked at her perfect handwriting and thought of all the times she made me feel self-conscious about writing on the whiteboard. It was coming up to lunchtime and she had spent hours writing each prisoner's name and details on the whiteboard, she had used a ruler to ensure that there was perfect symmetry. A group of prisoners arrived on the unit waiting to be assigned a cell. Ms Hook was in the toilet, so

I processed the prisoners. Standing back, I looked with pride at my large childlike and messy handwriting on the whiteboard. Six months ago, Ms Hook would have immediately come in and rewritten what I had written. I would love to see her dare try that now. She came in to the office, looked at the whiteboard in horror, looked at me, hesitated and then walked out of the office. The thing is every unit's white board is full of different officers' handwriting because every officer should be processing prisoners. Not on D3, but things were going to change. Ms Hook had disappeared into the smoking room.

"Ms Hook's going home," she said, the stress of D3 is getting to her. Mr Smith is still down the Block writing up that restraint.

"So you need to take over the move Ms Campbell, I'll ask Mr Jamu to help," Mr Potter said.

"Why don't you go and find an officer that knows what they're doing instead of asking illiterate Level 3 officers like me and Mr Jamu?" I said.

"Grow up, Ms Campbell," Mr Potter responded.

"But you're such an amazing prison officer, surely you can do it on your own?" I mocked.

Rot & Sherry

This morning at 7.30, I was going from cell to cell waking up the prisoners while the other D3 officers sat in the officers' smoking room eating breakfast as usual, all apart from Ms Rot who hung around the kitchen area. An OSG brought the prisoner breakfast trolley onto the unit, it was Sherry.

"Hi, let me help you with that," Ms Rot said as she held the kitchen door open. She then whispered, "So when can I buy you that drink?"

"What was that?" Sherry asked.

Looking behind her to make sure no one was around Ms Rot moved in closer and asked "What are you doing for lunch?"

"I'm going to the canteen."

"Can I buy you lunch? There's a nice kebab shop on Holloway Road which is really good."

"Okay."

"I'll meet you at the traffic lights on Holloway Road."

"Why don't we meet outside the prison and we can walk down together?" "Ms Rot," Ms Hook called out from the officers' smoking room.

"I'll meet you at the traffic lights fifteen minutes after the roll is called," Ms Rot said to Sherry, as she hurried away.

I got the Job

I got the job! Disability Liaison officer. After my interview with the new Race Relations

PO Lucas and Deputy Governor Rose, I ran back to tell everyone on the level, all of whom were waiting to hear the news in C3 association room. But I guess Mr King couldn't wait and met me on the stairs to congratulate me before he went off duty. Everyone was so happy for me, everyone apart from Mr Adie.

"You only got the job because you've been sucking up to Mr King. You'll owe him now."

"I won't owe him anything. Mr King put in a good word for me with Governor Rose, that's all."

"Oh, he put in a good word for you, did he? All that pillow talk he's been doing with Governor Rose helped you out, has it?"

"What pillow talk, what are you talking about, Adie?"

"That's Mr Adie to you."

"Mr Adie thinks everyone is sleeping with everyone," Maria laughed.

"Has it ever occurred to you, *Mr* Adie, that Mr King thinks I'm a fantastic officer and that I might have got the job on merit?" I said.

"Now that's something to laugh about. Merit is a fantasy BS concept. A bit like if we ensure that we keep the top 1% rich it will somehow trickle down to the rest of us, or if you get an education and work hard, you'll succeed. Don't tell me, Ms Campbell, you actually believe in that."

"Yes, I do," I said.

"Sorry to break it to you. Father Christmas isn't real either," Mr Adie said.

"Mr Adie, you have no faith. God is in control of our lives, trials and tribulations come our way, but we can rise above them if we have faith," Ms Hall said.

Mr Adie rolled his eyes.

"I'm in control of my life. I take responsibility for all my failings and I can succeed if I want to," I said.

"That's right, Ms Campbell. Ethnic minorities have made a lot of progress in recent years. I mean, I want to be offered a job because I'm good enough, not because I'm an ethnic minority," Mr Jones added.

"If we've made progress, why are you referring to yourself as an ethnic minority? Who gave you such an empowering label? I would love to meet the person who thought it would be easier to lump us all together and call us 'minorities'. Do you think White South Africans refer to themselves as ethnic minorities? No, because they're the founders, the pioneers, settlers, and founding fathers. Yet you continually refer to yourself as a minority," Mr Adie said.

"When I was in school, the Black kids were in the majority, but the teacher kept using the term minority as if to remind us of our place," I said.

Prison Induction

I had my lunch in the SO office with Mr King today, going over the Induction Programme for new prisoners I've set up.

"When the women get here, they're already often distressed. To spend that first week in prison not knowing anything about the rules and routines can be so traumatic for some that they want to end their lives," I said.

"I agree," said Mr King.

I went on, "Every morning, I take all the new prisoners, fifteen or so, out to a quiet room. I explain things like letting them know when they are expected to be up and dressed with their beds made, when and how they can have visitors, and also sort out urgent problems like child care issues."

"That's fantastic. It sounds like it's going really well"

"But this morning, everything went wrong. The Detox unit didn't get their women down until 10.30, and the overhead projector wasn't working. And the teachers from the education department didn't come down to do their enrolment. But it's early days. No one asked me to organise it, but someone had to," I said.

"I've been trying to get jobs and new skills workshops in the prison. I mean, most of these women come in here with nothing, no qualifications, no job and they leave with nothing. How can that be right?" Mr King said.

"No wonder we keep seeing the same prisoners come back here time after time. At least you care about the women. The sewing workshop you sorted out is really popular."

"Good. It's so nice talking to someone that cares about the prisoners as much as I do. I think you and I are the only ones in here that don't believe that the prisoners should be locked up twenty-three hours a day," said Mr King.

Investigation

Today, the Race Relations PO Lucas came to see me to tell me he was investigating racial discrimination by Mr Smith towards Mr Jamu. I wondered why my name came up as a witness. I was worried and Mr Adie came and sat in on the interview with me.

"You might be wondering why a White guy like me got the job as Holloway's Race Relation Priceable Officer," PO

Lucas said.

Mr Adie raised one eyebrow.

"I was wondering why I'm a witness in your investigation?" I said.

"Don't worry, I get asked about it all the time. I'm am ethnic minority officer because I'm Irish," he said in an English accent. "I understand what it feels like to face prejudice."

Mr Adie raised two eyebrows.

"Yes, Irish travellers' have a really hard time," I said.

"Oh no, I'm not a traveller. God no, they're the reason the rest of us have a hard time."

Anyway, the reason he came to see me was something about SO Smith shouting at Mr Jamu in the unit office, and Mr Jamu said that I witnessed it —but I honestly couldn't remember anything like that. I told him that some officers talk down and make fun of him, which Mr Smith is aware off. I really didn't want to get involved. Ms Hook, in particular, has made some derogatory remarks about his turban, as in: "Here comes the Turbanator", which everyone (except him) thinks is funny. At the time I said something to her and all the SOs. However, if the SOs won't deal with the situation, then the Race Relations PO needs to. Mr Smith has now put him on poor performance monitoring which is so unfair. I feel uneasy about the whole thing. I don't know whether I've said too much or too little. It's obvious that Mr Smith has singled-out Mr Jamu, perhaps, because he thought him an easy target.

7th July 2005

I was on a late shift today. I woke up late, so I was in a rush getting out of my front door. I set off to work at about 11.30 a.m. I didn't put on the car radio until I got to Highbury Junction when I was hoping to find out why the traffic was so bad. That was when I heard what had happened.

"Do not travel," the radio presenter repeated.

I thought "Should I turn back home now" but I was more than halfway to Holloway. So, I continued and became anxious sitting in the traffic listening to the faint sirens coming from every direction as emergency vehicles tried to get through. I became worried about my colleagues and the prisoners who I thought would be going mad.

"We're on lock down," Mr King said in a sombre tone as I grabbed my keys.

I ran in and was met by a deathly silence as I rushed to the unit. All I could hear was the sound of TV sets as prisoners watched to see what was going on. In the office, officers gathered round a spare TV borrowed from one cell. No one was talking, and no one was moving.

I went to the SO office and realised that many of the staff that were meant to start their shifts at 12.30 p.m. were not yet in. Mr King had already spoken to the staff on an earlier shift to see if they would stay the full day.

I've never felt so proud to be a Londoner. Two events both different brought up the same emotion. Yesterday, my city was chosen to host the Olympics. I am so proud that the eyes of the world will be on us. Then today, I believe that four bombs went off in the heart of our capital, striking the London Underground and a London bus as people travelled to work. Tonight, most people are walking home, only the sounds of emergency sirens linger in the air.

Investigation Continues

I spoke to Mr Jamu today and told him what I'd said during his investigation, and I also told Mr Smith what I said. Funny thing is, they were both happy. I have peace of mind now about this because I didn't lie or hold back on the facts or my opinion. It's plain for all to see that he is being bullied by our own senior officers, which is heartbreaking for me. To tell the truth, when I think about it, I've sat on the fence, and my reluctance to get involved, until this point, is just as heartbreaking. But what, I wonder, makes bullying turn into racially motivated bullying? I remember the first time I worked with Mr Jamu. One prisoner asked him for a pack of tampons. He walked back to the office and asked in front of four officers "what is a tampon?" Things like that have made Mr Jamu the butt of every joke on Level 3. But instead of our SOs dealing with it maturely, they have led the charge. Jokes about his turban and accent have been shamefully tolerated by Level 3 staff and our SOs.

I know what it's like to be the new officer that doesn't fit in; the one that everyone's mocking behind your back, to feel that others don't have confidence in your work. I don't know if I would have stuck it out if I knew that the SOs were leading the attack. Mr Jamu might not have their support, but he's got us – meaning Mr Adie, Maria, Mr Jones and Ms Hall and all the rest that never made it onto the D3 worthy list.

My position on the level is strange. I know they never accepted me into the D3 clique, which is now disbanded. But my closeness to our SOs suggests to the rest of the Level that I was. I know that for many, our SOs still embody all that was the old D3. However, my colleagues have not disowned me. Quite the opposite, as I am the bridge they need. For them, I have the ear of the SO's office. When Ms Hall wanted extra annual leave at short notice, she approached Mr King, who refused. It was no surprise. She didn't expect him to do her any favours, but thought that he might for me. I am more than happy to use my influence to redistribute some of the favour that the old D3 enjoyed. So later that day, I approached Mr King about it and I got him to bend the rules. So, when someone doesn't like where they are working, needs leave, or needs to change their shift they come to me.

"Ms Campbell, you're the backbone of Level 3," said an officer from another Level today.

Racism in the Workplace

I glanced at the SO detail sheet on my way out last night to see where and whom I would be working with today. I saw Mr Potter's and Ms Hall's name next to mine. Ms Hall, unlike Mr Potter, has an easy-going style of working. When she's not been shifted by the SOs to work in other areas in the prison, Ms Hall is a pleasure to work with on Level 3. The mother of three young children, she told me that at her last appraisal, Mr Smith noted that she has an "attitude problem". He had also raised concerns about her commitment to the prison because she is always eager to leave the prison at the end of her shift. I went into the SO office this afternoon. Under a hoard of papers and Mr Smith's gardening magazines, I found the detail sheet. I was not surprised to see that they had shifted her to work somewhere else in the prison. Alone in the SO office, I stared down at the SO Detail in anger. The office door burst open.

"Oh, hello, Ms Campbell," said a buoyant Ms Hall. "I'm working with you today."

"No, the SOs have moved you to cover staff on Level 4," I said. Her hopeful anticipation of what the day could bring turned into a sombre mood.

"Shifted again," she said. "It's not fair. Why is it always me?"

Flicking through the past month's detail sheets, I noticed a pattern that confirmed the injustice.

"It's not just you," I said. "They only shift Black and Asian officers." An alarmed Ms Hall whispered, "What?"

"Keep a watch on the door while I photocopy this."

Soon we walked out of the office armed with the necessary information, and then we rounded up the troops. Maria, Mr Adie, Mr Jones, and Mr Jamu were just about to go on lunch in the C3 association room.

"The SOs only shift Black officers," I announced.

Mr Adie rolled his eyes. "We know that. I need to go to the bank quickly, so if there's nothing else, Ms Campbell."

I blocked his path to the door. "But I have proof."

I unfolded the photocopied detail sheets, which caught everyone's attention. The room lit up.

"I knew it!" Maria said, snatching the sheets out of my hand for her own inspection.

Ms Hall said, "How long have I been working here? You know we get passed over for promotion too."

Mr Jones said, "They told me I have an attitude problem." Ms Hall and Maria both said, "They said that to me as well."

After thirty minutes of airing our complaints, our thoughts turned to what we would do about it. Mr Adie was first to put his pessimistic view on the table.

"They won't do anything, so what's the point? If you say anything, Ms Campbell, you won't be their golden girl anymore. You'll just become another Black officer with an attitude problem."

"This is unacceptable. The picerison service has policies against this kind of thing. I think we should confront Mr King and Mr Smith, if they won't do anything, we should take it to Governor Rose, if she won't do anything, then we go to the union. This needs to stop today," I said.

Ms Hall jumped to her feet like a pop-up doll that had just been pumped with a sudden amount of hot air "Yes, this ends today."

Me Adie deflated Ms Hall in five seconds.

"I've given over ten years to this place. I have a PhD in Criminology and yet, they don't see me. I've put myself forward for promotion five times and gone on every training course available, but they don't see me. They don't care about my qualifications, or aspirations, or what concerns me. I've seen it all, I'm telling you nothing will change."

Later that afternoon, I took a deep breath and knocked on the SO office door. With a warm smile, Mr King who was sat with Mr Smith welcomed me into the office.

"Sorry for intruding," I said. "But I just wanted to know why only Black staff were moved around the prison for cover?"

The question stunned them into an upright position. They looked at each other aghast.

I continued "It's just that it has a severe impact on morale. Not only the officers concerned, but the whole Level. I think it's divisive…" I stumbled over my words a little "… it's very difficult to settle down and build relationships with prisoners and officers on the unit if you're always being moved. I don't think it's fair."

Mr Smith must have just cottoned on to what I was actually saying and cut me off.

"Hang on," he said. "What are you trying to say here? We don't only move Black officers —"

Mr King then cut him off with, "No, Ms Campbell's absolutely right. And if that's happening, we need to look into it."

With a slight nod for encouragement, Mr King signalled to me to carry on.

"And why are Black staff who have been here for five or even ten years not being promoted? You should give experienced Black staff the opportunity to act up as SOs. That's not happening at all at the moment."

I then turned to Mr Smith. "There's also a concern that Black staff are being judged harshly on performance appraisals. Would you look into that too?"

"Yes," Mr King stated as he gazed at his colleague for backup. Mr Smith responded with a mumbled and confused "Okay."

Closing the SO office door behind me, I knew that that alone wouldn't do anything. But Mr King seemed generally willing to investigate any unfairness.

I sent the photocopied detail sheets to PO Lucas, the

Head of Race Relations. At teatime, I went to see Mr Lucas.

"Have you had a look at what I sent you? I think it needs to go to the governor. It's clear evidence that..."

"Slow down, slow down." He waved a hand at me. "I don't think it's clear evidence of anything yet. Leave it with me and I'll look into it."

I felt I was the last officer to leave the prison. Waiting for the night staff to relieve me, I sat in the unit office feeling a little deflated. On the way out, Mr Adie just couldn't help himself.

"So, when are we all going to be promoted to SO, Ms Campbell?" he laughed.

"Well at least you tried," Maria said on her way out.

21/10/05

It's been a slow week. I'm involved in setting up the Induction Programme, and it seems like I've been off the landing for most of the time—apart from doing the Transfer List every morning. Thursday evening was hell. There was a power cut and this one prisoner, Ms Renalls was a nightmare. She screamed out the hatch, "You bitch! Bring me some hot water NOW!" She constantly pushed the emergency button in her cell. At first, I tried to appease her, but she became more abusive and more demanding. I sat in the office with that deafening cell bell going all evening. I couldn't be bothered to go to the trouble of nicking her only for Governor Rose to tell her, "Don't do it again" or tell her she'll be given half an hour's loss of association. She refused to let me put her hatch up by sticking her arms out. She spent the evening shouting insults through the hatch and upsetting all the other prisoners on the unit. Sitting there on my own, I felt powerless, and I went home feeling depressed. The next day, she laid into Mr Jones in front of everyone. It's not personal. It never is. Some prisoners see the uniform and that's enough for them. This time, I gave her a warning (if a prisoner gets three warnings for poor behaviour they could lose privileges, like no TV for a few days).

SO Smith

I had a terrible argument with Mr Smith this evening.

A new prisoner arrived on D3, Ms Keller. The courts sent her to Holloway after being convicted of holding somebody at knife point. Just before the end of my shift the cell bell rung. The prisoner standing at the hatch said Ms Keller had called her the N word. I went to the SO's office to find Mr Smith with his feet on the desk flicking through a gardening magazine.

"Mr Smith, I've moved Ms Keller into a single cell and made her a high-risk prisoner after the women in her dorm reported that she called them the N word. I've written it all up, I just need you to do the risk assessment," I informed him.

"Why have you put her in a single cell? There's no need to go over the top, Ms Campbell. Put her back in the dorm we might need that cell later," he said as he returned to his magazines.

"What do you mean? This prisoner is a serious risk to other prisoners, let alone the risk to her. Are you seriously suggesting that I but her back into a cell with three Jamaicans?" I said in shock.

Irritated that I would not let him finish his magazine, he slammed it down on the desk.

"We might need that cell later for a high-risk prisoner, you're making a fuss about nothing," he insisted.

"This is a high-risk prisoner and risk assessment needs to be done on the prisoner immediately!" It all came out wrong and I knew that I had over stepped the line.

He stood up and yelled back at me so loud that I could feel my whole body cower in the doorway.

"Don't tell me how to do my job! You put her back into a dorm. That's a direct order."

I'm not sorry for questioning his decision, but I know I could have handled it differently. I wrote up the conversation and direct order from Mr Smith to cover my back. I then found a dorm with two white women and one Black woman (there were no dorms that had only White prisoners). I won't sleep easy tonight knowing I've put a violent racist in with a Black prisoner. Maybe I should have refused to move Ms Keller out of the single cell. Maybe I should have demanded that the governor on duty come up to review the situation.

"Tomorrow, try and get Mr King to do a risk assessment. You've done everything you can," said Maria over the phone from C3 unit.

Council flat

I bought some paint today, rolled up my sleeves and made a start on transforming this dark, old flat of mine into something that someone might want to buy. It will take a lot more than paint and filler to cover over the 1970s kitchen cabinets, the mould in the bathroom, and the freezing cold because I've got no central heating and the smell of shit when you walk into the block. But I plan to put money aside every month and do what I can.

Barking is where I'm headed. I'm hoping for a house with a garden. But I don't know the first thing about buying and selling houses even though I seem to advise everyone else about buying their council flat under the 'Right to Buy' Scheme. My mum has been paying Hackney Council rent for over twenty-five years.

"Sorry, but you're just not a priority. You and your mother could share a room and your two brothers should take the second bedroom. Or you could sleep in the living room," said one council officer.

I was sleeping in the living room. At the time I was so glad to move out of that tower block and into my own flat. Ms Hall and I have started going to church together on our weekends off. There are a few miracles I'm praying for, like getting out of my crumbling, tower block. It's my day off, and I did quite a bit. After I painted my bedroom, I cleaned the flat, washed and ironed all my shirts, put money on the electric meter and then read for an hour. After my hot bath, I've got my feet up to finish reading *Wild Swans* by Jung Chang. I still find reading difficult. I've never read for pleasure before, as it takes so much effort. But I enjoy learning and opening up my imagination to new experiences. There's so much I want to do, and so little time to do it. I want to go to China and Africa, buy a house, but it's all about the money. I also want to learn Spanish; I bought a beginner CD boxset in WHSmith and I'm starting with fifteen minutes practice a day.

Black SOs

I spoke to both Mr Lucas and Mr King again today about my concerns about the lack of promotional opportunities there are for Black staff. I want the prison to investigate why there are no Black Senior Officers at Holloway. The higher up the ranks you go the less colour there is. Starting at the bottom, I would say that 100% of the cleaning staff are Black; 80% of night staff; 65% of OSGs, like Sherry, that do not work directly with prisoners; 40% of officers; and 0% of SOs, POs and governors. And you can't say that the 40% of Black officers haven't been here long enough. Mr Adie and Ms Hall and a long list of others have been officers for over ten years.

"That's terrible, things need to change." Mr King nodded his head in agreement.

But Mr Lucas frowned unconvinced.

"The prison's HR policies are robust and ensure fairness. I'm sure that we do all promotions on merit only," Mr Lucas said.

Mr Jamu

"They're not going to do anything." Mr Jamu slumped down in the chair defeated.

"I told you they wouldn't, you shouldn't have bothered,"

said Mr Adie.

"What's happened?" I asked.

"The Race Relations guy, Mr Lucas, has finished his investigation and guess what? Mr Smith doesn't have a case to answer," Mr Adie replied with an anger in his voice. "The whole case has been dismissed and everything we said has been swept under the carpet."

"Don't worry Mr Jamu, God will—"

"Just stop, Ms Hall," Mr Adie cut her off. "I know you're trying to make things seem better but you're not helping."

I didn't know what to say. There was nothing any of us could think of to bring hope that things might one day change. We sat in the C3 association room. The walls seemed bare although they were plastered in public health notices. Posters about the dangers of smoking cigarettes and the benefits of regular exercise made the room feel more like a doctor's waiting room. Maria had brought in her Nigerian special spicy beef and jollof rice for us to share. There was little conversation over lunch other than statements of appreciation for Maria's cooking. Her food bought us comfort. C3 association room had become a place where we felt safe, a place where we felt free to complain about injustice and a place where we could find each other. At the end of his meal, Mr Jamu stood up.

"I'd better get back to work on B3," he said.

"I'll come with you. I need to get a box of pens," I said.

We walked in silence; he was grateful that I didn't fill the air with mindless chat. I stood at the unit office door, as Mr Jamu squeezed past Ms Hook and Mr Smith who were spread out in the office.

"Pardon me, please, I just need to get to the drawer, so I can get an extra box of pens."

They ignored him. He lent over Ms Hook and managed with a great deal of effort to get me the box of pens.

"Here you go," he said as he handed me the prized box.

"Put the kettle on, Mr Jamu. Milk, two sugars," Mr Smith said, as he repositioned his feet on the office desk.

I think something snapped in Mr Jamu in that instance.

"Why don't you make your own tea? I'm not your bloody servant" "What's your problem?"

"You're my problem."

"Now you watch it."

"Why, what are you going to do? You already have me on poor performance monitoring, you're building a case against me, so I'll lose my job and you want me to make you tea? No way. You think this is over? It's not. I'm taking this to the union."

"Come on, Mr Jamu," I urged, as I pulled him away.

"I don't know what's got into him," Mr Smith muttered to Ms Hook.

There was nothing I, or the others, could say to make Mr Jamu feel better. But telling everyone how Mr Smith looked like a rabbit about to be run down by a lorry when Mr Jamu stood up for himself made us all feel a lot better.

YOI

This evening Mr Smith put me to work with Ms Hall on the Young Offenders Unit (prisoners aged between seventeen and twenty-one) because the unit was short of staff. It was like working in a different prison – the prison from hell.

To say it's a slack unit is putting it mildly. They allow the youth to run around the wing uncontrolled. The staff on the unit are all themselves under twenty-one. This is a deliberate attempt by Governor Rose to have staff that can "relate" to young offenders. A young prisoner called Toni (unlike everywhere else in the prison, prisoners on this unit are called by their first names) wandered into the staff office and took notes of the information held against names of prisoners on the white board.

I asked her to leave.

"Who the hell are you?" she said. "You're not from this unit. You don't know how things are run round here."

One of the regular unit officers replied, "Oh, it's okay, Ms Campbell, Toni can come into the office." And then to the prisoner, "Toni, please don't talk to Ms Campbell like that."

"I can talk how I like," the prisoner said. "I run this unit."

The staff tried to laugh-off that damning comment. The office was soon flooded with prisoners nosing about the office trying to look for information about other prisoners while officers were being distracted.

I took a walk around the landing and left the regular unit officer to it. There was a commotion going on near the phones. The unit only has two phones, and with thirty-seven prisoners desperate to call their families in the two hours of evening Association time, the phones are a hot spot on every unit.

Ms Hall stood over a prisoner that looked through her like she wasn't there.

"Kelly," she said, "I'm afraid you will have to come off the phone now, as there are others waiting to make calls."

She turned her back on Ms Hall and continued her conversation, so Ms Hall moved to the other side.

"No, Kelly, you're going to have to come off the phone. Other girls are waiting." "Someone get this monkey out of my face," she said.

"If you don't hang up the phone, I will," Ms Hall said.

I asked a wing cleaner to get the other officer in the office. "Everyone back to your cells now!" I yelled.

While the other prisoners were being locked in, Ms Hall lowered her tone and lent in closer.

"Look, everyone is having to go back in their cells because of you. Come on, you know that it's not fair that one person hogs the phone."

Now surrounded by three officers Kelly said, "Go on. I dare you. I'll kill the three of you niggers if you touch this phone."

At that point, I hung up the phone. The nineteen-year-old punched me in the chest, sending me flying over a soft chair onto the floor. Then she gripped Ms Hall in a neck lock and smashed her in the head with the telephone receiver. I leapt back up, and we prised Ms Hall from her grip. The unit wing cleaners raised the alarm. Within seconds, officers from around the prison were on the scene, but the prisoner had already done the damage. Blood dripped from the telephone receiver and onto the floor below. Ms Hall had to be taken to hospital for stitches.

I felt awful. I wondered if I had handled it differently, or stepped in to help Ms Hall would it have escalated?

"I wish I never hung up the phone," I told Mr Adie.

"It's a thankless job. You don't know if you're going to get attacked just for wearing the uniform or whether you're going to get there just in time to stop a prisoner from committing suicide. You did the right thing, Ms Campbell."

Mr Adie put his arms around me. I felt comfort in his warm embrace. I looked up at him and without warning, he kissed me.

"What the hell are you doing?" I jumped back, wiping my lips shocked.

"Sorry, I thought..." He paused, confused and I waited impatiently. "I'm sorry, I misunderstood. It won't happen again," said Mr Adie.

To my relief, he put on his coat and left the office, sparing us both any further awkward embarrassment.

Amber's Blog 2018

Posted – 20th September 2018

Written in a campsite in Ghanzi, Botswana

Governor Rose introduced hot water flasks to allow prisoners to make warm drinks overnight. The flasks are made of metal and a few years later a prisoner would beat another prisoner to death with one of those metal flasks. I was not on duty at the time, but the staff member who was first on the scene that morning needed to take months off, such was the traumatic scene she witnessed. I've never really thought about the dangerous people we worked with, or that I myself was in danger. There was only one occasion when I felt intimidated by a prisoner, and that was whilst working shift on the segregation unit. There was a prisoner called Pryce, who was serving time for double murder on the segregation unit. Pryce had made threats to kill staff and was restricted to the segregation unit for her entire stay at Holloway. Together with two other officers we unlocked Pryce to collect her lunch. She had not seen me before, and eyeballed me as she slowly walked to the kitchen, picked up her lunch and walked back again.

Chapter 6

Finding What I Came For – Botswana

20th September 2018 6.00 p.m. - Ghanzi (Botswana)

The day before, we had an eight-hour drive to the campsite. From the moment the engine started until the end of the journey, they had the truck's speakers blaring out music at full volume. With the previous group, we would swop seats all the time so that no one could monopolize the rear seats where the music player is. In Livingstone, Tony, Scot, Marie and Mandy took control of the back seats and with it control of the MP3 player and the truck's speakers. I don't know if it's just me, but I find it very difficult to read and listen to loud music at the same time. At times, on the truck, it felt like I was trying to read in the middle of a rock concert. I struggled to hear Kelly, one of the other women on the tour, over the heavy metal that was playing.

"The music is too loud, don't you think? I have a splitting headache," said Kelly.

Three times, I got up and walked to the back of the unstable truck to ask them to lower the volume. Twice I was fobbed off with; "Yar, yar okay. We will." And on the third occasion, they laughed at me. I returned to my seat to reassure the others.

"Don't worry, I'll sort it, this will be the last time we have to put up with this."

The attitude of the back four has become fuel for my fire, but I've never been the type to completely lose it. Instead, I smiled and as I sat back in my seat, I plotted how I would sabotage the truck speakers and cut the MP3 player lead into little pieces.

Last night, I talked to one of the guys that work here. He said that he belongs to a tribe that has seven sub-tribes. Today in Windhoek, I bought two more books about tribes. Most of the time, I feel it's too much information. I'm going through changes sleeping in this tent, and tonight, we're sleeping in the bush again with *scorpions* crawling around everywhere. I'm constantly dirty, and I've realised that I'm not as low maintenance as I thought. I'm finding it all very stressful and emotional, but exciting at the same time. I experience a rainbow of emotions each day. Monday: anger. Tuesday: sadness. Wednesday: excitement. Thursday: frustration. Friday: pride. I have no one to share this rollercoaster with. This is my journey that I must do on my own.

21st September

4.00 p.m. - Maun (Botswana)

We've just arrived at camp. It's about twenty minutes from the town of Maun. We're going into the Okavango Delta tomorrow, which everyone's looking forward to, and I guess I am too. We had another Bushman walk this morning, but this was very different from the last one. It was a family of five and a baby who were *actual* Bush People. They were dressed in their traditional clothes of animal skins draped around their waist. The women were barechested. They walked shoeless through the dry bush covered in thorns. Even John the driver had boots on. They dug up things in the ground and explained to us what the plants were used for. It looked like weeds and roots that they where eating. They explained which ones were used for contraception, others for flavour, and some for medicine. The old woman said they no longer live the Bushman life and that they now live in the township. They were just re-enacting how they used to live. The older members of the family could remember the life in the bush. That, for me, so far has been the highlight of the tour. I felt I had received something I can take home.

22nd eptember

12.30 p.m. - Okavango Delta (Botswana)

They say the Okavango Delta is one of the most spectacular sights on earth. The 1,430 km long river starts in central Angola and enters this world of still water and never reaches the sea. It stretches out over 15,000 sq km, a maze of lagoons, channels and islands. We've just set up our tents under the shelter of the trees on our island in the heart of the Delta. There's nothing between us and the wild animals we can hear howling beyond the trees. Everyone's a little worried about hyenas or elephants wandering into the camp in the night. We got to the island by dug-out canoes, called a Mokoro. My dugout log was made of plastic. Some unfortunate travellers had the real thing filling up with water as we pushed through the long weeds.

23rd Septmeber

6.00 p.m. - Maun (Botswana)

As usual, it's been a non-stop day. I got back from the delta at about 12.00 p.m., it was fantastic. We had no water or toilets. Instead, we had black sand underfoot and mice running around everywhere. I eventually surrendered myself to the dirt. When I was a child, dirt never bothered me. Without a care in the world, I use to roll around in the stuff (probably because I didn't pay for my clothes). Anyway, like a child again, I sat in the dirt cross-legged listening to our delta guides sing African songs and I joined in the games around the fire. Dean did the Hacka, Scot sung the Scottish national anthem. Jackie and Karen sung the Dominican national anthem.

Of the nine British travellers, I was the only one who knew the words to 'God Save the Queen', but we struggled by. We then went on another walk. This time, we walked in silence behind our guide as he pointed out animal footprints and identified different animal dung. I could tell that some people in our group were bored, but I hung on to his every word. Inside I felt, if only for that moment, a part of their community, their great tradition was being handed down to me. For an hour, I forgot that everyone else was there. It was just me and my guide walking through the wild bush with herds of elephants in the background. As a mother hands down the tradition to a daughter, and father to a son, I was now taking the mantle. Through the weeds on the mokoro, I watched the sun set and I felt at peace that I got what I came for, and more.

The rest of the group are now playing volleyball. Sat at the bar alone, I must seem unsociable, but there's so much going on in my head. I'm desperate for a few minutes on my own to make sense of things. Our group of twenty-two is split into two between the loud types that stay up all night drinking, and the quiet types that are in bed by 9.00 p.m. I haven't bonded with anyone in particular, but I stick with the quiet types. I like that I'm not stuck with any one person, and when the truck stops in town for a precious ten minutes I'm able to do my own thing without compromise. The tour is pretty hard going, but I'm enjoying it.

24th September

12.30 p.m. - Kasane (Botswana)

I'm so glad I didn't go on the game drive at 6.00 this morning. I've had a bit of a 'lie in' and had a shower with a lizard and two frogs. I also had a late night yesterday knowing that I didn't have to get up at the crack of dawn like the rest of the group. Jackie and I went to the bar, which was packed with other travellers and all kinds of interesting people. We then got talking to a pilot, a young, White Kenyan man. He's at the camp site for another two nights, so I introduced him to Scot who is interested in learning to fly. I went into town this morning, wearing the traditional clothes I bought from the market, hoping to blend in as a local. In the supermarket checkout queue, I went off into a world of my own trying to work out the exchange rate. In the native language, the checkout lady yelled something at me. She had obviously been trying to get my attention for some time. With puppy eyes, I looked at her.

"Sorry, I only speak English," I said.

She then gave me the usual confused look as she worked out in her head; *Black woman + only speaks English = must be American.*

"Okay. That's 550," she said with a smile.

To the annoyance of everyone else, I continued to hold up the queue. I rummaged through my bag for the correct change. Getting a little stressed, I passed the checkout lady a handful of change. I looked up and there was the pilot. He was standing behind three people in my queue. I waved hello.

"Hi, how are you?" I yelled.

He gave me a blank look. Everyone turned and looked at him, awaiting his response. A single burst of laughter cut through the air. There were two White men sniggering behind him.

"Steve," said one, "I think that Black girl is talking to you."

He turned to them and said under his breath, "Shut it!" With that, the checkout lady slammed the till shut, and shook her head.

"He's not worth it," she said, as she handed me my receipt.

I wasn't sure whether she thought there was some kind of romantic connection between us.

"Oh no, it's nothing like that," I said.

However, I got the message that outside the walls of the campsite, even a social connection between races was rare and controversial.

6.00 p.m.

This evening, I put into action my plan of getting the MP3 player lead out of the truck. I knew it was risky. Everyone was busy preparing dinner and it looked like my only chance to have a few minutes in the truck alone. I seized the opportunity, creeping in with no one noticing. And there it was, the black MP3 player lead (the jack) that was connected to the truck's speakers. I scrambled over the back seats grabbing the lead that hung down from the overhead rack. I gave it a sharp tug. With a crash, books, water bottles and bags tumbled from above. The three-meter wire, ran along the top of the truck and was connected into the wall at the other end. The tremendous noise had alerted the group outside.

"Is there someone in the truck?" someone asked.

I froze. Footsteps coming my way became louder. I ran over to the connection point and ripped out the black red and blue wires. The truck door opened.

"What's going on in here?" said Tony. "You know you can't get anything off that shelf without everything else falling down."

We gazed at each other. I'm sure he suspected something, but the three-meter lead had dropped out of sight behind the seats.

Chapter 7

26th September 2018

3.45 p.m. - Livingstone (Zambia)

Last night, I removed the jack lead and put it in my locker. This morning, I was expecting to be interrogated, but no one suspected anything. So today, there was no music in the truck. I would have kept the lead till the end of the trip, but I felt that I had made my point, and keeping the lead any longer would have been unreasonable. We got to the camp at about 1.00 p.m., and as soon as we arrived, I spoke to the four at the back and told them why I had taken it. Scott and Marie seemed to understand what I was saying. Mandy doesn't really have an opinion of her own. And Tony gave me a hard time, just as I'd expected. He said I had forced everyone on the truck to have no music, even though everyone had their own MP3 players that they listened to with their own headphones. Then Sarah burst in with her great ability to make a bad situation worse.

"Why did you take the Jack? If you don't like the music, tough, majority vote rules," Sarah said.

10.30 p.m.

This morning, I went to Victoria Falls, one of the Seven Wonders of the World. As it was the low season, there wasn't much water falling over the top. But I can imagine how impressive it must be in its full glory. The Black family from London walked to the other side where they could get a better view, and as a result were three hours late coming back. Sarah, after ten minutes of waiting, wanted to leave them behind. But as we drove out the car park, the rest of the group insisted that we turn around and wait for them as they had no idea where the camp site was. I got out to look for them. When I got back, thirty minutes later, Jackie and her sister Karen were already back and we were now waiting for Karen's husband, John from London. I suggested that they go back to camp in a taxi since waiting around for three hours had pissed everyone off. Karen seemed fine with this suggestion. While she spoke to Sarah, I got on the truck and announced to everyone I had negotiated an agreement. Next thing I knew, Karen, a 46-year old professional, was sat on the steps of the truck with the door open and refused to let the truck take off. John the driver got out.

"You know you're being unreasonable! You're acting like an idiot, and everyone else has to suffer!"

I don't know what Sarah said to Karen, but whatever it was made Karen dig herheels in. Later, Karen told me she had tried to explain to Sarah why they had taken so long. Mimicking Sarah's harsh accent, she said, "I'm the tour leader, and you do what I say!" I had the impression that this middle-class Black family were not at all bothered by what we had seen in southern Africa. But Karen's reaction to what Sarah said may have been two weeks' worth of 'bottled up' emotion.

At the falls, there was also a market. I walked around with Sophia and Sally. Afterward, they were saying how the stallholders kept wanting to shake their hands. Sophia over-exaggerated by making it sound like these Black men were planning to drag her into a shop and rape her in broad daylight. Sarah then slipped in a side comment about how they'd better wash their hands.

"They touch your hands, you touch your face, then your food and say no more."

I later saw Sophia and Sally sterilising their hands with disinfectant.

I don't know how much more I can stand. The people on this tour make me want to scream, but I don't have a choice but to stick with it. I wonder whether I do in fact have a choice and I might be just giving myself excuses. I remember how Mr Jamu found the courage to take on Mr Smith. So maybe I could go it alone?

Hold Me, Thrill Me, Kiss Me

Christmas Day 2005

You would think Christmas Day in prison would be a depressing affair, and yes, there were a lot of tears. But overall, it was a jolly atmosphere. Prisoners packed the prison, as they always do at Christmas. A lot of offenders want to be here because they have nowhere else to go. Two weeks ago, Maria and I went around Level 3 and hung the unit Christmas decorations plus a small tree in the association rooms. This morning, the prisoners were unlocked to a full English breakfast, which they normally get only on Sundays. The unit stayed unlocked all day, and the sound of Christmas choirs drowned out the sound of tears coming from the women on the phones talking to their children. After church service, we switched on the karaoke machine in the association room, and, wearing my red Santa hat, I danced with the women in the dining room. Those whose families had long deserted them made a special effort to prepare the tables for dinner with loving care as if they were at home.

But a wedding on D3 unit made the day even more special. Technically it wasn't a real wedding, but I was there and no one can ever deny the reality of two people in love. The happy couple, nicknamed Thelma and Louise, didn't need a priest or a church. They exchanged rings and pledged their love to each other surrounded by convicts they regarded as friends and in the prison they regarded as a second home.

"Thelma, before I met you, I had nothing. No friends, no family. There's a reason for that. I've made some terrible decisions. Decisions that I've had to live with. But no matter how bad things get I know that I've always got you. You're the best thing in my life. Sometimes I can't believe how lucky I am to have you. I love you so much. I will always be here for you and I will always love you."

Thelma then unravelled a crumpled piece of paper she had been clutching. Her voice crumped with emotion as she read aloud.

"My beautiful Louise," her body shifted to one side and she stood unable to contain herself, "every day since I met you has been full of joy. This is the happiest day of my life. You bring laughter wherever you go. I'm grateful to be part of your world. Thank you for your love, your care, and your laughter. I can't imagine life without you and now I know that we will never be apart."

Ms Johnson

Things will get a lot better now that Ms Hook has been moved to B3. It all happened on the quiet. I came in one morning and Ms Hook was working on B3, which I thought was strange but paid no attention to it. However, she's worked on B3 unit every day for the last two weeks. Word is she can't handle D3. Nobody said anything, but the paper work on the SO's desk confirmed that she, not I, is now a B3 officer. What a turnaround! I'm now the most experienced staff member on D3.

"You look well," I said dishonestly to Ms Hall as we sat together in D3 unit office. She had returned to work after being off for some time. She repositioned her wig for the tenth time.

"Don't worry, your hair will grow back. A weave or hair extension will cover any scars,"

I tried to reassure her

"Get Mr King around here now," Maria said as she entered the room.

"She's a liar!" bellowed a voice from the landing.

Ms Hall stood paralyzed with fear.

"Ms Campbell," Maria barked standing in the doorway, "sit with her in the association room."

I found a young girl sobbing in the corner of the glass room. "You okay?" I asked.

I put my arm around her and she clung onto me sobbing

louder.

"I never touched her!" the dominating voice shouted from outside the safety of the glass room.

My radio, which was on the highest volume, then sounded an alarm. Officers ran onto the unit from every direction.

"It's okay," I said. "You're safe in here with me." I turned down the volume on my radio. A nurse in her reassuring uniform and Governor Rose came into the room.

As I walked out, the nurse turned to the girl and knelt at her feet.

"Lisa, can you tell me what happened?" the nurse asked.

I stepped out of a calm room onto the chaotic landing where four officers were struggling to restrain a prisoner.

"Ms Johnson, calm down!" they ordered, holding both her arms. "Screw you!" she screamed back.

"Down! Down! Down!" Maria yelled, forcing her to the ground.

Ms Hall sat in the office listening to her roar as they carried her off the unit. The officers placed the girl, aged seventeen, on D3 overnight because there were no spaces on the Young Offenders Unit. She alleged that the other prisoner in her dorm, Ms Johnson, had sexually assaulted her. The other women in the dorm of four confirmed that they were in the small box toilet together during the night.

Maria, Ms Hall and I spent the rest of the morning writing up reports.

"I thought they would have trained us how to deal with things like that during our training. When you think about it, we're unprepared to do this job," Maria said.

"Well, our training was focused on restraining prisoners. But, one thing they did tell us in training is that young offenders can't go into cells with adults. I'll love to see how Governor Rose will explain that one," I said.

"Ms Hall, are you okay?" Maria asked.

Staring down at a blank report form, a lost Ms Hall replied, "I'm fine."

"So, here it is." I pulled out of my bag a Tornado

application form and held it high in the air.

"How did you get that?" Maria asked with excitement.

"Prison service HQ sent it to me. Mr King thinks I've got what it takes."

"You've got what it takes and some, you know that. That's amazing, you're going to be a tornado officer," Maria bounced.

"That's right."

"You're going to be a tornado oficer," Maria said again with her hand over her mouth. Ms Hall started to hum the gospel song "All for Jesus" under her breath.

"Are you okay, Ms Hall?" I asked. "I'm fine, just a little tired that's all."

Mr Jamu

"I sat picking my fingernails. I think it irritated Mr Potter, but he tried to ignore it. After two minutes Mr Potter gave me a look that signalled that I needed to stop." Mr Jamu told me the story of how he took his complaint about Mr Smith all the way to the top. Mr Potter returned to reading a paper file on Mr Jamu's case, as the unlikely pair sat in silence in the grey office in the HR corridor. There was nothing on the walls to occupy Mr Jamu's mind, only a small window that opened to a brick wall. Mr Adie went with Mr Jamu some weeks ago to the union office.

"The union will take this up for you. It's discrimination," Mr Adie said to Mr Jamu as they march down the stairs.

"That's right. It's bullying and discrimination. I'm not going to let Mr Smith bully me out of the job," Mr Jamu said to Mr Adie.

Mr Jamu's new-found confidence went running back up the stairs when Mr Potter opened the union office door. The email informing everyone that Mr Potter had been elected as the new trade union rep for Holloway had not been sent out. This development put a spanner in the works.

"So, how can I help?" Mr Potter asked.

He sat slouched in the office chair with his legs spread

apart, one arm coked back. Mr Jamu looked at Mr Adie for reassurance, but what reassurance could Mr Adie give? It was a gamble. It was too late to change plan and Mr Jamu had little to lose.

"You need to put in a grievance. Don't worry, Mr Jamu, the workers united will never be defeated," Mr Potter said.

Now Mr Jamu told me how he sat in a poky little office with Mr Potter waiting for Mr Smith and the Head of HR to discuss the grievance. Mr Jamu told me he had never felt so alone.

"Sorry to keep you waiting," Mr Stewer, Head of Human Resources, said as he entered the room with Mr Smith.

"I don't think this will take long," Mr Smith said.

"No, I don't think it will," Mr Potter said.

Mr Jamu started to pick his fingernails again. "Why don't I start?" Mr Potter asked.

"Sure. We are only at the informal stage of this grievance. Let see if we can resolve matters," Mr Stewer said, as he adjusted his glasses and flicked opened the paper case file he had in front of him. Mr Stewer looked like someone who felt most comfortable in a poky, little office analysing numbers and writing reports. He looked up at Mr Potter.

"The only way this will be resolved is if Mr Jamu is taken off Poor Performance Monitoring immediately and if you take Mr Smith off Level 3," Mr Potter said to Mr Stewer.

"That's ridiculous," Mr Smith said.

Mr Stewer took off his glasses and rested them on the paper file.

"Well," Mr Stewer said, "from what I've read in the files there is certainly some justification for Mr Jamu to be on Poor Performance Monitoring. Coming in late, forgetting to update the Observation Book before his shift ends, not completing reports properly. Unless we see improvements in these areas, I'm afraid Mr Jamu will have to get a final written warning. Perhaps we need to put in place a support plan over the next few weeks and see if Mr Jamu can improve."

Mr Jamu told me he wanted to give up at that point. But Mr Potter responded quickly to Mr Stewer.

"And what happened when Ms Freeman was late for her shift? Or when Ms Hook forgot to update the Observation Book? What happened when Ms Rot didn't complete a report properly? I'll tell you what happened, Mr Smith had a quiet word in the smoking room," Mr Potter said.

"You're trying to say I'm a racist. That's ridiculous," Mr Smith said.

Mr Potter turned to Mr Stewer.

"Mr Smith's behaviour is evidence of discriminatory practices in the way he manages staff. Whether or not he means to, it is a fact that Mr Smith treats Black, Asian and Minority Ethnic staff differently. That is discrimination. I have fifteen statements from BAME staff on Level 3 all stating that they have either witnessed Senior Officer Smith turn a blind eye to racist bullying at Mr Jamu or Mr Smith has himself discriminated against them," Mr Potter said.

Mr Potter pushed a pile of statements towards Mr Stewer and Mr Smith sitting on the other side of the desk. They both braced themselves as the small but not insignificant tower of papers came towards them. Mr Potter picked up a statement that sat at the top of the pile and read aloud.

"I, Ms Hall, am a Level 3 officer. I have witnessed officers make inappropriate jokes about Mr Jamu's turban. These jokes have been made in front of Mr Smith and he has not challenged the behaviour. I can recall one particular incident—"

Mr Stewer interrupted Mr Potter.

"I think we've heard enough. I get the picture and I find this very concerning," Mr Stewer said.

Mr Jamu sat tall in his chair. He had fifteen officers and a feisty trade union rep by his side. In that moment, he knew that he had won and that his battle against Mr Smith was over.

Move to Barking

I think I've found my dream house!

I spent all day yesterday looking at properties. Things were not looking that good. The houses I viewed were out of my budget, or had a bathroom downstairs and needed too much work. Anyway, the last house I saw today was in Barking; three bedrooms, a garden to die for, a back porch, and a bathroom upstairs. It was perfect. The kitchen's small, but l can live with that. I put in an offer within five minutes of walking through the front door. A young couple with their 18-month-old baby put in an offer for my flat after a week of it going onto the market. I'm not surprised, after a lot of hard work I would be happy to stay in my beautiful flat with brand new central heating, laminate wood flooring throughout and a stylish Ikea kitchen.

On the Phones

I moved to Barking a few weeks ago and the first thing I did was sign up to help Barking Labour Party with campaigning. I can't believe that the BNP won a council by-election here a few months ago. When I was packing up to leave my flat, in my wardrobe I found: one pair of jeans, one t-shirt, a pair of trainers, one nice top for clubbing, one pair of shoes for clubbing, one tracksuit for sitting around the house, that's all the clothes I have. Why do I need clothes when I have a uniform and my whole world is my job? That's something I want to change. There is life outside the prison that I can't ignore. Racists threaten to take over my borough, I can't sit back and watch that happen. My estate, called a ward, is typical of the change that has occurred in Barking over the last decade. When I moved in, my neighbours grilled me.

"And where are you from?"

"Hackney." My answer was less exotic than they were expecting.

What was once an elderly ward with a high level of unemployment, has turned into a young multicultural area that is dead during the day, as everyone's at work, and commuters pack the buses during the rush hour.

The elderly lady that lived next door moved a few weeks before the election after living in the house for over fifty years.

"I don't feel safe here anymore," she told me.

The figures show no rise in crime in the area, but facts mean nothing to her. A large Asian family from Tower Hamlets bought the house.

On the phones is where I get the most candid responses from BNP supporters. Going down a phone list of people who said they had supported Labour in the past, an elderly man said today; "I'm not racist…" they always start with that line when they're about to say something racist "… but three more darkies have moved into my street. I mean, where do they get the money?"

I find it almost amusing watching the political parties trying to rationalise the motive for BNP support in Barking. Some people are keen to justify this resident's comments about housing for "darkies" into a rational complaint about the lack of social housing in the borough. When in fact, the majority of Black families are not council tenants, they have either bought or privately rent the house. Even if they *were* council, the point of his grievance is that the families are Black. If there were 1,000 social houses available for "local residents", he would still have a problem with three Black families moving into his street.

Some Labour councillors and MPs are calling for council housing policy changes which would give "local residents" preference over "outsiders". This would include residents having to prove that they have lived in the borough for ten years before being able to apply for council housing regardless of need.

I find this to be a populist quick-fix attempt that only legitimises an irrational myth that "non-White outsiders" are getting council housing; a myth that has racism at its heart.

I wonder to what extent the Labour Party will match the BNP "sons and daughters housing policy", the only aim of which is to keep the borough White.

Ms Brown

The day started as normal. I put down my coat, put the kettle on and had a cup of tea with Maria and Ms Hall. OSG Sherry announced over the radio that the prison roll was correct at 7.45 and I unlocked the wing cleaners Ms Brown, Ms Black and Ms White to help me unload the breakfast trolley.

"I will start unlocking," I said to Maria and Ms Hall, I opened the door of Ms Aziz cell.

"Get back!" screamed Ms Brown as she pushed me to the floor. Ms Brown then screamed in pain as the scolding hot water mixed with sugar dripped down her back. Ms Aziz's planned her attack with care to inflict as much damage as possible. I pounced to my feet. I lunged at Ms Aziz with no hesitation, disarming her. Maria was there in a flash. Ms Hall froze again, so Ms Black stepped in to help restrain Ms Aziz as she punched and kicked. Ms White raised the alarm.

Later that morning Ms Brown stood in the door of C3 association room with Ms Black and Ms White.

"It's only a surface burn. Here, look, it's just a small patch," she pulled down her top to reveal her right shoulder and the square white dressing that the doctor had put there. "You know I've got your back, Ms Campbell."

"I don't know what we would do without you there," I said.

"The Lord will bless you for your faithfulness. I'm so

sorry I didn't—"

"Don't you worry, Ms Hall," Ms Black interrupted "We all know what you've been through. You're a good prison officer. You remember that."

"What I want to know is how did she keep the water hot over night?" Maria asked.

"Ms, I wouldn't worry yourself with all of them kind of questions right now. All that matters is that you're safe," Ms Brown said.

"That's right," I agreed.

We carried on working that morning but something didn't sit right with Maria.

"What can I get Ms Brown to repay her?" I asked when the wing cleaners were out of sight.

"Ms Brown has a lot of stuff already. Considering that her family in Jamaica have disowned her and she has no one in the UK to send her money, I wonder how she can afford two packs of cigarettes a day. I mean, just look at her cell, it looks like a sweet shop."

Strip Search

In the afternoon, the segregation unit called me down to help with the strip search of a prisoner named Ms Long. I'm now an experienced officer but I hate doing strip searches and while the governor was briefing us on the situation I fidgeted. Ms Long has been in here for a few months. Her Unit report was good. She kept to herself and was polite. The courts had found her guilty of child cruelty, and had strict restrictions over who she could contact. This afternoon, the prison was alerted to the fact that she had got hold of a phone card and was calling the victim. Ms Freeman led the way into the cell and spent twenty minutes trying to persuade her to give up the phone card. "You will have to take it off me," the 55-year old said whilst sitting on the bed.

Two officers then took her arms, one on either side, and pulled her to the ground. Ms Freeman gripped her head. She struggled and fought as I pinned her legs down while the other three removed the top half of her clothing. After covering her top half with a dressing gown, they then removed the bottom half of her clothing so she was never completely naked. I felt uncomfortable listening to her cry out, "No! No! Please, no!" as we held her down and removed her clothes. Keeping her legs pinned to the floor, I consoled myself with the thought of the child she had been threatening today, and the torture she continued to inflict even from her prison cell. We retrieved the phone card from her knickers.

I went to the landing still troubled. While I was down on the segregation unit the prisoner opposite Ms Aziz's cell complained to Maria about how much she hated the wing cleaners.

"They'll get what's coming to them. Everybody hates a grass. They think they're better than us and as for that Brown, well…"

"Amber, I found out how Ms Brown can afford all her treats." I perked up to listen to what Maria had uncovered. "She's been trading hot water for cigarettes, sweets and God knows what else."

"No," I said in disbelief.

"Oh yes. And she gave Ms Aziz hot water this morning for a pack of fags."

I stood over a sobbing Ms Brown as she packed her bags. She and the other wing cleaners had slightly larger cells that were isolated in a little corner, the best cells on the unit. Now she would be move to Level 5, fired from her job as a wing cleaner in disgrace, both officers and prisoners will shun her.

"I'm so sorry Ms Campbell, I didn't mean for anyone to get hurt. I swear I didn't know Aziz was going to attack you with the water." Tears streamed down her face. "Do you think, maybe in a few months if I prove myself, I could get my job back?" she asked with hope.

I then remembered one of my favourite episodes of *Sex and the City*, where Carrie Bradshaw breaks up with Big for the second time. Carrie says a killer line that fit this situation perfectly. I turned to Ms Brown and recited the line.

"It's over. It's so over, we need a new word for over."

4.00 p.m.

We only had twenty minutes but it was enough time to go through the basics with Ms Hall. She was buying her council house in Dagenham under the 'Right to Buy', unlike me; she had no intention of ever moving.

"It would be nice to leave the kids something. Did you know the mortgage will be cheaper than the rent I pay to the council?" Ms Hall said.

"But you'll be responsible for all the repairs. You can't call the council if the boiler goes and if something big needs doing, you're on your own. It's worth getting some home emergency insurance cover. You should also pay a little bit extra on the mortgage every month as well. An extra £100 or even £50 a month will take years off your mortgage and save you thousands."

"Okay, I'll make sure I do that. God is so good, I'm truly blessed. When it all goes through the first thing I'm going to do is paint my door blue. I've always wanted a blue front door."

I leant over the office desk to inspect the of paper work and application that Ms Hall had brought in to show me. The alarm on our radios sounded.

"Immediate assistance required on Level 5. Immediate assistance required on Level 5."

I took thirty seconds to sprint up the stairs from Level 3 to Level 5. When I arrived, there were already several offices on the scene and I could barely see over the shoulders of the officers. A prisoner had tipped her bed on its legs and hung herself, it was Ms Brown.

"Let me through," I asked as I pushed my way through. I stood at the cell door helpless and watched two officers do CPR on Ms Brown. Out of the corner of my eye I noticed her suicide note. It was one line.

It's over. It's so over, we need a new word for over.

I held the doorframe, as my legs seemed to give way beneath the weight of the consequence of my flippant comment. I could never forgive myself for this. How could I carry on knowing that my stupidity cost Ms Brown her life?

"She's breathing," an officer said.

I gasped for air. A nurse pushed me out of the way when she rushed into the cell.

"There's too many officers here. Can you move away to allow the paramedics to get through?" the nurse asked.

I stumbled my way to the stairwell. Alone, I held the wall for support and cried aloud.

"God forgive me. Please Lord forgive me," I whispered through my tears so that only God could hear my prayer "Please let Ms Brown be Okay".

Thelma and Louise

7.00 p.m.

I returned to the unit and stayed on autopilot hoping to get through to the end of my shift. It was 7.00 p.m., only two hours to go.

"Lock Down. Lock Down" The prison siren rung out "Lock Down. Lock Down" OSG Sherry commanded over the radio.

The command was not one that I had heard before and I hurried the women into their cells. I masked my panic with reassuring words to the prisoners.

"Thelma and Louise have gone missing," Mr Adie told Maria, Ms Hall and I. "They are going to be moved to different prisons, Ms Hook told them both this afternoon. Thelma's going to a prison in the north."

"That's terrible, they won't see each other for years. Why can't they stay together?" Maria asked.

"Louise has a longer sentence for aggravated robbery. And after pulling off this stunt when they're found, they will definitely be separated," said Mr Adie.

"Well I hope that they've made it over the wall," I added.

"If they wanted to stay together, they shouldn't go around robbing shops with metal bars. If you can't do the time, don't do the crime," Mr Adie stated. "I suggest you get comfortable. No one's going home until they're found."

"What! I need to get home to my kids," Ms Hall protested.

I sat at the desk on D3 and watched Ms Hook running around in an excitable state, which I guess for her is normal behaviour. Every inch of the prison had to be searched. I was left on the landing, doing boring stuff and not knowing what was happening, but I was at least in the warmth. Ms Hook had to do a Fixed Post outside for an hour. With a hot cup of tea in my hand I could see Ms Hook from the office window shivering outside. Anyway, by 10.00 p.m., she broke down crying (as usual). She was in Mr King's office for an hour and twenty-three minutes being comforted. I couldn't bear it any longer so I banged on the office door and opened it before Mr King said 'come in'.

"Sorry, I didn't mean to interrupt," I said.

Ms Hook had her head in her hands crying and he sat on the other side of the desk looking disinterested.

"Campbell, if you don't mind," Ms Hook snapped.

"Ms Hook was just leaving," he turned to her. "You're okay now, aren't you?"

She walked out leaving me in the room with Mr King. I had forgotten the made-up reason I knocked on his door.

"Come in, close the door. I've been meaning to speak to you after what happen down on the block the other day. You were amazing. I'm making a coffee, do you want one? I think it's going to be a long night," said Mr King.

Governor Rose had ordered pizza for all the staff. I looked at the half-eaten ham and pineapple sat on the desk, undecided.

"Go on, have a slice."

"I'm okay, thanks."

"Just to let you know Ms Brown is doing fine," he said.

I brought my hands to my face to hide my tears. Mr King

pulled me into his embrace and wrapped his arms around me tightly.

On the other side of the prison, Ms Rot was searching the prison's large kitchen with a group of seven other officers and two OSGs.

"Look, it doesn't take seven of us to search this room, I'm going to walk the wall and then go back to control. I'll take one of the OSGs back with me," Ms Rot said to Mr Smith. She looked at Sherry and asked if she wanted to go back which she agreed to. They walked round the prison talking about various things, guided only by the moon light.

"What happened to your eye?" Sherry asked.

"Oh, nothing really. I just wrestled a prisoner with a knife to the ground and then saved her from a burning cell. No big deal," Ms Rot answered.

"Yeh, it's the kind of thing I do every day," Sherry replied

Maria stayed with Ms Hall on C3, where Ms Hall had just put down the phone to her husband.

"I hate this job."

"You don't mean that. Your one of the best officers this place has got."

"Come on Maria, if the wing cleaner wasn't there this morning to help out, you and Amber could have been seriously hurt."

"You've just lost your confidence, that's all. It's okay to be afraid. A prisoner attacked you. You could have died. It takes time to recover after going through what you have. Trust me, you're one of the best officers this place has got and I pray that God shows you how valuable you are."

"I've lost my faith. I always lose faith when I need it the most."

"Don't worry, that's what I'm here for. I'll pray for you."

Inside on D3, Ms Hook found another officer to cry to. Mr Jones had just walked past and saw her crying in the smoking room. An hour later he was still there comforting her.

"We're getting a divorce. I'm so sorry to bore you with

all this, Mr Jones," a tearful Ms Hook said.

"No, Ms Hook, it's fine. I think your husband's mad, if I had a woman like you, well... why don't you come to mine for a drink tonight? I'll cheer you up."

"Okay," Ms Hook agreed.

Outside, Ms Rot and Sherry were still walking around the prison wall "We better get back to control," Sherry wondered.

"You're beautiful you know," Ms Rot said.

"Thanks," Sherry replied. "I've heard so much about you, well about you and the other D3 officers."

"Don't listen to any of that. That isn't me, when I'm with you, this is the real me," Ms Rot moved in closer and attempted to touch her face.

"Sorry," Sherry backed away, "it's just that I'm not really."

Ms Rot took both her hands. "It's okay, I know, it's okay you don't need to explain. Let's just be friends for now and see where it goes."

On D3, I was still in Mr King's office. Over an hour had gone by, I lent up against the windowsill sipping my coffee with a cigarette in one hand. He leant up against the office desk, as we talked, our bodies almost touched.

"I saw a different side to you, Ms Campbell, on the segregation unit the other day. You're a lot braver than I thought," he smiled.

"Well, there's a lot more to me than meets the eye," I laughed. "I've applied to be a tornado officer," I said, as I took another sip of my coffee hoping for an encouraging reply. He leant in and took the coffee out of my hand. His breath was fresh and brushed up against my cheek as he placed my mug on the windowsill. His nose touched mine and I longed for our lips to unite. The phone rang, we ignored it and then over the radio we heard "Can all SOs call the control room". We ignored it. Then finally, over the radio "Can SO King call the control room immediately". He reluctantly let me go.

Outside Ms Rot and Sherry walked hand in hand.

"What will happen if they find the women?" Sherry asked. Ms Rot shrugged her shoulders. "I hope they make it over the wall."

"I think they've found the women," Ms Rot said. "How you getting home?"

Looking at her watch she said, "Well, I think I'm going to miss the last train."

"I can give you a lift home," Ms Rot said.

"Okay," Sherry answered.

"Ms Rot," SO Smith said, as he approached.

Ms Rot let go of Sherry's hand and backed away.

"We've found the women, you're needed back on the 3's so we can get the hell out of here."

They found the prisoners about midnight, hiding in the education department. The prison fell silent and listened to the two women's screams as prison officers separated them.

Amber's Blog 2018

Posted – 27th September 2018

Written in a campsite in Livingstone, Zambia

I moved to Barking from Hackney in the winter of 2005. Hackney had a large Black Caribbean population, a population that had been increasing since the 1960's. A 30-minute bus ride away, Barking was part of my playground as a child. As an adolescent, I worked at the Barking Fair every year in exchange for free rides. During that time, there were no borders, Hackney and Barking all looked the same to me. However, Barking, unlike the rest of East London, was mainly white. In a short period of time, first-generation West Africans moved into Barking transforming the area. Now Barking looks like the rest of the East End.

The far-right capitalised on people's fears about the rising Black population in the area. When I moved in, the Labour Party sent me a letter asking if I wanted to help campaign against the BNP. I jumped at the chance.

Even with the threat of a far-right controlled council, Barking Labour Party struggled to find volunteers to help with the fight back. If we were to convince residents to vote for Labour in the local elections, something had to change.

The 2006 local elections were a year away and the selection of candidates that reflected the community was the first battle that needed to be won by the local party. As a party member, I took a great deal of interest in which candidates would be for my ward. Anyone that had been a party member for a year could apply to stand, although not everyone knew what to do. A small number of gatekeepers tightly guarded the process.

"I'd be grateful for your support at Monday's meeting," said the son of a councillor to me over the phone.

The other candidates didn't even know that they could contact members directly to ask for support. After the selections had finished, I was disappointed that our councillor candidates were not reflective of the diverse community that there was in Barking. I knew then that Barking Labour Party would struggle to engage the whole community.

Chapter 8

Going it Alone (Zambia)

27th September 2018

2.00 p.m. - Livingstone (Zambia)

We arrived at camp today at about 1.00 p.m. after setting off at 7.00 a.m. In the truck, for a good four hours no one dared put on the music. Scott asked me and the others, on behalf of the four at the back, if it was okay to have some music. They put on something of Jackie's, and then asked everyone if the sound level was okay. After the initial drama last night of me taking the jack lead, we all chilled out and I spent most of the night with them at the bar. I couldn't be bothered to stay angry at Tony or Sarah.

I've just come back from the village tour, and I've now got the rest of the afternoon to relax. The village here in Livingstone is amazing. It was interesting to see how the majority of Black people here in Zambia live. Funny thing is, it's exactly how I imagined an African village. There's a tree in the centre of the village, which is the meeting point, and mud huts with straw roofs. There are up to five small huts within a large straw circle. They showed us one family circle that had five huts with twenty-two people living within that circle. However, the colourful huts are only used for sleeping and keeping things in. Living and cooking are all done outside within the privacy of the high walls of the straw circle. The family and community structure seems *so* strong. They have agreed to let me spend two nights in the village on my own. I'm excited, but nervous at the same time. But this is my chance to experience the real Africa. It's the last dinner with most of the group tonight. I'm sad, as the people I feel most comfortable with (all the quiet types) are the ones that are leaving, but I'm sure I'll be fine.

28th September

4.00 p.m. - Livingstone (Zambia) Mukuni Village

I'm here in the village, sitting on the floor overlooking a dry, golden Africa. There are a few huts to my left, and it's just so peaceful. In the background, I can hear the faint sounds of African drums and people having a good time in the main village. I was worried about coming. I thought I would feel awkward, and I do a little bit. But I've only been here an hour. I also thought I'd be imposing on the family that I'm with, but it's been okay. I'm staying with a young lady called Fairway, aged twenty-seven, who was my village tour guide yesterday. She lives with her two sisters (about ten and eight years old) and her four-year-old son. She is supporting her whole family, plus an orphaned ten-year-old boy. Her circle has two huts. The huts seem different from the ones I saw yesterday. They just had sleeping mats inside. She has a sofa, an armchair and cabinet, like a living room. The hut is divided into two by a curtain behind which she has a double bed. They live in one of the sub-villages close to the main village where the chief lives. There are 110 sub-villages around the main village which all make up Mukuni Village. In total they have a population of around 7,000 people. We will soon see the prime minister of this village. Each sub-village has an elected headman or headwoman who reports to the prime minister, like an MP. The prime minister reports to the president, and the president reports to the chief, who is part of a royal family. It's not quite a democratic system, but I was told that they have a committee looking at the chief's performance, and if the chief isn't up to scratch, they'll poison him so they can get a new chief. I'm not sure how often it happens, but I don't want to bombard my host with too many questions tonight.

29th September

7.00 a.m. - Livingstone (Zambia) Mukuni Village

I woke up this morning to my host Fairway's stereo, coming from the other side of the divide, I could hear the soulful Nigerian song *'African Queen'*. Even though they have no electricity in the huts, I think most people have battery operated TVs and stereos, as Fairway does, and everyone has a mobile phone.

Yesterday evening, I went to see the prime minister of the village, and I also went to see the female chief of the village. Before I entered her hut, Fairway explained that I had to kneel with a bowed head and clap my hands twice. With immense concentration, I did this simple thing nervously. The female chief is not married to the male chief as I had assumed. This is because there was once only a female chief ruling and when she married a chief from another village, they agreed that their daughters would also become chiefs. I was told that Mukuni Village is the only village in Zambia that has two chiefs. The conversation with the female chief was awkward as I didn't know whether it was appropriate for me to question her about her role, so I played it safe and didn't say much at all. She asked me if I was a "negro", on seeing my puzzled facial reaction, she asked Fairway.

"What is she?" the chief asked Fairway.

She tried to clarify her question. "I call myself an African. What do you call yourself?" said the chief to me.

"Black" I responded.

I couldn't understand her confusion as I have dark skin with prominent Black features. But born in England to Jamaican parents, 400 years away from the continent, did I still consider myself as an African? I had felt sad when reading Ekow Eshun's experiences of being bullied at school at the hands of Caribbean children because his parents were African.

*'Born in England to Jamaican parents, it seemed to me

they drew from their dual heritage without angst – in the patois they traded and the exercise books they stickered with the Jamaican flag. In their height, and the swagger with which the proceeded, three abreast, down the school corridor, I saw a self-assurance I could never match. For Dwayne and his crew, being West Indian and British brought with it an ineffable cool... Thanks to that generation, black people were garnering a level of popular respect in Britain they'd never before held. Unless you came from Africa - in which case you were still nobody' (Eshun, 2005)

I realised that I have very little knowledge about an important part of my identity. Ekow Eshan said that he saw *Dwayne* some years later and he had become a "born-again African". Eshan concluded that he was searching for an idealistic homeland that doesn't exist. I have no illusions about the reality of Africa as "home". I have accepted that my home can only be Britain. However, I'll never forget that feeling I had when I first stepped off the plane in Cape Town, it's a feeling that many Black people born in Europe and America experience. The Black American Nathan McCall describes his experience thus:

"... That is why Black Americans like me constantly search for belonging and that is why we are naturally drawn to Africa - because, technically, it is our home. Our ancestors were forcibly torn from here. Even as I know that Africa is "home", the curious glances I get from Cape Town blacks everywhere indicate that they recognise me for what I am - a foreigner, puzzling hybrid who stands out as a kind of contradiction in terms - a black American." (Makgoba: 2000)

Everyone in the village seems to know each other. After seeing the chief, Fairway and I walked back through the village, back down the long strip of dirt road. The sunset lit up the sky with bright oranges and golds. There were people in the streets with music coming from every direction. Fairway and I went to a bar and sat outside in the warm air as everyone does. We sat in a circle with four of my host friends. We had one bottle of beer and one glass, which we passed round. I spoke mainly with James who was one of the village tour guides. We talked about Tony Blair and Gordon Brown. I don't know why I was so surprised that he knew so much about British politics. After all, they have full access to the news. I guess it must say something about my preconceptions about African villagers.

Fairway cooked "Shema" ground rice, spinach and a tomato soup dip. We also had two little pieces of sausage each. I never for a moment thought they were poor until I saw those two little pieces of sausage meat at the bottom of my tin bowl. The meal was delicious. I made a complete mess with my food. It found its way all over the floor, the table and even on my clothes as I'm not use to eating with my hands. Fairway's sisters found it hilarious as I tucked in enthusiastically, regardless.

10.00 a.m.

Fairway went to work this morning at 8.00 a.m. and said that she'll be back by midday. She's left me in the care of her two sisters and her twenty-five-year-old brother, Kevin, who's come over with his two-year old son to entertain me. He lives in another sub-village about fifteen minutes walk from here. I went into the main village with him and Fairway's sisters. I'm beginning to recognize faces, and most people recognise me. I bought a traditional African wrap in the village, and Fairway gave me one last night as a present. I feel that these twenty-four hours will change me both inside and out.

12.30 p.m.

Kevin and I went back into the main village where we had a game of pool in one of the bars. I was a terrible player, but by the end of the game, the poolroom was full with about twenty guys all joking and pushing each other on to challenge the winner, Kevin, to a game. A drunken man tried to say hello but he was intercepted and dragged away quickly by one of Kevin's friends.

I needed to change some of my US dollars last night, so they took me to see one guy who I met at the craft market the day before. He's intent on making me his second wife, and he's a joker in this community. He took me to one side and pulled out a handful of cash—he's also the village money exchange bureau. Again this morning, I needed to change money so I could buy my wrap in the market. I went to see him again, but this time he took me to his boss. She was an overweight woman wearing a tightly-fitted Jamaican T-shirt. In the shop, from behind the counter, she looked me up and down and said; "How much does she want?" She seemed to prefer to talk to the man rather than directly to me. Later, in the pool room, a young boy, aged about ten, ran in looking for somewhere to hide a small bundle he had in his hand. He shoved it behind my chair. The women in the Jamaican T-shirt burst into the crowded room, screaming in rage. I later unwrapped the cloth bundle to find a small loaf of bread that the boy had stolen from her shop. She screamed and shouted trying to justify her anger to everyone. The room emptied until it was just Kevin and I sitting there when he said, "Let's go." Walking back through the village, I saw the boy.

"I think you forgot something," I said, as I handed him the bundle.

In general, women selling their wares mostly ran market stalls, there were also several little grocery shops, also run by women. The men, meanwhile, seemed to be occupied in the craft market or involved in the production of the manufactured goods being sold. This community's structure, like the Bushman's, seemed to be very different from western society. The responsibilities of working and family seemed to be shared within the community, and equally between the genders. Each village has a function, like the main village does craft and the other smaller villages do farming. Fairway explained that in a farming village, you might sell some of your crops in the main village so you have money to buy the things you can't grow. Shop keepers in town only need money to buy the crops from the farmers, and so the cycle continues. I work not just for food, but also to pay for my car, my clothes, my house, pay my general bills and to keep up with the Joneses. It makes me realise how simply you can live and be happy.

6.30 p.m. - Campsite

I've arrived back at the campsite, and I thought I'd be happy to be back as I didn't want to impose on my host for too long. But as soon as I entered the camp, I once again felt cut-off and isolated from the Africa that I so long to see. On seeing my new group, I felt even more depressed. From the "old" group, I'm left with the loudest and most irritating: Tony, Mandy, Scott, and his girlfriend Marie. Six young women have joined us, all in their early-to-mid twenties (three Australians, two New Zealanders and one English). They all began their trip in Johannesburg five days ago. We were having our first dinner when Sarah said that she foresees trouble in town. Zambia is in the middle of elections (which so far have been very peaceful). But she said that one candidate was "anti-tourist". The rest of the group thought this was ridiculous as the country is "dependent" on tourism and that villages like Mukuni wouldn't be able to "survive" without the tourist dollar. I informed everyone that Mukuni Village, which is seven hundred years old, is made up of 110 self-sufficient villages and the village was not at all "dependent" on tourism. Silence followed my little speech. If I felt frustrated by the group before, then the next three weeks with this lot will be interesting.

This afternoon, the elections captivated everyone in the village. Even the kids, just ten- year olds, huddled around the radio eager to hear the announcements and promises of each candidate. MMD have been ruling the country for fifteen years, and the current president has been in power for five years. Most people in the village were rooting for the 45-year old who also is the richest man in Zambia. I think the majority were supporting him because of his tribal connections. Election talk consumed the village all day, it was the talk of the pool room, the market, and the school playground. The excitement was infectious. From the Livingstone Camp site, I could hear the noise from the main town, as people were celebrating when the results started to come in.

30th September

4.15 p.m. - Lusaka (Zambia)

We're now at another campsite near the capital of Zambia, which is Lusaka. As usual, we're located away from everyday people, which makes me feel trapped.

All day, I've been thinking about the village. I told Kevin, Fairway's brother in the village, that a flight to London would cost about £700. That worked out to be 5.6 million kwacha. I'll never forget the look on his face when he saw the amount on my mobile phone calculator. It might as well have been 5.6 million *pounds*. It was a figure that was unobtainable. I don't think they would want to live my life, if they really knew what it consisted of, anyway. In many ways, I envy the life they have. But the things we in the West take for granted, like electricity and running water for each home, could make things so much easier. And toilets! It's not possible to compare my perceived "wealth" with their "poverty", which I'm tempted to do. Our ways of life are different and are set up to achieve different goals. We can learn and exchange lessons from both worlds. Technology has and should continue to benefit such communities, but there is so much we could learn from them, such as a return to a way of life that works with nature and not against it.

1st October

10.30 a.m. - Chipata (Zambia)

Last night, I was considering leaving the tour. It is depressing enough to be imprisoned in the campsite, unable to leave, as we're miles from any town. We were sitting around the fire, as usual, when Sarah asked the group what they wanted to eat as she was going shopping for the week. I suggested an African meal, which we could eat in the traditional manner (with our hands). She seemed okay about it. John the driver then shouted; "Well I'm going to eat somewhere else, I'm not eating any of that shit!" Most of the group has no idea what an African meal consists of, so he suggested it was chicken feet and worms—which got everyone's imagination going leaving the group looking disgusted. I said that it didn't matter if he liked it, the purpose was to introduce the group to some traditional African food.

"It would be like going to Italy and not trying a pizza, or returning from home after six weeks in Spain and not even knowing that paella was a traditional Spanish dish," I insisted.

On seeing my enraged bloodshot eyes, John tried to retract what he had said, claiming that he was only joking. But it was too late. The damage had been done. I heard anarrogance in his voice, an arrogance that wanted to undermine African culture. I couldn't bear to even look at him, and I wished I could nurse my anger towards him forever. But after about an hour, I had to let the matter go. I'm glad I made a stand. At the end of the evening, I thought about what I was getting out of this tour when it was an uphill struggle just to get some African food.

Last night, instead of storming back to my tent in a rage, I stayed with the group and played the games that the guides taught us in the Delta. I'm wearing my African wrap, which I've been wearing since I got back from the village. The colourful African prints have for me become a way of expressing what I feel. Or maybe this African print skirt is in fact a way of me hiding the way I feel.

"I need to find myself," I had told my husband before I left.

After all these years of marriage, and the years married to the job did I really need to explain why I need some me time?

A solo trip through Africa is what I need to do. Maybe I need to rediscover the me that loves exploring.

Chapter 9

2nd October 2018

10.30 p.m. - Kande Beach (Malawi)

We're now in Malawi, at Kande Beach where we will stay for the next four nights. We arrived at camp at around 5.00 p.m. after leaving at seven this morning. The ten-hour drive didn't seem too long as the scenery on the way was stunning. Every thirty minutes, we seemed to be driving past a roadside village. And if for only for a few seconds, I saw a snapshot of their lives as people went about their 'day-to-day' routines. The earth was a rich terracotta that stood out strong among the other sandy browns and dark oak colours of the land. Their huts didn't clash with God's beauty. Instead, they used the land and were part of it. As we got closer to Kande Beach, the water breathed life into everything. The red earth faded, and lush green hills that looked like they were covered in dense forest surrounded us. Listening to the soothing hum of the truck wheels against the dirt road, my mind wandered back to the more difficult times in the prison service.

'Where do Broken Hearts Go?'

Ms Bennett

13th April 2006

I had to restrain Ms Bennett today. Ms Bennett is an 18-year old Black girl. Like most teenagers, she has a spotty face and a tiny waist. The system has already given up on her because she is so addicted to drugs. At lunchtime, she threw a chair at Mr Jones when she was told there was no second helpings. I don't know whether it's the drugs that have fried her brain, or because she is so young and immature. She is constantly in and out of Holloway. Six months here, three months there. This time, it's for shoplifting. A few days earlier, I asked her what happened.

"A stupid old lady grassed me up," she said.

From her way of thinking, the reason she is in prison is the fault of a member of the public who had reported her for stealing goods and not because she had done anything wrong.

We can't put her on the youth offending unit or any other landing because she is too much to handle, so she will stay with us on D3. In a way, I feel sorry for her. She's got no one on the outside, and she's so young. I took control of her right arm. She fought all the way, and we had to carry her down the stairs to the segregation unit.

The Argument

In passing, Mr King said to me, "I can meet you for lunch later on Holloway Road if you like."

"Sure," I replied.

I was on induction again this morning and was counting down the minutes to lunch time. I was doing Induction with an officer from Level 4. I said to Mr King that I'm supposed to be training Level 3 staff to deliver the programme, so I'm not the only one that can do it. So he put Mr Potter with me. Well, Mr Potter told me he's not doing "liberal shit" and refused to do it. Mr Potter made his opinions known to Governor Rose, who was walking through the unit. Next thing I knew, Governor Rose had put me back with the officer from Level 4.

"Why have you taken Mr Potter off the 'Induction Programme'?" I asked Governor Rose.

"It's my decision and I don't need to give you an explanation," she said with her nose in the air.

"As officers, we need to explain our everyday decisions to prisoners. Not because we have to, but because we know it's important that they understand our reasoning."

"Ms Campbell, I don't need to give you a reason for my decision. And I don't appreciate being questioned," Governor Rose insisted.

"The fact is, it was easier for you to tell me that you don't have to explain yourself than to tell loud mouth Mr Potter to go on induction, wasn't it?" I asked.

Later, Mr King called me in and said that my questioning of the Governor was "rude and disrespectful".

"Governor Rose said that you were aggressive, it's clear that you have an attitude problem."

As I sat there in complete shock, I tried to stop a fit of the giggles coming on that would have further enraged him. I mean, you either laugh or cry.

"Do you think this is funny?" he said.

"No, it's not funny at all. I work so hard. I'm never late. I'm not rude. And I don't talk down to people. It's quite hurtful when I think of all the rude people I have to work with. But as soon as I open my mouth, I'm the one with the 'attitude problem'. I can't believe that she described me as aggressive."

"Get your priorities straight. You need to get back to basics." His voice became raised. "Maybe you need a break from induction?"

"You can't take induction off me. I've built that up from scratch," I said. "Well I'll put you on B3 then, where you can get back to basics," he said.

"Okay, I'm sorry I pissed off precious Governor Rose, but if the pair of you had the guts to stand up to Mr Potter instead of tiptoeing around him like—"

"That's enough!" he snapped, thumping his fist down on the desk and I knew then that I had gone too far.

"Do what you're told, no questions. Is that clear?"

"Fine," I replied. As I went to leave, he stopped me with the final blow.

"Ms Campbell, I've denied your Tornado application, you're not ready to be a riot officer

– come back to me when you've learnt some manners."

I could say nothing, the injustice of it all was too much to bear. I opened the office door and went to walk out.

"Ms Campbell" – I turned around to face him but he didn't look up from the paper work on his desk – "I can't meet at lunch I'm busy" he said.

"Fine," I replied.

Hackney 1996

I remembered what high hopes I once had. How I believed that all I needed was hard work and determination.

But people couldn't see beyond the sixteen-year-old with no qualifications that stood in front of them. I knew that I could do an advanced course, but I also knew that the college admissions department would take one look at my application and dismiss me. The reality of my position was that I would often struggle to spell my name and address. I would carry a card with basic information in case I was asked to complete a form or something. With my grades, I would be lucky to get onto an intermediate course.

I put together a video presentation of all my work on the eight-week City & Guilds course that I had just completed, references from the evening English GCSE course teacher and the independent dyslexia specialists that I had seen. Without an appointment, I took the bus down to Hackney College. I stood at the gates rehearsing a pitch.

"Sorry, all applications should be sent to the admissions department," the head of the media department said as he continued to walk past me.

"Please just watch this," I said as I flung the video tape into his hand.

He looked at me and maybe he saw there was more to me than what would be on the application form.

I didn't have the money to travel out of east London. I had made copies of my work and stood in the rain waiting for the college tutors of each college. On Monday, I received a rejection letter from Newham College. On Tuesday, the letter from Barking College started with 'Unfortunately' and I didn't read the rest. On Wednesday, the letter from Walthamstow College came they said I could do the foundation course. Why was I disappointed? I knew that I did not have the grades to get on to an advanced course Only Havering College and Hackney College hadn't got back to me. On Thursday, a letter came. On Friday, I still hadn't opened the letter that had come on Thursday.

"Hello, am I speaking to Amber Campbell?" the voice on the other end of the phone said to me.

"Yes."

"Hi Amber. I'm the college tutor from Hackney College. You gave me a video of your work as I left the college last week."

"Yes."

"Well, your work and determination really impressed me. So, we would like to offer you a place on the advanced media course here at Hackney College."

After the call, I opened the letter that had been sat on the table for twenty-four hours. It was from Havering College also offering me a place on their advanced course.

Mr King and Ms Rot Promoted

Things are not too good at the moment. Governor Rose has promoted Mr King to Principal Officer. The first thing he did was promote Ms Rot to Senior Officer and things are going as I expected with her in that position.

"How can Mr King promote Ms Rot to Senior Officer over Mr Adie and Ms Hall. She has only been an officer for five years and Mr Adie has been at Holloway for over ten years and Ms Hall seven years?" I complained to Mr Lucas, the Race Relations PO.

"Well, Ms Campbell, it's not as simple as that. Ms Hall's only part time and she's had a total of two years off on maternity leave. Mr Adie, well I don't know, a lot may have to do with his poor attitude. A PO needs to pick people he feels he can work with," said Mr Lucas.

"If a PO can choose people based on who they feel they can get along with, then they are just going to keep choosing officers that they sit in the smoking rooms with and go to the pub with."

"Are you saying that Mr King is racist?" Mr Lucas asked.

"No, but maybe the system is racist. And there's no chance for Ms Hall. Her service seems to count for nothing. It's just jobs for the boys," I said.

"Maybe you should talk to Mr King, as this seems to be a Level 3 issue," Mr Lucas suggested.

I had spoken to Mr King on several occasions, before he made PO, about the glass ceiling that had stopped Black officers moving up the ranks. Maybe Mr Adie was right? Mr King was no different from all the other POs before him. Even if I thought Mr Adie was wrong, my 'day-to-day' relationship with Mr King was now just a series of cold business transactions.

That evening, I overheard Mr Smith giving Ms Rot a pep talk.

"You're a Senior Officer now, it's completely different from being an officer. If you're going to get the respect of officers, you can't show any weakness. You think you're going to have a hard time with Ms Campbell, Mr Adie and that lot," Mr Smith went on with on foot on the desk and a cup of tea in is hand. "No, you're going to have a hard time from Ms Hook and Mr Potter, that's who you need to win over – you've got to get their respect."

Ms Rot looked worried. "I'm not as tough as everyone thinks, there's a side to me that they don't see," she said.

"Sure, you're tough enough. I know you are, just don't let anyone see any weakness," Mr Smith said.

I walked into the unit office at teatime today to find Ms Hook sitting opposite Mr Jones with a smile on her face. I don't think I have ever seen her smile. The range of her facial emotions that I had become accustomed to were: angry, upset and miserable. The smile seemed out of place on her face and did not suit her at all.

"Some of the prisoners have come down with the flu, it won't be long before we all get it," Ms Hook said to Mr Jones.

"I was feeling a little off this morning, but you've turned me on," Mr Jones said.

Ms Hook threw her head back and cackled.

"Oh Mr Jones, you're so funny," Ms Hook said.

"It wasn't that funny," I said.

"You've got no sense of humour, Ms Campbell," Mr Jones said.

"I do. I just don't find cheesy over used chat-up lines funny." "Wooo," Mr Jones laughed.

Ms Hook didn't find me funny, which was just as well because I didn't mean it as a joke. Her face returned to its usual bitter look.

Governor Fox

Ms Bennett is back. This morning, Ms Rot sent me down to the segregation unit to calm her down after she had kicked off in reception, but there was nothing I could say to her to calm her down. She hung her arms out of the cell hatch refusing to allow staff to close it, spitting at anyone that walked by and shouting abuse.

"The new governor is on his way down," Mr Jones announced.

That remark raised some eyebrows and a few smiles in

the office. The prison ranking system has what we call the Number One Governor. I've never seen the Number One on the landing. In fact, I've spoken to him only once, and that was when I reversed my car into his in the staff car park. Governor Rose is the prison's deputy governor. Below her there are about five junior governors responsible for different areas of the prison. The governors might walk round once a day. Today, we got a new junior governor, Governor Fox.

"So, what's with the new governor?" I said, feeling very much out of the loop. "You'll see," they told me.

A six foot-plus man in his mid-sixties with slick back greying hair burst into the office. He was muscular and full of energy.

"So, what's going on here?" Governor Fox said in a strong, northern accent.

After a short debrief, Governor Fox said, "Well, come on then" and he led the way to Ms Bennett's cell.

Confused, I whispered to another officer, "Where's he going?" and followed. When we got to the cell, he stopped and looked at the problem prisoner.

"Right, Ms Bennett. You need to take your arms out the hatch now," he demanded. In response, Ms Bennett spat in his face. With that, he sprang into action and grabbed both her arms, forced them together and pushed her body back into the cell. Then he slammed the hatch shut.

The other three officers and I stood speechless. "Has anyone got a tissue?" he asked.

I have never seen a governor being "hands on" with a prisoner. Governors normally stand at the other end of the unit "observing" and inching backward if there's any sign of blood. It was also weird to see a working-class governor.

Over lunch, the other Level 3 officers gathered in the association room to hear what happened. I told them like it was the stuff of folk legends.

"They say he came up through the ranks as a prison officer," I said. "A proper prison officer; like you and me," I went on.

"It can't be true," Maria said as the other disbelieving officers shook their heads. "It's true, I tell you," I insisted. "I've seen him with my own eyes."

By the afternoon, rumours about the new governor had engulfed the prison.

"Hey, Ms Campbell," said a Level 4 officer. "Have you heard about the Silver Fox?" "The Silver Fox?"

"Yeh, the new Irish Governor who's eight feet tall and single-handedly restrained two prisoners on segregation this morning?"

The prison, however, is a much calmer and safer place than it once was. I mean that no one, other than Mr Smith, want us to go back to the 1980s when prisoners were being abused by staff. However, Governor Fox's arrival has created such a stir because the prison leadership is comprised of supermarket managers and twenty- year-old university graduates who treat prisoners like customers. I wouldn't mind if I felt it was working and if I didn't see so many offenders back here again—and, more to the point, *glad* to be back. This softly-softly approach needs teeth.

Ms Rot strolled down Holloway Road 'hand in hand' with Sherry.

"I know you wanted to take me out for my birthday but my mum and dad are laying on a big family get together, so I'm not going to be around all day. It would be nice for you to meet my family. I'm not hiding you or anything. I'm getting used to this myself. My family are going to be pretty shocked that I'm now gay," Sherry said.

"It's fine. You can introduce me when you're ready. Maybe you're not gay, straight or bi. Maybe we're just two people that have fallen in love?" Ms Rot said.

"Yes. But it's not right. I'm not ashamed to be with you and I want to tell everyone, all my family, that we're in love," Sherry said.

"Whenever you're ready. I need to pop into the bank. Are you okay to walk back to the prison on your own? I'll meet up with you after my shift," Ms Rot said.

"Sure."

Terry

It surprised me to learn that an old friend of mine from school is a BNP member. Terry is in his early forties and is a popular character in our predominantly Black church in Barking. He works all the hours God sends as a security guard and has been dating a mixed-race friend of mine. I couldn't understand, while helping him to serve the teas and coffees after Sunday service.

"I'm not a racist, but it's not fair that I'm still on the council waiting list while all these foreigners get places before me. The next time you go into Tesco's, look at how many White people there are at the checkout. I bet there's hardly any. These foreigners come over here and take all our jobs it's not fair," Terry said.

I struggle to believe that a man that I've known for so long is just a racist. Maybe I was wrong, but the lack of working-class jobs and adequate housing also seems to be masking deeper issues. Terry has a job he's happy in and the council has just given him his own flat, but he's still a member of the BNP.

He said twice that it was "not fair", and what I got from him was a deep sense of injustice. He feels he has the right to housing, a job and a good standard of life. However, what he was saying was that he has *more* of a right to those things because he is White British. I watched him trying to work out the puzzle in his own head. "How can you have non-White people doing well when White people are struggling?"

Terry slipped me a monthly magazine that he gets from the BNP. It's called; "IDENTITY". He claimed that White working-class people have lost their identity, and in a Britain, which is now a classless society, they are irrelevant and dismissed with no voice.

23/11/05

I've been thinking about my conversation with Terry last

weekend. If you go beneath the surface of housing and jobs, you'll find the issue of race at the heart of it, but go deeper still and you'll find the issue of identity at the core. Since the end of the Second World War and the end of empire, what it means to be British has changed, with globalisation and the end of traditional working-class trades. By the time I was born what it meant to be working class had changed, but changed to what?

The colourless and classless Britain may only exist in the minds of White middle-class politicians. Identity is not something that can be achieved through a quick fix populist policy, but has been defined from the bottom up.

Ms Locksmith

I had a dream last night that I had to restrain a prisoner on my own while Ms Hook and Mr Potter looked on. In the dream, I got the wing cleaner to press the alarm. When Mr King came running around, I told him what had happened, but he didn't seem that bothered and said nothing to the two officers that just stood there. Well, my dream kind of came true today.

I'm now Ms Locksmith's personal officer. I first met the teenager on night duty when she tried to kill herself, I then saved her again when she attempted suicide on the Vulnerable Prisoner Unit. Ms Locksmith is a serious and constant self-harmer. She mopes around the unit with her head hung low, and her greasy brown hair draped over her face. I found out that she is fluent in German and I used her to translate when talking to a German-speaking prisoner. I asked Ms Locksmith if she had lived in Germany, but she said that she had learned it in school—where she finished with 5 GCSE's grade A*. She's in for arson. Mr King asked me to search Ms Locksmith whenever she comes out of the bathroom to make sure she doesn't take razors back to her cell. When she came out of the bathroom, I informed her that I needed to search her. She refused point bank. Mr King said that there's nothing that we could do, because I should have been watching her in the bathroom.

"With only two officers on the landing and thirty-six other prisoners to oversee, I was supposed to stand in the bathroom with her? If she's going to refuse to let me search her pockets, she's hardly likely to let me watch her take a bath," I said.

The thing that upset me was why did he ask me to do something that he knew I couldn't enforce? Mr King then came out of his office and started joking around with her. Suddenly, I was the bad guy, and Ms Locksmith has never had a problem with me. I was furious and at the end of my shift, I went around to the SO's office to tell him he should have backed me up.

"You should have been doing your job properly in the first place!" he said. And that was that.

Ms Rot

Standing in line to collect her keys in the morning Ms Rot looked at Ms Hook, as she approached her.

"Congratulations, mate," Ms Hook greeted Ms Rot.

"We on for lunch later?" Sherry said to Ms Rot from behind the glass.

"What?" Ms Rot said.

"You know this OSG?" Ms Hook asked Ms Rot.

Looking back at Ms Hook and Mr Smith who was also standing in line, Ms Rot replied "No". She then grabbed her keys and hurried away.

Ms Rot showed her true colours again, but this time in front of Mr King. As Ms Locksmith's personal officer, all I wanted to do was to give her a job as a wing cleaner. I think the job would give her some encouragement as she refuses to go to education, or interact with others. Her self-harm is increasing, and I want to push her a little. At the same time, she would still feel safe on D3. Ms Rot said Ms Locksmith had done nothing to deserve the post. In the SO's office, when I tried to reason with Ms Rot, I was calm and respectful. But she got defensive and took up an unreasonable position. As we debated back and forth, I knew that if I could just hold out a bit longer, I could come out of it smelling like roses. Mr King sat there listening, as I probed her just a little bit further. I also knew he was on my side, or he would have spoken up against me. I think he was waiting for me to leave before he spoke to her. It would be unprofessional for a PO to disagree with his SO in front of an officer. But she blew her chance to be spared that humiliation when she barked, "I said no! Get it into your thick head, no!"

At that, I looked at Mr King whose face was red with anger. He stood up and barked back, "Ms Rot. You won't be a senior officer for long if you talk to officers like that. I won't have it, you understand!"

He turned to me and said, "Tell Ms Locksmith, she can start the job today." Walking away from the closed door of the SO office, I could hear him yelling at her.

Later that afternoon, when the prisoners were locked in their cells waiting for their evening meal, I joined Maria, Mr Adie, and Mr Jones as usual in C3 association room. Ms Hook, Mr Potter, Ms Freeman and Mr Smith went to D3 smoking room as usual. It was common for the Level 3 SOs to go to the D3 smoking room for their break. When Ms Rot approached the small room, Ms Hook stood in the door way with her back up against the door frame and her leg stretched out.

"Where have you been sneaking off to on your tea breaks for the last four weeks?" asked Ms Hook.

"Rumour has it you've bagged yourself an OSG," Mr Potter laughed from inside the room, rolling a cigarette.

The sound of the lift doors opening interrupted her.

"Oh, here she comes now," smiled Ms Hook. "Excuse me," Ms Hook yelled out to Sherry.

Sherry approached.

"Leave it out, Hook," Ms Rot said.

Ms Freeman and Mr Potter stepped on to the landing to hear what Ms Hook was going to say to Sherry.

"Sorry, but rumours are going around about you and our senior officer?" Ms Hook asked Sherry.

Sherry looked at Ms Rot.

"I haven't been keeping up to date with the latest Holloway gossip," Ms Rot said.

"So, it's not true?" Ms Hook asked.

"No, of course not," Ms Rot said.

"No, I didn't think it was true." Ms Hook then turned to Sherry. "I mean, why would a senior officer have anything to do with an OSG?"

Ms Rot looked at Sherry with regret. An announcement that "the Prison Role was correct" sounded over the radio, which meant that the officer's break was over. Ms Hook and Mr Potter went back to the office.

"I think you've just made a big mistake," Ms Freeman said to Ms Rot.

Ms Rot paused for a moment alone on the landing. She raced to the landing door, ran down the stairs and ran to the trolley route. She could see Sherry coming out the lift at the other end.

"Sherry!" she yelled. "Sherry!" Ms Rot yelled again Ms Rot grabbed her saying that she was sorry. "No! Get your hands off me," Sherry said.

Ms Locksmith

Ms Locksmith attacked Ms Bennett today. The attack was unprovoked and out of character for Ms Locksmith. Walking down to the segregation unit to see her I knew that there must be more to this than she was telling me, but she said nothing. Mr King went down to see if she would open up to him. Ms Locksmith broke down and told Mr King everything. Mr Smith had asked her to beat up Ms Bennett because she had been disrespectful to him. At first, she refused because she knew that she would lose her wing cleaning job on D3. But Mr Smith continued to press her saying that if she didn't do it, he would have her transferred to Durham. On hearing that she agreed to attack Ms Bennett, Ms Locksmith thought Mr King did not believe her, but she realised that his silence was anger.

"You can trust me. Don't worry, this will stop," he reassured her.

This evening, Mr Smith was walked to the gate. Being "walked to the gate" is the walk of shame that an officer has to endure when a governor, flanked by two or three senior officers, come to get you on the landing, strip you of your prison keys and escorts you to the prison gates. It all happened so quickly. Mr King reported him, and spent the rest of the evening hiding in the SO office while two POs and Governor Rose escorted the proud Mr Smith off the landing. Mr King was scared to leave the prison because Mr Smith was waiting for him in the staff car park with a baseball bat.

While Mr King was busy sorting out Mr Smith, I was on my own. I had to deal with the unit that suddenly went mental. Ms Davis slashed her body repeatedly with a razor. Ms Weavers then also wanted to kill herself and Ms Bennett screamed obscenities from her hatch.

Fast Track Programme

Since Mr King rejected my application to become a tornado officer I've been walking around the prison in mourning for the prison officer that I had hoped to be. Talking about it with others just makes me feel more angry. Thinking about how all my dreams have now been thrown down the drain so easily makes me cry. And I'm powerless to do anything about it.

"Put it to the Lord in prayer, and move forward," Ms Hall advised.

But how can I move forward when management think I have an attitude problem. I can't even look at Mr King now without the sudden urge to either attack him, or burst into tears.

I was on Induction again today. The last few days have shown me how much I care about the Induction Programme. When I take up a project, I get so involved—which I don't feel is a negative thing. I just have to learn how to reign it in a little. I confronted Governor Rose because I want the Induction Programme to last beyond me. The hurt in me wants to give up, but the fight in me won't let it go, and I'm determined to prove that I am more than capable.

I sat in the C3 association room with Ms Hall, Mr Adie, Mr Jamu and Mr Jones eating lunch, an excited Maria walked in.

"I've printed out the application for the 'Fast Track Graduate Programme'. I'll make a start on it today. The closing date is next week. You never know, in twenty-four months, I could be a prison governor?" Maria said, hoping for encouragement.

I thought if I can't say anything positive, it might be best not to say anything at all.

"You'll never get through. They want posh 21-year olds from top universities, not Black immigrant prison officers," Mr Adie said.

"Maria has a Master's degree and has prison service experience," said a defensive Ms Hall.

"They'll tell her she's over qualified then," laughed Mr Adie.

"Don't listen to Mr Adie, Maria. If you're good enough you'll get through," said Mr Jones.

"What's being good enough have to do with it? If merit has anything to do with it, then why is Ms Campbell being prevented from applying to Tornado?" Mr Adie asked.

Sitting in the corner, with my Pot Noddle, I was hoping not to get drawn into the conversation. I thought I would struggle to say anything that would encourage Maria to apply, but as the words left my mouth, I thought this could happen for Maria. Who cares if I can't be a tornado officer? My best friend has a good shot at becoming a prison governor and it was my job to do all I could to encourage her.

"My situation is completely different. The application is just the first stage. Maria will need to pass all kinds of test before she even gets an interview. The interview panel will be senior people from the Home Office, not some off key prison officer from Holloway that's only going to promote their mates."

"And the prison service have said that they want to encourage people from a more diverse background to apply," Maria said

"That's right. So, I think as long as you can get through the application stage and those really difficult tests, you should be a 'shoe in' at an interview," I added.

Ms Hook and Mr Jones

At lunchtime, Ms Hook met with Mr Jones on B3 in a store room. "I've told my husband."

Doing up his shirt, Mr Jones replied, "Told your husband what?"

"About us. I've told him I'm with someone else," Ms Hook said. A moment's silence interrupted Mr Jones relaxed state of mind.

"Well say something," Ms Hook demanded.

"You know I like you, but..." Mr Jones said.

"But what?"

"Sorry, I can't do this, I thought we were just having a bit of fun. I never said this was serious," Mr Jones said. "We've only been fooling around for a few weeks. What's the matter with you, are you crazy? I never told you to tell your husband."

"They're right about you. You really are a **bastard**."

Leaving the store room in a hurry, Mr Jones bumped in

to me. I clocked what was going on when I saw a tearful Ms Hook inside the store room that he was running out off.

"Mr Jones," I demanded, following him as he stormed around to C3 unit.

"Not now, Ms Campbell."

Once in C3 association room he sat down next to Mr Adie, Mr Jamu, Ms Hall and Maria. I burst into the room.

"Mr Jones, have you been sleeping with the enemy?" I asked. "This is ridiculous," Mr Jones said.

"What?" Maria asked.

"He's been sleeping with the enemy. Ms Hook," I said.

Mr Adie laughed.

"She's still married," Ms Hall said.

"How could you after all that woman has put me through?" I said.

"Sorry, but this is none of your business. I don't have to explain myself to you," Mr Jones insisted.

"How could you, Mr Jones? Ms Hook is a racist," said Mr Jamu.

"She's no racist. If she was, I knocked it out of her last night – if you get what I mean," Mr Jones said as he looked to Mr Adie for approval.

"That's disgusting. Don't ever talk to me again," I said.

"Don't talk to me either," Maria said.

"And don't talk to me," Ms Hall said.

"Fine. You guys are so childish," Mr Jones said.

"Who should I sleep with to stop you all from talking to me?" Mr Adie laughed.

Black Vote

The local elections are in a few months, yet I've been finding it difficult to mobilise the Black vote in my area. I wonder why we are at risk from the BNP when this ward has a 35 percent Black population? Black voters on the doorsteps seem either disengaged from the whole election, or are contemplating voting Conservative.

"The Conservatives are not even putting up a full slate

of candidates," I said to one lady.

What's making things worst is the Christian Party are also canvassing the Black vote, which may split the Labour vote down the middle. The only thing we are certain of is that the BNP vote will stay rock solid.

My ward has three large Black African churches, one boasting a membership of over 6,000. They have three services on a Sunday, each sitting around 2,000 worshippers and drawing their congregation from across the borough.

Before I started helping, it didn't even cross the minds of the local councillors to stop by and introduce themselves to these churches. I decided today just to say hello. The churches presented me with a list of complaints with which they had been battling the council for several years. One of the main issues was planning permission. The council refused them planning permission for a place of worship for what we might call a "traditional" church building. This was because it was in a residential area, and there were fears that the noise would disturb residents. Now they are in a warehouse that has been empty for years and far away from residential homes. Again, they were refused planning permission, this time, because the council has marked the area for industrial use only.

"We're being harassed and threatened by the council all the time," they told me. "We've been fighting for planning permission for four years. Where are we supposed to worship? They won't help us because it's a BNP council."

I had to tell the pastor that the council was in fact, controlled by the Labour Party, which didn't help my case. Some churches in the borough refused to meet with our MP or councillors. I feel victory slipping away right in front of us.

It feels like a constant struggle trying to canvass voters who are disillusioned and telling me they can't be bothered voting at all. I feel that the voter turnout will continue to fall, as the national political parties seem to roll into one. From the conflicting views I have heard from residents, not wanting to vote for a mainstream political party doesn't mean that they are not politically engaged. I wonder why there is such a lack representation of social – economic backgrounds within politics when it's clear to me we want to play a part in how our communities are governed. Diversity in our parliament and council chambers would do more than engage Black and White working-class voters. It would get us voting.

Ms Bennett

It is uncommon for three officers to accompany a prisoner to the hospital, but this was Ms Bennett who was going into hospital to have her second baby, a planned C-section.

In the mini-van, the taxi driver looked back at the four of us in his rereview mirror every five seconds. I wanted to reassure him that Ms Bennett, who was thirty-nine weeks pregnant, would not try to strangle him from behind.

"Ms Campbell, am I allowed a burger from the hospital canteen as a special treat," I frowned. She tugged at my arm like a seven-year-old. "Oh please, please, Mr King said that I was allowed."

"We'll see."

Ms Bennett then lunged forward, the taxi driver gripped his steering wheel and filched to one side.

"Oh, l love this song, can you turn it up?"

"No," Ms Hall said gently, guiding Ms Bennett back to her seat.

Three social workers met us at the hospital entrance. There was Ms Bennett's social worker, the unborn baby's social worker and a senior social worker. Ms Bennett greeted them warmly and as we waited to go into surgery we chatted about the weather.

"Ms Bennett, are you sure you don't have any questions about what will happen after the baby is born is afternoon?" Maria asked, concerned that she seemed so detached.

She rolled her eyes. "No, they've told me what's going to happen a hundred times."

I wondered whether we should go over it for the hundred

and first time, but Ms Bennett turned the conversation to *EastEnders*.

"I hope I get back in time, everyone's saying that Grant is coming back."

"God willing, you'll only have to stay a few nights."

"A few nights," Ms Bennett said. "Well at least I have a TV in here. Can I put the TV on?"

"No," the three of us said, united. I lay Ms Bennett back on the bed.

In the operating theatre, Ms Bennett hummed the latest pop song. She lay still on her back with a drip in her arm and the doctors cutting and pulling at her belly behind a blue curtain.

"Do you want to see the baby, before they take it away?" I whispered into her ear.

"I don't know." Her face looked at me for an answer.

It was as though it was the first time that anyone had asked her what she wanted. Her baby's cry then filled the room.

"It's a girl," a nurse said, as she placed the baby in her arms Ms Bennett fumbled as she struggled to hold the baby amongst the wires, almost dropping her. I offered a steady hand just in time. They wheeled Ms Bennett out into the recovery area where Ms Hall and Maria were waiting.

"She's beautiful," Maria said, leaning in.

"7 pounds 4 ounces," Ms Bennett said holding her proudly. "Praise the Lord."

"I'm going to call her Kayia." Ms Bennett stroked Kayia's head and examined every finger and toe with care.

The social workers loomed outside.

"I think it's time to say goodbye to Kayia now," I whispered, but my words were too loud for Ms Bennett. She held Kayia tight to her chest and looked at me alarmed.

"Why can't I take her to the Mother and Baby unit at Holloway? I promise I'll be good." I knew that she was told that she would not be allowed on the Mother and Baby unit because of her violent behaviour that might put her baby and other babies on the unit at risk.

"I promise I'll be good. I won't fight with anyone, I promise." Her tears broke me. "I'm not doing crack no more. Can't you tell the social workers?"

Ms Hall lay a hand of comfort on Ms Bennett's shoulder, but she tightened her grip on her baby.

"No. I'm not going to give her up for adoption any more." Her voice became raised. "I want to take her back to Holloway with me."

"Sssh Ms Hall placed her finger to her mouth. "You'll scare her."

Ms Bennett then returned to her beautiful daughter. She looked at her for the last time and kissed her cheeks. I nodded to Maria who then let the social workers in the room. As Ms Bennett placed her baby in their arms, she bit her lip in agony.

"I don't want to scare her," she wept.

The social workers left the room with Kayia, the door slammed shut and Ms Hall grabbed Ms Bennett, as she let out a cry of anguish from deep down inside. She screamed and punched the air in a helpless rage. Ms Hall wrapped her arms around her holding her up as her legs collapsed beneath her. Maria helped to lift her up from behind and I held her head to my chest. Yet the three of us could not contain her distress. We had no words of comfort to offer, only tears. Our shift finished at 9.00 p.m., but we stayed overnight. Ms Bennett cried without relief until she fell asleep in the arms of Ms Hall. The job of a prison officer is difficult, undervalued and sometimes dangerous but Ms Hall that night remembered what a difference she could make by just doing her job.

Amber's Blog 2018

Posted – 3rd October 2018

Written in a campsite on Kande Beach, Malawi

It was in dark prison cells that many prisoners reflected on how their lives had been stolen by drugs. The women who were drug addicts at Holloway tended to be in their mid-twenties, but looked like they were in their mid-seventies with missing teeth and the skin hanging off their bones. The system had given up on them and they only cared for what drug substitution medication they would be given while they waited in line.

No government seems to be able to fix the broken link between prison, drug rehabilitation services and probation. It is clear to me that something bold is needed to cut the link between repeat re-offending and drug abuse. I believe that people with drug misuse problems, should not be sent to prison but to secure drug rehabilitation centres. It is accepted that short-term sentences do not work. It would not work in a rehabilitation centre either. Ensuring that someone spends longer behind bars that would under today's sentencing guidelines only serve six months of a twelve month sentence is a controversial idea. But being tough on the causes of crime means being tough on drugs. I believe that we should treat this as a public health issue first and foremost. I see secure drug rehabilitation centres not as places were prisoners would waste time behind bars costing the tax payer thousands but a place where they can receive specialist intensive support. Such centres would operate like open prisons.

Chapter 10

Kande Beach (Malawi)

3rd October 2018

1.10 p.m. - Kande Beach (Malawi)

I'm sitting here at the bar overlooking Lake Malawi with its golden sands and blue waters. I've upgraded for the next four nights, and this morning, I awoke in my cabin to the sound of the waves from the beach; a sound coming through the bamboo walls of the cabin. I open my eyes and just lie there knowing that this isn't a dream I was on a beach in the heart of Africa.

After dinner, our group exchanged the funny clothes that we bought each other in the market yesterday. The guys got dresses, and I had to wear a pair of cycling shorts and a horrible blue jumper. The atmosphere is relaxed, and I'm starting to appreciate some of the characters we have in our group. Afterwards, we headed for the bar. It's been an easy day. Most people just chilled out.

4th October

1.00 p.m. - Kande Beach (Malawi)

We went on the village walk this morning. It differed greatly from Mukuni Village in Zambia. Here, they no longer use the traditional African style of hut that many associate with Africa, which is made of mud and straw. Instead, they have small brick houses with a traditional straw roof. The house I saw comprised of four rooms with a separate block outside for cooking. These grey cement blocks seem dull in comparison to the colourful red and patterned huts at Mukuni. Most were just grey brick shells, with little character. The village also seems to be built on a rubbish tip, and I feel overwhelmed by the poverty. At first, the square brick houses seemed to distort the village structure that I am familiar with. In Mukuni, the structure was very visible, but here, it resembles a township rather than a village. We went to the village health centre first where they said that the biggest local cause of death is malaria.

They don't have the correct drugs to treat people and instead, have to send patients home with painkillers. Here in Malawi, primary school is free for 6-13-year olds, but secondary school is not. We went to the secondary school first. It was a private establishment that accepted pupils aged 14–18 years and was run by local volunteers. The school has seven teachers and one hundred pupils. Sixty of the pupils are orphans, for which admission is free. In the crumbling school building, they said that they would appreciate any donations. After we left, four of the young women that joined us in Livingston complained that they were being asked for money.

"Well if their situation makes you feel uncomfortable, why come? I don't think they care if *you're* comfortable or not," I said.

One of the young women, a 23-year old Australian named Stacey, looked at the children as if they were rats, and when about twenty children surrounded her wanting to hold her hand, she pinned her hands to her chest and shrieked, "They're so dirty!" The four thought the African dinner we had the other night was disgusting and didn't understand why they had to be subjected to it in the first place. Faced with such poverty in a primary school where there are one hundred children per class, I looked for signs of compassion or anger in their eyes, but it seemed to reinforce their own sense of superiority. The people on my tour were relieved to be back behind the safe walls of the campsite.

I asked the head teacher if I could spend the day tomorrow at the secondary school. They seemed happy to have me as a guest for the day.

5th October

11.00 p.m. - Kande Beach (Malawi)

I spent the day as a guest teacher at Kande Secondary School. The school is a single grey block shell divided into five classrooms, most of which have crumbling walls and broken windows. I had prepared a little something on Black British history, which I thought would explain where I was from, as most children looked confused when I told them I was from England. But when I arrived, the head teacher wanted me to talk about the First World War. I had about fifteen minutes to prepare from a textbook. I entered a class of about twenty-five students between the ages of fourteen and twenty.

I was so nervous, what with the deputy head teacher taking a front seat and expecting greatness. They had no maps of the world, so I began by drawing a map of Europe on the black board. In a squiggly blob, I drew Britain and Ireland first. I got the students to shout out what countries were in Europe. Some said things like "Japan" and "Australia", but in the end, we got there. I went through the main reasons the First World War broke out. Trying to make it interesting, I compared the Triple Alliance (Germany, Austria, Italy) with the Dual Alliance (France and Russia) as warring factions.

The students were interested and motivated. I had only three girls in the class that didn't contribute, but the boys were sharp. The whole class (except the aforementioned trio of girls) were full of questions and showing immense interest. The lesson lasted three hours. The deputy head (an English teacher) was full of praise. I felt my afternoon class wasn't as successful as the first. I had a much older group, meaning people in their forties. There were only about six people. Four were women, but once again it was the men who were more interactive. I felt that my material on oral and family history too basic for them. I had teenagers in mind when I prepared it.

The school is vital to the village. It also acts as a community adult learning centre. It's run, managed and staffed by the locals of Kende village. The head director of the school, a local businessman, showed me the plans for a new school building they were raising funds for. During our lunch break, together with the head director and Paul, I sat on the street corner watching the local market. It was Thursday, and every Thursday, the neighbouring villages come together to buy and sell. Colourful clothes and local produce lined the streets. It was wrong of me to compare Mukuni Village with this village, as maybe every village has its own style. But that same strength of community can be found here.

We're leaving Kande Beach tomorrow morning. Kande Beach is like a dream paradise hidden behind the high walls of a camp site. On the other side, we're surrounded by a bleak reality. Although, in that reality is where I'd rather be. One of my favourite students of the day was a boy who came to both my classes. He didn't know how old he was. He told me that his parents were "ignorant and foolish" as they didn't record the year he was born. At first, I thought how terrible it was that he didn't know his own birthday, but now I think it's terrible that he thinks his parents are ignorant and foolish.

There are benefits from knowing *exactly* how old you are, but it's not the end of the world. The Bushmen we met in Botswana didn't know how old they were, but their way of life did not call for importance to be placed upon such things. I'm seeing how African communities can also compare, judge and value themselves through western eyes.

I think Sarah's come to not only accept, but appreciate my input in the group. She said that I had made her think a lot more about and value African culture. This evening at dinner, I sat next to her and Tony the Australian. We had a discussion about other tour groups who have White tour guides. Tony said that I wasn't "*really*" European, and Sarah wasn't "*really*" African because his head can't get around the colour of our skin. However, I made a very firm point of saying that Sarah was "African" and I appreciated having her as my tour leader instead of someone European. Under the old apartheid system in South Africa, to say you were an "African" meant you were "black", but she knew what I was trying to get at. I'm now the European, and she is the African. Maybe if Sarah could embrace that word "African" she might not see African culture as being separate to hers.

I told the group today that I was no longer going to be part of their tour. I was going to make my own way to Kenya. Part of me feels like this a crazy decision, but I know I can do this.

Chapter 11

7th October 2018 Africa - Tanzania

I crossed the border today into Tanzania on my own after I hitched a ride with a group of German backpackers. The big news is that I quit smoking yesterday. This is my second day without a cigarette. Since Monday, I've been trying unsuccessfully to stop. On Monday I had three, Tuesday four, Wednesday six and on Thursday I had about ten. It looked like it was going to be another failed attempt. But on Thursday evening at dinner, John the driver, who loves his cigarettes, announced to the group he was going to give up smoking too. I arose from my bed on Friday morning determined that he would not beat me to it. Reading my prison diaries has been a great distraction.

With a Little Help From my Friends

RMT meeting

Today, I addressed the RRMT meeting (Race Relations Management Team) and gave my first presentation on disability. After a shaky start, I think I did well.

"We desperately need wheelchairs, basic mobility and training for staff on supporting prisoners with disabilities. We need a stair lift in the education department."

I gave examples of current prisoners with mobility problems that didn't have access to the prison library. The response from Governor Rose who chaired the meeting was, "Well, we don't have any money for that. Write to the Primary Care Trust. It's their responsibility."

"I already have," I said. "They told me it's the prison's responsibility." Looking at her watch, she said, "Next item on the agenda please."

The meeting dragged on and on. The head of each department read out pointless data. Governor Rose ticked a box on her spreadsheet as we went through the meeting. After two hours, I finally got the chance to raise my concerns about the lack of Black senior officers at Holloway.

Mr Stewer, Head of Human Resources, woke up.

"I don't think this is a problem, Governor Rose. Overall, the prison's work force reflects the prison's BAME population."

After lobbying him for months, Mr Lucas said the magic words: "This is institutional racism."

I wanted to punch the air as the meeting exploded. We couldn't get off the subject. I feel so privileged to have been in that meeting; privileged to raise such an important issue.

After the meeting, although the governor seemed to be in a hurry to get off, I approached her to press my concerns about the conditions of disabled prisoners again.

"Disabled prisoners are confined to their cells and most of them are on suicide watch."

I guess rethinking what she might say to the media if disabled prisoners started to kill themselves, she turned to me and said, "Okay, I'll see what we can do."

My Own Office

My workload has exploded. I'm struggling to keep it together, but that's only because I'm not yet organised. Governor Rose has given me my own office, the only officer to have their own office in the prison. Everyone is happy for me – except for the obvious ones.

They're finally moving me to B3. Ms Rot had the honour of telling me, no doubt hoping to see me breakdown in disappointment. But to be honest, I'm quite happy with the move. B3 is only next door, but is a mile away from D3. It's a quiet unit, which will give me more time to do my disability work. D3 has been a bit much lately with the new roles that I've taken on. Change is hard for me. Everyone knows me as a D3 officer. But the change might do me good this time. After all, I'm not being shafted because bullies want me off the unit, or because I can't handle it.

23/3/06

Mr Smith is back at work, but has been moved to the prison's detail office, away from contact with prisoners. He gave me the whole afternoon off the landings to work on disability, but I saw only two disabled prisoners, which is disappointing. I need to prove to Mr King that I can do the job of disability officer and being a good landing officer. I think I will have to do most of the work in my own time, as one afternoon a week isn't going to cut it.

Mr King has promoted Ms Freeman and Mr Adie to Senior Officers. Mr Adie is now my line-manager. We're all so proud of him, although there's something brewing between us as I sense that he's unhappy that I have my own office.

Ms Freeman

Just got back from another mad day at the office. Mr Smith in the Detail Office wanted to give me the day off. I would have welcomed it a year ago, but I've got too much disability work to do. I've become a victim of my success after creating awareness about such issues. I've been flooded with referral forms. Because I haven't had any proper time to do the work, some officers are complaining about me not seeing the women that they have referred. I've been doing the best to meet women in my lunch breaks.

Today, I spent an hour with Ms Johnson on Level 5. I remembered Ms Johnson as she was restrained on D3 unit some months ago after being accused of sexually assaulting a young offender that had been place in her dorm. She went on about how she can't have a bath, about how it's a struggle to use the toilet, and so on for over an hour. Then I had to see a disabled woman on the Post Detox Unit who's been in for a month, and no one told me. Injecting drugs into every vein in her body over two decades has left her bedbound. She can barely stand, let alone walk. Her face was black and blue from where she had fallen over. I then found out that the wheelchair I had promised Ms Richards on B3, (the third of only three wheelchairs we have in the prison), has a puncture, so I will have to try and get to the bike shop. Ms Richards has numerous physical and mental health conditions and is known for her attention- seeking behaviour. She's short, fat and helpless, meaning a big target for bullies. Ido my best to look out for her. Simple things like checking in on her every hour or so and making sure she's at the front of the dinner queue. Half the battle has been to bring it to the attention of the prison governors and make them understand that these are serious issues that require some level of thought and money.

At 4.30 p.m., I was called down to the segregation unit where two prisoners had seized control of half the unit through a dirty protest. The incident had been going on since 3.00 p.m. The prison alarm wasn't sounded. I guess lessons have been learnt from what happend with Ms John where she stood at the unit door with a bucket of shit as officers ran onto the unit.

After unsuccessful attempts by Ms Freeman to regain control, Governor Fox was brought in to take over. He immediately called for more officers.

"Don't worry Ms Freeman, you're a new Senior Officer and finding your feet. Some people are naturally better at some things. This is a major incident that requires tactical thinking and strong leadership," Governor Fox said rolling up his sleeves. "But I hear you're a good shoulder to cry on. Some of these women need a grandmother figure like you in their life."

I wasn't told it was a dirty protest, but as soon as I unlocked the unit door, I knew what I was walking into as the foul smell of excrement hit me.

Governor Fox ordered me to put on a white forensic one-piece suit, latex gloves, and plastic goggles. I could hear the chants of the two prisoners goading us on, and then their celebrations as tired officers retreated from their barricade. I was fresh-faced, but certainly not ready to go. A new batch of officers started to put on their riot gear, navy overalls, stab proof vests, shin pads and heavy riot helmets. Zipping up my white suit, it was clear that I had drawn the short straw.

Governor Fox then revealed the plan. The two teams in navy would remove the barricade, and the two teams in white would restrain the prisoners. I spent most of the briefing thinking about how I could get onto the navy team, but before I knew it, we we're all lined up and ready to go.

Before the prisoners realised what was going on, we had them "twisted up and bundled away," as Governor Fox put it. With speed and aggressive force, the two teams in navy removed the barricade that jammed shut the dividing unit fire doors. We could then clamber in and pin down the women before they used their sharpened broom handles.

In total, we had the unit back under our control in less than ten minutes. As I charged into the danger zone, my mind became focused. It weeded out every unnecessary sound and the smell of excrement, and my eyes narrowed in on the weapons in the cell. I seemed to go into autopilot and the control-and-restraint techniques, which I normally over-think, came to me without a second thought. My only concern was getting myself, the other officers, and the prisoners out into a safe place.

My heightened senses now alerted me to danger that could bring me harm. Restraining a woman that had covered herself in her own excrement didn't process until I got home and showered.

BNP Ripping us Apart

The council local elections are less than eight weeks away. I know my ward well now, I know who are BNP sympathisers, and I understand their reasons. I know who's going to vote for the Labour Party, and I know the faith groups and the local businesses in the area. The leader of the BNP, came down to canvass the ward the other day. It almost felt like an intruder had broken into my home and I could not do anything about it.

He got a cup of tea in my local bakery, talked to residents on the shopping parade and went into my local pub. I feel like he's ripping the community apart. It's like he's pitched neighbour against neighbour.

A wave of BNP material has come through our door. This seems to have rallied the community behind the local Labour Party. During the week, I met with volunteers from the churches and went out knocking on doors.

Demands on my time have been growing as polling day draws nearer. I've been running canvassing sessions and hand delivering literature. The local party office is full to the brim of volunteers stuffing envelopes with letters aimed at first time voters, women, pensioners, and so on. In the evenings, I'm also making phone calls to residents who live in tower blocks asking them to vote Labour on 4th May.

Arguments

It's been an okay weekend at HMP Holloway—apart from the office politics that I can do without. At the end of my shift, I let Mr Adie know that I was unable to get the Regime Monitoring Form done, some new useless form that Governor Rose wants. He said that he wasn't surprised that I didn't do it. I didn't bother arguing with him in front of Mr Jones and Maria. I also had my Spanish course that night and just wanted to get off. And I had an argument that afternoon with Mr Jones over a TV aerial. It happened in front of Mr Adie who goaded on Mr Jones. In the car home, the weekend's bickering sunk in. Everyone comes to work with their own issues and insecurities, even Mr Adie who's trying to make his mark as Holloway's first Black senior officer. He doesn't understand why I got the disability job or why I have my own "special" computer and my own office. I just wish he wasn't my line manager. Other than that, I don't care what he thinks.

I overheard raised voices coming from the SO office.

"I won't have my senior officers overburdened with useless paper work, when they should be on the unit," Mr King said.

"I'm not here to ask for your opinion, or debate the merits of the policy. This form needs to be completed by all staff," Governor Rose said.

"No. This is just another piece of useless paper work. I won't have it."

I could hear a thump as Mr King's hand band on the desk.

"Matthew, please. I don't want to argue with you. I need this form to be completed. Prison Headquarters have asked for this information. I can review it in two weeks, and if it really is taking too long for staff to complete, I'll pull it."

"Fine."

Waiting for the night staff to relieve me this evening, the sound of Governor Rose calling Mr King by his first name 'Matthew' unsettled me. I stumbled across a play that I think one of the prisoners had written in the office. It was a comedy. Reading through and laughing to myself, it gave me some light relief taking my mind far away from Holloway. I remembered how much I loved the theatre.

"Why don't we go out next weekend, to the theatre?" I said to Ms Hall and Maria.

Ms Richards' Wheelchair

It's been a frustrating day. I was given some time to do my disability officer work, and I got very little done after getting stuck on the segregation unit for a nicking. I placed Ms Bennett on report for "fighting with another prisoner". The incident happened a week yesterday. I knew that the governor would give her only a slap on the wrist, and it wasn't worth the hour I spent filling in the forms. It took three officers to restrain her, and two other prisoners got hurt, so I hoped that Governor Rose might raise the bar a little. But two night's loss of association is hardly what I call a deterrent.

I then tried to take Ms Richards' wheelchair to the bike shop to get some new tyres fitted, and my new car got clamped. I seethed in frustration. After paying £115 to get my car back, the wheelchair didn't even get fixed. So I wasted three hours of my precious disability time. I wanted to cry. Other than being a waste of my time, it's the money that kills me the most. By the time I *walked* back to work, I lost the will to do anything else.

There's no space left on the set of nights I needed for that extra week off work. That extra week off and my two weeks annual leave would have given me three weeks clear in January. I'm sure it will all work out. Where there's a will there's a way, etc— or so I keep telling Mr Smith in the Detail Office. Because of all the women on twenty-four-hour suicide watch—which now includes Ms Richards'—the prison is now paying staff overtime to sit by their cells and watch them continually.

Maria and I got a nice little pay packet this month from all the overtime hours we've been doing. Maria will put her extra money towards debt repayments and mine will go towards my 'Travel the World Fund'.

On the Doors

I've been knocking on doors asking/pleading with people to come out and support the Labour Party on 4th ay. The key thing is accurate data. I was told that in the 2004 by-election when the BNP won a seat, Labour activists just assumed people would vote Labour because this is a working-class area. Come polling day, they were reminding people who were in fact BNP voters to vote. It was a sign of the complacency that the local Labour Party had for this safe seat. They took the voters for granted.

On the doorsteps, people are open with their views when asked directly. On one street that we went to yesterday, everyone who opened the door said that they were going to vote BNP. I've stopped asking "why" as whatever I say it's not going to make a difference.

Today, one lady told me she "didn't want her child to be the only White child in the class". That may sound ridiculous, but she told me that "…in Tower Hamlets, it's happened. Some of their schools have only four or five White children in the whole school." I couldn't and didn't want to promise her that her child wouldn't be the only White kid in the class.

"Kids are all the same when they put on the school uniform. The important thing is achieving the highest standards in our schools, that's something a Labour council would be committed to," I said.

Ms Richards' Wheelchair

On Wednesday, I'm going backpacking for three weeks through South America. So, if anything should happen to me between now and then, let it be known I have my bags packed for Rio. I desperately need a day off to get my hair done for the trip. I'm getting single plait waste length extensions put in, which is an all-day job. Mr Smith in Central Detail just keeps throwing it back in my face that I could have had Monday off.

"What was I meant to do? Leave Ms Richards without a

wheelchair?" I asked him.

I guess I've been well and truly stitched up with this crap job. Some days I feel like I'm making progress, and then nothing. Disability is an issue that I care so much about. Maybe that's the problem; that I care about it too much. I've got wheelchairs coming out of my ears. I think my head will explode if I hear the word wheelchair again.

We've got nine prisoners who are confined to their cells for twenty-four hours a day because of mobility problems. They are suffering, and because I'm the Disability Officer, I'm supposed to do something about it.

Letter

I've just returned from my backpacking trip through Argentina, Uruguay, Paraguay and Brazil. Considering that I've never really learnt English, I knew that learning Spanish would never be easy. I was surprised that I could understand and communicate with people in the Spanish speaking countries on my trip. It was the middle of carnival season, and every night, the whole continent seemed to party till dawn. Needless to say, I had an amazing time. I feel like I can accomplish anything. This morning, I decided that I was going to stop smoking.

First day back at work was as expected: a nightmare. As soon as I walked through the prison gates, the officers on Level 5 told me that Ms Johnson had been counting down the days on her cell wall waiting for me to return to work. Her wheelchair, which I think is about twenty years old, is broken once again. The officers on the unit then tried to imply that it was my fault that Ms Johnson has been bedridden for three weeks. I received a letter from Ms Richards with all her complaints, to do with having a crap wheelchair and being confined to her cell for several months. Before I went away, I encouraged her to write a letter that I will give to Governor Rose. I felt she needed to channel her distress and I'm still concerned that she is a suicide risk. Reading through the letter, I know I will have to write a statement covering myself. I also had a furious argument with Mr Jones after he described a prisoner as "stupid and obviously dyslexic". At the end of my shift, I shook hands with Mr Jones, but changing everyone's attitudes towards disability and ensuring that everyone takes responsibility is going to be quite a struggle.

Another argument with Mr Adie

I've managed to wind down after a hectic day. I was a Disability Officer, and was in the middle of moving offices. Consequently, for a while, I had nowhere to work. Ms Freeman said yesterday that I could use the SO's office just for the morning. I'm now trying to make an induction pack for disabled prisoners. Just my luck, that Mr Adie was
SO this morning. He didn't care where I went that he said was my problem. He just wanted me out.

"I've got to get this done by the end of today, I only get a few hours a week to focus on disability," I said.

"I don't care. Look at the sign on the door it says 'Senior Officer'. Has Mr King promoted you to SO?"

"Oh, that's just great, the power has gone to your head already. Are you going to run the Level like a dictator?"

"Don't talk to me like that. I'm not your sweetheart. Go running back to Mr King, he'll find you somewhere to work."

"What's Mr King got to do with it? It was Ms Freeman that said that I could work in here for the morning."

"I know how you got the disability job and your own office. Come on, Ms Campbell, I've known Mr King for a long time and I know he don't give nothing for nothing."

"You're so insulting. I've got no respect for you whatsoever."

"Whatever, pack your shit up and get out of *my* office."

I picked up my stuff, my bag in one hand and my papers in the other, and heard the door slam shut behind me. I realised that I had nowhere to go. Ms Freeman was working downstairs on the healthcare unit.

"Maybe Adie's just having a bad day," she said. "It might be best if we try and find you somewhere else to work this morning."

She came up with me and helped me to get the rest of my things out the office and was a friendly face. As we walked up the stairs, I wished she were Mr King going up to kick Mr Adie's ass.

Arguments with the SOs

I was on an A Shift today: 7.30 a.m. – 9.00 p.m. It felt like one hundred years. I was working all day with Mr Jones. I really needed to take Ms Richards' wheelchair to the bike shop for repair. For months, the poor woman has had a dodgy wheelchair, and now it's completely broken. She's confined to the bed in her cell twenty-four hours a day.

"It's completely unacceptable," I raged to Ms Freeman. I added, "I'm still waiting for the Primary Care Trust to order her a new one, and the prison won't pay for it. But they can spend £10,000 on video games and PlayStations for young offenders."

Anyway, I couldn't go. Ms Freeman didn't have the balls to tell Ms Hook who was working on A3 to cover me for thirty minutes while I went to the bike shop. There were four officers on D3 unit, but Ms Freeman rang me to say "The officers on D3 were busy doing something."

I felt bad about the situation, not that I was sorry or anything, but I did not want to be arguing with both my SOs.

Ms Freeman came around to "clear the air". But I was still mad. Ms Freeman has been supportive of the work that I'm trying to do as a Disability Officer and has been a relief from Mr Adie. After I continued to kick up a fuss, Ms Freeman covered for me on the landing, and I finally got Ms Richards' wheelchair fixed.

This afternoon, I saw Mr Adie in the office today talking to Maria, their conversation seemed strained. When Mr Adie saw me approaching, he left the office.

"You okay?" I asked Maria.

"I'm fine," Maria said.

"Listen, if Mr Adie is trying to rip you off, you don't have to stay in his flat. You can come stay with me for a bit till you find somewhere else," I said.

"What are you talking about? Mr Adie is a good landlord," Maria said.

"Sure, he is. His tenants have nominated him for landlord of the year several times," I said.

"Really?" Maria asked.

"No, of course not! That was a joke," I said.

For Evening Duty, I was with an officer from another landing who sat in the TV room all evening while I ran about sorting out canteen orders for tomorrow.

To round off the day, 'Crack Head' Ms Phipps called me a "bitch" because she couldn't hand in her canteen order form in the morning. In saying that, Ms Bennett also called me a "bitch" this morning for waking her up. So, the prison service got their monies worth out of me today.

Visits

Today was a nice easy day; just what I needed in this long stretch leading up to my next day off. I was down in 'Visits' where everyone is chilled. I was on an early shift. Ms Bennett said sorry for calling me a "bitch". She said she was having a bad day. I was with Ms Baxter who has been placed back on duty after being walked to the gate after allegations of bullying.

Overseeing the happy reunions of prisoners and their families, she filled me in on all the gossip, something to do with a love triangle between her, Mr Night, Ms Tate and Mr Sands. It all sounded very complicated. After three hours with Ms Baxter, I'm still none the wiser about who was sleeping with whom out of the four officers that all work together on D3. I'm glad to now be a boring B3 officer. Mr Darkin, a Level 5 officer, sent me an email today saying that he likes me. I thought it childish, and after listening to Ms Baxter on 'how out-of-control' it can all get, I think I'm going to pass on the question of dating a Holloway officer.

Local Election Day 2006

Election day has arrived. I was up at 5.00 a.m. this morning after having had only four hours' sleep. I've had over thirty volunteers at my house from the local churches in the ward. It's a day that I can only describe as electrifying from start to finish.

The Labour Party turned my house into a military command centre for the ward. Volunteers were once again on the phones calling people in tower blocks reminding them to vote. All four polling stations in the ward were well marked, and then at 10.00 a.m. I took the first team out to canvass.

It was a carnival atmosphere on this sunny day. People everywhere were hooting their car horns in support. Every door I knocked on this time said, "I'm voting for Labour". When I got back to the house to see how the results of the phone canvassing was getting on, I read LABOUR, LABOUR, LABOUR. This evening, when the shopkeepers locked up early to come out to help us, most people said, "I have *already* voted, and I voted for Labour". At 9.45 p.m., fifteen minutes before the polls closed, two men flagged down Maria and I in the car (which was covered in Labour posters) by jumping up and down in the middle of the road. They said they couldn't find their polling station. Looking at the map, we saw that their polling station was on the other side of the ward, so they got into the car. I wouldn't advocate giving a lift to two complete strangers, but such was the urgency of getting the last voter to the polling station before the doors closed.

12 BNP Councillors Elected

I hoped that the 2004 by-election, when a racist was elected to the council, was a fluke. But it was just a warning sign for Barking & Dagenham. I wonder how this could happen?

When I think of Barking, I think of a place where I feel safe. I think of home; a place that's growing and that has a lot of potential. When I think of Dagenham, I think of a strong working-class community into which they welcomed my mum during the 1970s when she worked at The Ford Motor Company. Today, the media paints my borough as racist, poor and ignorant. That, however, is not who we are.

The feeling of disillusionment from mainstream political parties is clear. Somehow, the BNP has an additional victory that they have been able to bring to the attention of the media and politicians, the forgotten White working class.

I'm so busy at work, and, to be honest, my shifts don't make it easy. But I need to do whatever I can do to fight the BNP and find out why people in my own street voted for them.

1997 General Election

My course at Hackney College is wicked! At the moment, I'm making a documentary about the General Election. The other day we had some politicians come in to the college to talk about their policies. I've been talking to students about what they think, and everyone's fired up about voting, and they're voting for Tony Blair.

I can't wait to vote for the first time. The politicians have been trying to target first time voters with what they think are "student" issues. Everyone's getting heated over the introduction of tuition fees, which the Labour Party said they will introduce. All I care about is the economy and getting a job when I finish my studies.

The minimum wage would benefit me, but the Conservatives say that it would hurt small businesses, and therefore, hurt the economy. I'm also worried about the breakup of the UK, if Scotland, Wales and Northern Ireland get devolution. I'm sure that the students of Hackney College will risk all for a change and the hope of having some kind of future. Some people say that politics changes nothing, but if Labour win the election in a few weeks so much is going to change. When I grow up, I want to change the world. I bet every eighteen-year-old says that. My Labour Party membership card came through the post today so maybe I will make a difference in the world someday.

Preparing for Diversity Week

I had a 5.30 p.m. finish but stayed on until 9.30 p.m. to start work on Diversity Week, which is next week, I'm cutting it a bit fine. Organisation is not one of my strengths, so I'm happy to have the help of Ms Hall and Maria, who began organising it three weeks ago. My focus is Disability Day, which takes place on Wednesday, and a fashion show which will happen on the grand finale, Friday afternoon.

Today, I spent my lunch break sorting out Ms Johnson's commode, and then spent my tea break with Ms Butt, a new disabled prisoner. In saying that, I've got tomorrow off, but I've decided to go in to sort out the wheelchair basketball and the Introduction to Sign Language workshop for staff and prisoners.

Fireworks

After tea, Maria locked in the women for the night and she was on her own for what she must have hoped would be an uneventful evening. She walked around the unit checking in on a few prisoners who were on constant suicide watch and then went to check on Ms Jackson who was not on suicide watch. She had spent some time with Ms Jackson during the day as she was feeling down. It was her son's birthday; a son that had been taken into Care some years ago and with whom she had no contact. At tea, she told Maria that she would be okay as she was in prison this time last year as well, but Maria thought she might like some company. Maria was shocked to find she had tied a ligature around her neck and had barricaded herself inside her cell. She called on the radio for help, Ms Freemen and I came running. We did all we could to get the cell door open as Maria tried to talk Ms Jackson down, but she was hysterical. Maria called again on the radio.

"Immediate assistance required. Code Blue."

The three of us tried in vain to prise open the cell door. Out of nowhere, Mr Potter flew in.

"Stand aside," Mr Potter said.

He rammed the cell door four times with his shoulder. We and the ten prisoners in the dorms opposite watched with our jaws dropped, and I think our hearts must have jumped just a little each time he ran at the thick steel cell door. He managed to get it open just wide enough so I could get through.

"I guess you can take it from here," Mr Potter said to Maria.

"Yes, thank you," Maria blushed. Maria settled Ms Jackson in a cell near the office and sat down to write up the incident in the unit Observation Book.

"Do you need any help?" Mr Potter said, standing in the doorway.

"Oh, hi," Maria looked up.

Mr Potter sat down. "Someone's having a good time," he said looking out of the window. He flinched as another firework went off in the distance.

"You don't like the fireworks? I find them annoying as well..." Maria said. "They remind me of Iraq," Mr Potter said.

"Sorry, yes you were in the army. I didn't know that you served in Iraq."

"I only did a six-month tour. I left the army as soon as I got back to the UK."

"Okay," Maria said.

There was a pause in the conversation.

"I couldn't take it. That's why I left. I'm a coward really. I left my friends over there getting shot out for nothing," Mr Potter said.

"You can't be a coward. Anyone that joins the army, joins to protect their country. That's why you joined, because you're brave. This war isn't about protecting us, it's about oil."

Captivated, Mr Potter responded, "You've got beautiful eyes."

"Thanks," she said coldly.

Letter

I lit a cigarette this afternoon defeated, as I sat down to respond to Ms Richards' letter that she gave to me months ago. It was a failed attempt to quit smoking and I should have known that Ms Richards wouldn't get a reply from Governor Rose. I told her to write it only because I was angry at the way she had been treated. Now I'm having to respond in my capacity as Disability Officer, but I cannot defend the indefensible. The reality is that I can do little but inform the prison management of the situation and make recommendations. In the future, I need to be careful not to raise expectations too high amongst prisoners, and even myself, otherwise only disappointment and frustration will follow.

I attempted to give a pep talk to a prisoner who's the same age as me the other day "You're really talented. You can get a job anywhere," I said.

Looking down at the letter she received, she said, "What job could I ever get?"

At fourteen, she was written off by her school as stupid, not knowing that she was dyslexic. Her story could have been mine. She has been in and out of prison for nine years never able to read her own letters.

£5,000 for Disability

The good news is that today I ordered £5,000 worth of equipment after Governor Rose decided that the number of prisoners on suicide watch was a corporate risk. Judging from the amount of referral forms I get from all over the prison, my aim of putting disability on the agenda has been a success.

The RRMT meeting today also put in place actions to address the issue of staff of colour not getting opportunities to act up and moved around the prison. All managers will now have to go on a refresher diversity training course every year. I think the training will help senior officers to think more about unconscious bias and how it might impact on their 'day-to-day' decisions.

The bad news is at the meeting Governor Rose has concluded that Holloway is doing okay with promoting staff on merit. This is because they have just promoted three BME officers to SO, Mr Adie, and an Asian officer and an officer of Turkish heritage.

"We also have enough BME staff that have put themselves forward for the Fast Track Programme, which would put us in line with the percentage (32%) of Black prisoners," Governor Rose said.

At lunchtime today, Mr Potter hovered around the C3 association room uncertain. "Are you okay?" Maria asked.

"I was wondering if I could have a word?" "Sure."

"I've got tickets to a live comedy show next week. I thought you might like to come with me."

"Sorry, I'm just not in a space where I'm ready to start dating. I've got a lot on…" Maria said.

"We don't have to call it a date," Mr Potter said.
"I just don't think I'm ready…"
"We can take it slow."
"No. It's not the right time for me," she stated.

Out Clubbing

Maria and I went clubbing with officers from Level 3 this evening. We took a bit too long getting ready and didn't arrive at the club in the West End until 1.00 a.m., which was just when things were getting warmed up anyway. Maria spent the night killing men with dirty looks across the dance floor if they dared to even look her way. I spent most of the night dancing with Mr Jamu. As I walked over to him, he became nervous and started looking around.

"Mr. Jamu," I said, yelling over the thumping music. "You wanna dance?"

"Yes!" he yelled back, putting his drink to one side. Then he leaned in close and said, "Ms Campbell, I bet Mr Adie told you to ask me. But you don't have to if you don't want to."

I could see Mr Adie and Mr Jones at the other end of the bar giggling like two school boys whose practical joke had just fallen into place. Anyway, we danced together for a few songs, which wiped the smiles off their faces.

Mr Jones came over with his chest puffed up and with a few dance moves of his own. He tried to manoeuvre himself between Mr Jamu and me.

"Ms Campbell, you wanna dance?" Mr Jones yelled.
"What?" I said.
"You wanna dance?" he repeated, reaching out to put his arm around my waist. I moved back and yelled, "Nah, you're all right."

"Do you want to dance?" Mr Potter asked Maria.
"No," Maria said.
"Can I buy you a drink?" "No," said Maria.
"You're a tough nut to crack," said Mr Potter.
"I don't need cracking and I don't want to talk." Maria

picked up her glass and went to walk away.

"Maria, I know what happened between you and your ex-boyfriend." Maria faced him in shock. "Everybody knows. It was obvious what was going on. I'm not perfect but I'm not him. And I'm not one of those racists that made your life hell in Germany. I'm just a guy that really likes you. Wants to buy you a drink, dance with you and make you laugh."

"I don't think we have anything in common," Maria said.

"Look, I know that we don't hang around in the same circles. When I came to Holloway, I wanted to fit in. I felt like I had abandoned all my mates in Iraq and I was at a pretty low point. Hanging around with officers like Ms Hook was a mistake. Here I am starting again trying to fit in with you lot. People change, I've changed, you can change too," Mr Potter said.

"As I said, I don't need cracking and I don't want to talk," Maria said.

Ms Richards

I stood at the window and watched beautiful white snowflakes fall onto the prison exercise yard. It had been an exhausting day. A3 unit had reopened after being closed for the weekend for refurbishment and Mr Adie put me in charge of getting the landing settled. The office was a state. The women were arguing over rooms. Everyone was unhappy with something, and I couldn't find anything in the office. We had to move twenty-five women today only a few yards. It was a nightmare that took all afternoon. "We should have thought it out better. Some prisoners, we know, would find it stressful. We should have moved them on a separate day," I complained to Mr Adie.

On B3, I moved Ms Richards to a cell near the office so she could ask me all the questions she likes without me having to get up. Things were so busy this afternoon trying to get the landing sorted out that I don't think I even checked on her when I started my shift. When everyone was locked in behind their cell doors, I thought I might sort out the unit office. At last, it was quiet. What a difference TVs make. But before I could pour myself a cup of tea, cell number seventeen's emergency bell went off.

Emergency bells are normally pressed for a cigarette light, and I invariably prepared to issue a warning. It took me five seconds to look at our new board to see who was in number seventeen, which was on the other side of the unit around a corner. I saw the name Richards. I raced there my heart in my mouth certain that this might well be a true emergency. She had pressed the emergency bell and had then waited for me to arrive at her cell door before she jumped off the windowsill with a noose around her neck. I lunged for her but was unable to break her fall. Searching my belt, I had nothing I could use to cut her down. I was still waiting for my strip knife to be issued. All I could do was call on my radio for immediate assistance. I screamed for the wing cleaners, Ms Black and Ms White, but they couldn't hear. I held her up with both my arms wrapped around her, but I could see the panic in her eyes as she tried to loosen the noose around her own neck. She could only cry "Miss!" and I could only say, "Don't worry, I'm here now!" The thundering sound of prison boots coming from every corner of the prison got louder and louder.

"You hear that, Ms Richards?" The noose around her neck was squeezing the life out of her. Her laboured breath grew silent, I tried to loosen the noose but it meant letting her go. All I could do was hold her up.

"Ms Richards, Ms Richards stay with me," I cried.

Officers rushed into the cell and cut her down, then the nurse started CPR, but I knew that she was dead.

10.00 p.m.

The night staff was checking the landing and there was nothing left for me to do but go home. But I was still there alone in the office. In the office door way stood the only man in the prison who could understand how I was feeling.

I rushed into his arms and cried "Mr King". Mr Adie ran on to the unit to offer me comfort. When he saw me in the arms of Mr King, he paused and then turned back.

Amber's Blog 2018

Posted – 10th October 2018

Written in the hotel room in Stone Town, Zanzibar, Tanzania

So much has changed over the years. I've seen violence in prisons skyrocket. The government has tried everything, privatisation, bringing in the third sector, a drive to reduce short-term sentences. Yet re-offending is still high and prisons are still failing. All these new initiatives cannot off set the cuts that the prison service has had to endure.

I believe that the prison system has always failed women. I do not take the view that we should not send women to prison at all. My years in service has exposed me to the many complex reasons women end up in prison. There was an overwhelming theme that the women were victims themselves struggling to get the support they needed or pawns in a larger game.

I have tried to think of an example that could illustrate how education, employment and skills training can transform the life of a person in prison. Unfortunately, I could not think of one example, not because there are none but because it's currently the exception and not the rule. Education in women's prisons is mainly therapeutic with a narrow range of subjects and some basic English and Maths. We see employment and skills training as the role of probation. We almost expect women to come out of prison and remain dependant, instead of being given the tools they need to find work. Many of the courses in prison are too limited. Local colleges could partner with prisons to offer a full range of interesting and useful courses that they can start in prison. We should encourage adult learning to be continuous. Some adult prisoners may benefit from taking an art course in prison that should be identified and not just taken because there is nothing else on offer.

Employment and skills training need to be just as important in women's prisons as it is in male prisons. The focus on finding work is also not just for the probation service but the job hunt should start in prison. There's so much more that the government can do to incentivise employers to take who could be considered as high-risk employees. The fact is if an offender re-offends it's not only the cost of imprisonment that needs to be considered, but also the cost to the community and the victims. The state has a duty to do all it can to end the cycle of crime that many of these offenders feel trapped in by providing access to employment and skills training and all the help they need to stand on their own two feet when they leave prison.

Diverting women with mental health and drug substance misuse issues away from prison and into secure centres that can deal with their issues is not being soft on crime. These individuals need to access the support that they need to move forward with their lives and contribute to society. In addition, if women have access to a wider range of quality education, employment and skills training in prison we may well see numbers come down considerably.

Chapter 12

A New Africa(Tanzania)

10th October 2018

6.00 p.m. - Stone Town (Zanzibar, Tanzania)

I arrived yesterday on the Tanzanian island of Zanzibar on my own. I'm on day three of not smoking and I'm feeling it.

Anyway, yesterday I entered Stone Town at about 1.00 p.m. and my impression is that it's different from what I've so far seen in Africa. I noticed a change when we entered Tanzania. The women no longer wore wrap skirts with African prints. I saw lots of silks and prints that were of an Asian or Arab influence. The country has a high Muslim population. There are women covered completely, but there are also a lot of women without the hijab. In Stone Town, they tell us that that, as women, we have to have our shoulders and head covered when walking around the streets. I took a cab outside the enclosed old town. The memory card in my camera needed to be cleared onto CD, the hostel said there somewhere in the market that could do it for me. I was planning to walk to the market, as I was told that it wasn't far.

"Please, please, sister, let me take you to the market," the friendly taxi driver who had driven me to Barclays Bank that afternoon said to me. He was a chubby little man about five feet four inches tall in his early fifties. I was glad he drove me as it was a little farther than I had expected. Once we arrived at the market, my taxi driver insisted on coming with me to find the shop. I had planned on first browsing for a good hour, but he ignored my refusal. Once out the car, it was clear that it wasn't the best place for a woman to brows the shops alone. My taxi driver went from shop to shop in the massive market trying to find a photo store. We went down many alleyways of 'back-to-back' shops and stall holders, behind the meat and clothes markets. As he weaved through the crowd, I kept a nervous eye on him and struggled to keep up. From the traders to the buyers, all I could see were men everywhere, most of who looked at me with disgust as I hurried by in my western clothes. As we made our way through the back alleys, I felt so uncomfortable. I realised that I had entered a new very male- dominated world.

11th October

11.00 a.m. - Zanzibar (Tanzania)

I've got the whole day to myself. I'm at the north end of the island where it's stunning. It's like those holiday brochures that have a picture of an empty beach with white sands and clear water. I always think that such images are staged or enhanced on a computer, and if it was real, then I certainly wouldn't be able to afford to go there. But here I am sitting in that perfect picture overlooking an empty beach with white sand and clear warm water.

It's day *six* of not smoking! I think I'm over the worst of it. Day *three* was by far the worst, and day *four* wasn't that much easier. After dinner, at around 8.00 p.m., I've been desperate to get to bed because I just can't stand the craving. Yesterday was a little better.

I would hire a motorbike to do some exploring, but I couldn't be bothered. After lunch, I just wanted to relax on the beach. Under the shade of a tree, I overheard another group on a similar tour but going the other way. They were discussing the "Africa problem". It bothered me somewhat, as I wondered what has changed since the 1400s when the Europeans came and saw Africa as "the problem" and ourselves as the "solution". Is it an ingrained belief that we have of western superiority? Our minds seem to be conditioned into believing that Africa is helpless. Such a viewpoint seems to be all around me disguised as innocent conversation.

"I wonder if they know how to make sausages. I guess they would have to get them from South Africa," one lady said.

12.30 p.m.

I've come back to Stone Town. I've hired a bicycle instead of a motor bike or a car. The bicycle cost ten dollars. I've noticed here that women don't drive the little mopeds.

They don't even ride bicycles. I haven't seen one woman on a bike. Only men. The women walk or sit on the back of a bike with the man driving.

12th October

11.15 a.m. Zanzibar (Tanzania)

Before I left Zanzibar this afternoon, I wanted to ride back to the market to take a few discreet photos. However, that proved impossible as I seemed to be the first woman in Zanzibar to have ever ridden a bicycle. Everyone was staring at me in shock- horror. I've been unable to explore freely the maze of shops and alleys. Yesterday afternoon, I shopped till I dropped. I was on foot, and because of that was constantly hassled and harassed by men. Not just hassled to buy things, but "hitting" on me. In the afternoon sun, one man in particular, every time I walked past, would follow me down the street saying; "My sister, you think you are too good for me!" Each time, he became more aggressive. Nowhere on this trip have I experienced this kind of harassment.

Last night, I was so glad to have my bike. At 7.00 p.m., I got on it and rode as fast as I could down the dark, narrow streets to the Italian restaurant that was ten minutes' walk away. Men shouted out aggressively "What are you doing?", "Where are you going?", "Stop that woman" as I sped past them. Other women in my hostel have not had this hostile reaction to their presence. This might be because they are

White or because they do not go out alone. I have enjoyed being mistaken for a local woman on this trip, getting the local price for goods, but not being treated like a tourist here has also answered my questions about why I have seen no women in town.

I remember watching a programme on TV about how it's human nature to assimilate and how we are programmed to conform. That is what culture is: a pattern of behaviour that is copied. There are no laws against the women riding bikes or laws stopping women walking through the streets and markets. Maybe it's just a cultural thing that has developed over time. Like blue for boys and pink for girls. We have developed gender codes, which have become accepted. Each culture has developed different codes around gender most of them I think illogical. I have a friend that refused to buy his four-year-old son a doll, when he had asked for one. Why? Because "it just wasn't right" he said. My friend told his child it was a "girl's toy". Cultural codes change over time. However, comparing girl's toys and boy's toys is not quite the same when "culture" is being used to oppress, harass, and confine women. I feel uncomfortable, even scared, to go out on my own here.

On my first day in Tanzania, it was day three of 'no smoking', I saw a giraffe cross the road. I wasn't in a game park or anything. The animals were simply free to roam the countryside. I didn't expect Africa to be so diverse. I'm not sure what I expected. I wanted African culture, but in my mind, I had a preconceived idea of what that culture was.

Chapter 13

15th October

4.45 p.m. Arusha (Tanzania)

I could go into the Serengeti tomorrow. I've got another five days before my trip ends and I'm excited at what I'm learning. It's as though my journey is just beginning. When I started in Southern Africa, my lack of knowledge and understanding was frustrating. With five days to go, I wonder just how much more I will learn? I've almost finished reading my prison diaries, where I'm hoping to find answers.

One Week in 2006 Monday

You Mean the World to Me

I had arranged to meet Ms Freeman at 6.30 a.m. this morning, an hour before the start of my shift, she had agreed to give feedback on a proposal that I was writing for the prison service. Waiting for her in the D3 smoking room Mr King showed up with a box of chocolates for me. He asked if he, instead of Ms Freeman, could look at my proposal. Ms Freeman had set me up.

"Ms Campbell, we have to work together. This distance between us isn't professional. I said some things that you might have found hurtful. I know you're disappointed about not being put forward for Tornado, but I think it's for the best."

"Disappointed?" I couldn't contain my emotion. "You've taken away all my hope. The hope that I could become good at something."

"You're good at lots of stuff. Look what you've done with the prison induction programme and now with this stuff on disability. I just don't want you to get hurt."

"I wonder how many male officers you've turned down for Tornado because they might get hurt. Please Mr King, don't worry about me, I can take care of myself. I just wanted my application to be considered based on my ability to be a riot officer," I said. "Anyway, what do you care if I get hurt?"

"How can you say that Amber? You mean the world to me," he said.

Footsteps approaching the unit office interrupted our argument. We sat in silence waiting. It was Mr Adie.

"You guys want any breakfast from the canteen?" Mr Adie asked. "No thanks," we both replied.

"Yah, the canteen's going downhill." Pulling up a chair, Mr Adie went on "I might go down to Holloway Road..."

"Adie, can you give us a minute?" Mr King said.

"Sure, sorry." Adie got up. Just before he left, he looked at me concerned.

"Yeah, I'm fine," I said. Mr Adie then left the office.

I said to Mr King, "It's okay, I'll get over it. I'm fine."

"You're the best officer I've got on Level 3, I don't want to lose you. So, what's this proposal you're working on?"

"It's a proposal to prison service HQ suggesting that they train all prison officers in how to support prisoners with disabilities, particularly hidden disabilities like dyslexia."

Mr King pulled up his chair next to mine and started to read through my draft proposal with excitement. He lavished compliments on me and listed several ways that I could improve the draft. Sitting with him that hour I realised how much I valued his opinion and enjoyed his company. Maybe Mr King was right, there were other things that I was good at. It was clear that Tornado was not going to happen for me, so I had to find a way to move on.

Diversity Week

Diversity Week is here. I heard that this morning's opening

in the chapel was a disaster. Very few prisoners turned up, and those who did were heckling Maria and Ms Hall. I'm glad I wasn't there. I got my hair done and then rushed into work this afternoon for a fashion show rehearsal. Ms Weaver's wheelchair has broken. Ms Johnson is still waiting for a new commode, and I haven't met with either of them yet to go over their presentations for Tuesday's Disability Day. It's all a bit up in the air, but my fashion show is the talk of the prison, with expectations running high.

Prison life revolves around routine; the same old same old every day. This week—and for one week only—all that will change. I've brought in all the saris I bought in India. There's one prisoner in the whole prison who knows how to wrap a sari. Ms Singh, a young fragile woman who was too scared to come out of her cell a week ago. She has not only taken charge of fitting the saris, but also enlisted the help of Ms Bennett to make all the other costumes for the show.

I was just about to leave the Senior Officer's office when Governor Rose marched in. "Ms Campbell, just the person I want to see. Ms Bennett cannot be part of your fashion show or play any part in the diversity week. We have a number of high-profile guests coming down from HQ and I don't want to risk prisoners like Ms Bennett embarrassing us."

"Ms Bennett has calmed down quite a bit, m'am," I said.

"I don't want a discussion about it, Ms Campbell," Governor Rose said.

I looked at Mr King, who looked on in silence.

"Okay," I said as I left the office holding in my frustration. I placed my ear to the closed door hoping that Mr King might intervene.

"I see that even 'Crack Head' Ms Phipps has been drafted in. This is an important week for the prison and I can't allow this to become a freak show," Governor Rose went on/ "I might have Ms Phipps and Ms Bennett transferred."

"This week is supposed to be about engaging prisoners, not promoting your career," Mr King said.

"I don't like your tone," Governor Rose said

"Ms Bennett's made a lot of progress; if anything, she's a prisoner that you could show off to show how Holloway under your leadership is making a difference," Mr King suggested.

"Fine. If there's any trouble, I'll know who to blame."

I've got a group of women working on the set design for the gymnasium, and a separate group of women doing hair and makeup. For over a week, the ten women I selected to take part in the show have been practising their dance moves on the landings. Day by day, the excitement for the event has been building. I see this as I walk through the prison with the women singing at the top of their lungs one of the songs that will play during the show; Carl Douglas's "Kung Fu Fighting".

Today, I was reminded of why we were putting so much effort into "diversity week". One of our eighteen-year-old YOIs said to me, "Ms Campbell, my family is a bit racist…" but after spending time with Ms Singh and some other Black prisoners from different cultures, she told me, "My family are so wrong…"

Maria and Ms Hall are rightly pissed off that I've been a little blinkered by the fashion show. The hype around the show seems to overshadow the hard work they've put into the entire week.

"I've organised all the events for tomorrow, and I've organised the Windrush exhibition in the prison library for the week," I said.

Ms Johnson

I gave Ms Johnson a new commode this evening. A few days ago, she received her new, extra-large wheelchair. However, the officers on Level 5 are refusing to push her in her wheelchair to activities around the prison because they say she is "too fat", and they say it takes two of them to move her. They're now seeking advice from the union. "You have to consider health and safety," Mr Potter said.

The whole thing is ridiculous. I don't know what she's in for this time, and I don't know the details of her disability, but she's a shadow of the loud and intimidating woman that I first met many years ago. Trying to comfort the broken woman this morning, as she begged for help, I reflected on the victims of her crimes and her bullying behaviour for which *she* showed little sympathy. In the past, prison never bothered Ms Johnson, but now she cries herself to sleep every night. By day, she depends on the mercy of other prisoners to help her get dressed and move her around the prison.

"It's a humiliation worse than death," Ms Johnson sobbed.

On the D3 unit, Mr Potter looked up from the office computer to find Maria stood in the doorway. Maria told me she laid in bed awake at night going over what Mr Potter had said to her in the nightclub.

"Can you still get tickets for that stand-up comedy show?" Maria asked Mr Potter.

Tuesday

Disability Day

Today, I had my Disability Day. It was flat; far from the awakening that I wanted. I think the prisoners enjoyed the wheelchair basketball, and the sign language class went well, however, I spent most of the day running around sorting out problems. I had outside guests from the Prisoner Service HQ. Our own governors didn't even bother to show up to open the day, or come to any of the events, which was embarrassing for me and disappointing for the prisoners who put so much work into the day.

"I hope that you've enjoyed this morning," I said looking around the half empty gym. "Please refer to your programmes for workshops this afternoon on Hidden Disabilities." My special guests from the prison service HQ flicked through the four-page programme with little interest. Mr King gave me a slight nod of encouragement and Mr Adie had merely come down to see me crash and burn. The women, although small in number, hobbled together with their walking sticks, walking frames and sat in their wheelchairs. I looked at Ms Johnson, she was tired, battered and bruised from the constant struggle of life. I held the microphone tight.

"I know that having a disability isn't something you can put down and pick up when it suits you," I said. "It's not a choice, when you don't have access to education or the tools to work with or create because of your disability. It robs you of your humanity. Discrimination comes in many forms; some might say it's hidden and hard to stop. Well, if you've got a physical disability you can be turned away from public spaces and no one will think anything of it. Those of us with learning disabilities or mental health conditions are treated like we need to apologise for the inconvenience that we cause to everyone else. Would it be easier if we were all just hidden away? Progress is slow. I was on a train the other day, crawling along. Looking out the window, I saw people walking faster than the train. I got up from my seat and yelled 'Driver, can't you go any faster?' He said 'I can go faster but I have to stay with the train'. I know you want to go faster, but I urge you to stay with me, together we can push this train up the hill of progress."

At lunchtime, everyone for some reason or another was not around. So, I opened a Pot Noodle in D3 smoking room alone. The lime green walls had turned yellow and the smell of cigarette smoke radiated from the soft blue chairs. The kettle was broken, so I headed to the SO office. A plain, black folder sat between the kettle and the biscuit tin. I opened the folder and there was page after page of short plays. Comedies, thrillers and romances. Reading through, my mind was again transported out of the prison by the work of the playwriter. One play was a workplace romance, where the main character is in love with her dashing boss who is a bit of a prick. She overlooks the fine qualities of her boring yet trustworthy colleague. In the end, her boss is exposed and she of course ends up with the boring colleague, which left me with the warm glow of natural justice.

The office door swung open.

"What are you doing in here?" Mr Adie demanded.

I jumped to my feet. Over an hour had passed and I had barely touched my Pot Noodle. "Nothing, I'm just leaving," I said.

I wondered if it might be the work of a prisoner, but why would it be in the SO office? Mr King was probably my mystery writer. He was a hopeless idealist. I pictured him sat at his writing desk and perhaps, overlooking his garden, while writing romances.

On the Stairs

Mr King bumped into Governor Rose on the stairwell. It was her fault, she was in a rush, as always, to get to a meeting on Level 4. Her meeting papers that were organized in a black folder spilled out over the floor. Bending over to pick them up she huffed and puffed. Mr King kneeled down to give her a hand.

"It's okay," she said.

But Mr King continued to assist her.

"You missed Ms Campbell's Disability presentation," Mr King said.

"I was busy in meetings." Governor Rose stood to her feet. "I hear it was good. Sorry, I have to dash."

She continued to walk up the stairs at a brisk pace with Mr King behind her. "All these stairs are keeping you nice and fit," Mr King said.

Governor Rose whipped around.

"Mr King, that's completely inappropriate."

"Yes, maybe it is, given you're a Governor and I'm just a low-down Principal Officer." "That's not what I mean. Our rank has nothing to do with it. I won't be undermined," Governor Rose said.

"I'm not undermining you. I'm just saying these stairs are keeping you in shape. Is that so bad?" Mr King said.

"I think you're pushing it and you know you are." Mr King gave her a cheeky wink and she smiled.

Ms Bennett

Ms Bennett has surprised herself; she has found her talent in sewing.

"Look at this," Ms Bennett said, as she laid out a brightly coloured dress across the office desk. "It's in the Jamaican flag colours. It's not finished yet, but I'll have it done in time for the fashion show on Friday."

"It's beautiful," I said. "You're really good at this.""You think?" Ms Bennett asked.

"Yah. You should take it up when you get out of here. Maybe go to college or something."

"I won't get into college. I never get through rehab and I always end up back out on the streets."

"How many times have you dropped out of rehab?" I asked. "Twice."

"Twice? You're in and out of here at least three times a

year. Who's sorting out your rehab placement for when you leave prison on Friday?" I asked.

"I'm not going rehab when I leave here. I'm going to bunk at my mate's flat Friday night. I'll have no money over the weekend, so I might have to suck—"

I interrupted her, before she could finish her sentence. "Okay. I'll do what I can," I said.

SO Exam Revision

At lunchtime, Mr Adie met with me, Maria, Ms Hall and Mr Jamu in the C3 association room like he had done for the last three weeks.

"Exam question one, you're the senior officer and you're short of staff, the prisoners have been in their cells all day. What do you do?"

"If you only have one member of staff on each unit, I wouldn't let the prisoners out because the officer's safety comes first," Mr Jamu said.

"I agree," Ms Hall added

"I think," Maria paused to think. "I think, the prisoners have to come out of theircells in the evening. The women need to take a shower and to call their families, if not, we would have trouble very quickly. I would stand down as senior officer and just become an officer on the unit. That way, there would be enough officers on the unit."

"What do you think?" Mr Adie asked me

"I would let half the unit out for an hour and then let the other side out after. If things are really tight I could do it thirty minutes at a time. That way the women get to use the bathrooms and make calls, but still maintain safety."

"That's right," Mr Adie confirmed.

Wednesday

Debt free

"Here's to Maria and being debt free, praise the Lord" Ms Hall said, raising a can of coke in the air as we sat down for lunch in the C3 association room.

"I'm finally moving forward. Oh, and did I tell you, my offer on the flat in Dagenham was accepted," Maria said.

"Praise the Lord," Ms Hall said.

Maria had paid off over £40,000 of credit card debt, car and personal loan debt. She had sold all her designer handbags and shoes, worked every weekend and lived on pasta. I thought she would find it hard to sell her beloved designer collection, but the glow on her face told me it was an act of liberation. A new, financially responsible person replaced the old indulgent Maria, although I knew that she had kept just one or two of those bags for special occasions.

"Now, instead of paying £700 a month just in minimum payments you can put aside a proper emergency fund of three to six months of expenses. You'll never ever have to take out a payday loan or use a credit card again. Then comes the fun stuff, saving and investing and all that money every month – you'll be loaded."

"What do you mean, invest it?" Maria ask me.

"Well, just say you invested £500 a month in a fund, with compound interest you'd retire a millionaire," I said.

"That's incredible," Maria said.

"We should go out clubbing on Friday night?" I said.

"And church on Sunday morning," added Ms Hall.

Thursday

Ms Bennett

I wished Ms Bennett good luck before she entered the office where a greying old man sat polishing his glasses, next to a woman in a suit. I hoped that my presence might encourage her, but I now fear that it might have just made her more nervous. She knew that I had pulled every string to set up the interview.

"Good afternoon, I'm Tony. I hear you're quite a talented dress maker."

Ms Bennett looked out through the glass door at me. She held in her hand the brochure about the rehab placement that I had found for her in Leeds. This morning Ms Bennett couldn't contain her excitement, looking back at her through the glass door I wondered where her enthusiasm had run off to.

"So, we might be able to help you back into Further Education, is that something you would be interested in?"

Ms Bennett shrugged her shoulders. "What are you writing?" Ms Bennett asked. "We're just making some notes."

"Notes about what?"

I could feel the tension from outside the room. Ms Bennett stood to her feet and yelled at them from behind the desk. I was about to rush in when she stormed out. "Sorry to waste your time, Ms Campbell," she said as she pushed past me.

I chased after her but she was reluctant to tell me what had gone wrong.

"I spent hours sorting out that interview for you. Those people have come all the way down to London to see you at short notice and you can't keep a lid on it for twenty minutes. What the hell is wrong with you?" I said.

"Well you didn't tell me I'd have to sit an exam."

"What exam? They only wanted you to write a sentence or two about yourself."

"I'm not writing anything. They can stick the rehab place up their ass."

The penny dropped. Ms Bennett can't read or write.

SO Exam Results

The SO exam results came out today. Ms Hall, Maria, Mr Jamu and I agreed to open our letters together. We met in the C3 association room in the morning after the women had left the landing. I held my white envelope to my side dreading the moment that I would have to open it in front of an audience. I would have preferred to open mine on my own in the toilet, but Ms Hall full of faith insisted that we shared the moment.

"On the count of three. One, two, three," Maria said as though we were starting a race. We tore open our envelopes. There was a moment's silence as we all read the first line from the Governor that started with "I am pleased to inform you…" Ms Hall and Maria let out a joyful scream of surprise. Maria threw her arms around Mr Potter. "Yes! I knew that you could do it," Mr Potter said to Maria.

"Oh my God, I can't believe it. I've passed," said Mr Jamu.

"Don't cry, Mr Jamu. Please don't cry." Mr Jones laughed.

My letter started with "unfortunately…" Maria and Ms Hall were still bouncing up and down. I smiled and joined their celebrations. My disappointment was clear only to Mr Adie.

"Let me see your letter, Ms Campbell," Mr Adie asked.

At a glance of the letter he added "You should take it again next year. You only failed by a few points on the maths section."

Ms Hall and Maria then realised that I had not passed. The jubilant high of the room then crashed down as they all turned to me. I put on a fake smile and lifted my head. "It's okay, Mr Adie's right, I only failed by a few points. I'll take it again next year."

That was a lie. There's no way I'm going to put myself through this again next year or any year again. Ms Hall and Maria seemed to accept failure as a minor setback instead of the devastating blow that it was for me. The mood in the room returned to celebration, although slightly muted.

Mr Adie seemed determined to return the mood to that of depression.

"I wouldn't get too excited. They'll use any excuse not to promote you. Ms Hall, they'll say they can't promote you because your part time. They'll make up some stupid reason why you can't be promoted if your face doesn't fit."

Ms Hall and Maria shrugged off Mr Adie's scepticism and spent the rest of the day humming gospel songs and when they thought no one was around the odd "thank you, Jesus" slipped out. I was on an A shift and was struggling to see how I would keep up my act until 9.00 p.m. I must have knocked on Mr King's office door seven times hoping to catch him this morning.

"Mr King's just called and asked if you could go around to his office," Ms Hall said after dinner.

As I walked around to his office, I had to stop myself from running, I had to stop myself from crying. Mr King was the only one who would know that I was shattered, not because I had failed the SO exam, but because it was a sign that I could not overcome my dyslexia.

"I heard that you failed the SO exam," Mr King said.

But before I could close the door behind me, he stood up from behind his desk.

"I haven't got time to talk to you now about it, I'll come around to B3 this evening if that's okay. Keep your chin up you can go for it again next year. Come here."

He gave me a shallow hug with one arm. I wanted to sink into his embrace, but he pulled away.

"Keep your head up, my girl," he said with a wink before, he left the room.

9.15 p.m.

The roll had been called and the night patrol had relieved

me of my duties. While the night patrol walked on towards A3 unit carrying a bag full of midnight snacks I sat on B3 waiting for Mr King. I heard footsteps approaching the office so I flicked the kettle on and got two cups ready.

"Two sugars, please," Mr Adie said standing in the doorway.

"I'm waiting for Mr King," I said moving the cups away from his reach.

"Mr King has gone. He rushed off as soon as they called the roll fifteen minutes ago," he replied, sitting down stretching out his legs.

Drained of the will to hide my true feelings any longer, I put on my coat and my eye searched the office for my bag.

"You know I failed the SO exam the first time around," Mr Adie said. "I took it again the year after. But you're not going to do that, are you. What I want to know is why, I mean you're no quitter are you, Ms Campbell?"

I stood in the doorway with my bag on my shoulder and wondered whether to tell Mr Adie of all people why I wasn't going to take the SO exam again.

"I'm not a quitter but I know when I'm beat. I gave it my best and I still failed. I studied for months, I gave it my all and I still failed. You can't win every battle and sometimes you have to choose which battles are worth fighting. I've learnt the hard way that if you're going to fail, fail fast and move on. That's what I need to do now. I need to move on."

"Move on to what?" Mr Adie asked. "I don't know," I said.

My face crumpled and I could not hold back the flood of tears that had been building up since this morning.

The sound of my whimpering filled the room as Mr Adie struggled to find any words that could offer comfort.

"When I joined the prison service thirteen years ago, I was so ambitious, like you. I thought I would climb up the ranks and be a governor in five years. I had it all planned out. One year as an officer, two years as and SO, two years as a PO and then governor. When I failed the SO exam I was gutted but it was only a minor setback, I passed the year after. But I didn't get promoted to SO that year, nor the year after that, nor the year after that. After four years of watching other people get promoted over me, I began to wonder if I would ever be promoted. Maybe I shouldn't have relied so much on the prison service to fulfil all my ambitions. So, I began to do stuff that I enjoyed outside of work. I bought a rundown house that hadn't been lived in for years did it up and sold it for a profit."

"I thought you were a landlord?" I asked, puzzled.

"Well I own one flat that I rent out, but I don't really make a profit on that because I try to keep the rent as low as possible. No, I do up houses. I might buy one a year, do them up really nice and sell them at a profit. There's something satisfying about renewing an old house to make it somebody's home. I also sit on the board of a small local theatre company. I love the theatre. We do lots of stuff within the community and local schools. Did I tell you I write plays?"

"No." I looked at Mr Adie in amazement.

"I write the odd church play that we perform to the homeless at Christmas," he said. Mr Adie then gave me the best advice that I had ever received.

"What I'm trying to say Ms Campbell, is don't put all your eggs in one basket. This is just a job, there's lots of other stuff out there that you can do."

A light went off in my head as everything he said made perfect sense. I also could not believe that the comedies and romantic plays that brightened my evenings came from Mr Adie. His revelation was unexpected and I was unsure how to respond.

"Thanks," I said.

Friday

Ms Bennett

"Have you got your train ticket?" I asked.

"Yah."

"Don't just say 'yah'. Check." "Calm down, miss. Look. I've got it."

"Okay, do you know who you're going to be meeting when you get there? Have you got their number? Have you got the rehab number? And don't forget to call your probation worker as soon as you arrive."

"Yah, yah yah."

Ms Bennett could have been my only daughter that I was waving off to university. I was full of worry about whether she would complete the course, whether she would be safe on her own and so far away from all that she knows in London. Yet, I looked at her through water filled eyes of pride, full of hope for her future.

"Thanks, miss."

"Come here, give us a hug." I stood at the prison gates with my arms open. "I don't want to see you again."

"You won't," she said.

I lingered around the gate area for a while until I could no longer see her walking in the dimmed evening light.

After avoiding Ms Johnson for two days when my shift ended, I went up to Level 5 to see her for a few hours. It's a thankless job, as I've learned, But I'm grateful that I am the one there to listen to these women when they're at their lowest. In most cases, I can't do or even say anything, in most cases they feel that their world has ended and all I can do is be there.

Saturday

Mr Jones

Mr Jones was "walked to the gate" this morning and is now under investigation after a prisoner made an allegation that he had sex with her. Word went around like a flame that he was about to take the long walk of shame down the long and only straight stretch of corridor in Holloway Prison. It almost felt like a funeral procession. I wasn't able to pay my last respects. It has since emerged that the prisoner has made several malicious and unfounded allegations against staff to whom she had taken a dislike to. Mr Jones wasn't even working in the prison on the day that she claims he had sex with her. However, the prison management has to be seen to be conducting a full investigation, so they have taken Mr Jones off landing duties. I saw him in the prison car park broken and humiliated, I couldn't bear to look him in the eye worried that I might cry.

Sunday

Fashion Show

The Fashion Show was a success! I'm so proud of myself and the women. At the last minute, it all looked like it would fall apart. The textiles teacher wouldn't give me the rest of the costumes that Ms Bennett and Ms Singh had made and told me two hours before the show was due to start, that she was bringing her own prisoners to model them. Plus, I lost the CD with all the songs on it for the show. We couldn't do a dress rehearsal in the morning because the gym stereo system had broken down. I also got the dreaded call from Mr Smith in Detail saying it would have to be cancelled because so many prisoners wanted to go to the show that they were having problems finding the extra staff needed to supervise. We packed the gym with prisoners and extra staff stayed on for the show. In the end, the five women that the textile teacher brought down went on first and served as a fantastic warm up act. When the women that I had worked with went on stage, the gym erupted. We could have been in a rock concert at Wembley. All the time, effort, stress, and late nights showed in the quality of their performance. We had dresses from West Africa, and saris from India. Ms Hall did a great job as MC and Maria helped with some African dresses. Maria wowed the audience by modelling one of her dresses, as she walked down the catwalk, Mr Potter looked on.

It's been so rewarding over the last few weeks seeing these ten women blossom. From 'Crack Head' Ms Phipps with her big mouth, to Ms Locksmith, who burst into tears because she thought she wouldn't have an African dress to wear to Ms Black and Ms White, who were both determined to feature in every section of the show and also did a Jamaican section that took the prison roof off. Ms Singh was happy to stay backstage and manage everything. I would not have done it without her. I also can't forget how Ms Bennett started jumping on her bed when she found out I had selected her and that I was coming up to get her to be part of the show. For the past two weeks, how can I forget all the women singing at the top of their voices in their cells every night; "People of the world join hands, start a love train…" that echoed throughout the prison. It was the final song played in the gym this evening.

As the prisoners joined hands to sing together, I stood backstage and caught the same look in the eyes of Maria and Ms Hall. The three of us had worked together to make the first ever Diversity Week at HMP Holloway a success.

Mr King told me that I've been invited to prison service HQ to talk about implementing a national disability policy throughout the prison service. It's a direct result of what I thought was a failed Disability Day.

On the way back to Level 3 from the gym that evening, Mr King stuck his head around the door of Governor Rose's office.

"Have you come to gloat?" Governor Rose asked. "Gloat about what?" Mr King said.

"You were right about Ms Bennett. The guests from headquarters were very impressed with her," Governor Rose said.

"I bet she made you look good."

"Yes, she did. The whole week made me and the prison look good." Governor Rose put a stack of files in to her briefcase that she would read through at home. "I'm off. Are you going to the car park?"

"No, not yet. I just need to go tie up a few loose ends on Level 3," Mr King said.

I sat up in my chair in the C3 association room still buzzing from the fashion show, my head exploding with ideas.

"I think we need to do stuff outside of the prison service. Ms Hall, why don't you think about becoming a school governor at your kid's school. Maria, you've got a Master's degree in Finance, why don't you go on a Board or something? We've got so much to offer, but if the prison service won't use our talents here, we should put them to use elsewhere," I said to Maria and Ms Hall.

Ms Hall had to dash off. She hoped to get home to see her kids before they got put to bed. Maria and Mr Potter left the prison 'hand in hand' like teenage lovers. Mr King appeared in the doorway of the C3 association room. He handed me a piece of paper.

"What's this?" I asked

"I've approved your application to be trained as a tornado officer." I looked confused.

"I think you're a good officer, I've always believed that. I just thought you needed more time. You know what this means. If you get through the training, they could call you to any prison in the country," he said with concern.

"Yes, I know," I said.

"You will be called to male prisons as well."

"Yes, I know," I replied.

"You could get hurt," he said with even greater concern.
"Yes, thank you," I replied.

Amber's Blog 2018

Posted – 17th October 2018

Written in a campsite in Arusha, Tanzania

The structured daily prison routine is designed to manage time, not to instigate a change of behaviour. Therefore, in my view, prison does not rehabilitate or even punish those that will eventually once more become our neighbours.

The responsibility for rehabilitation should, I believe, lie with the prison service itself and not the multiple agencies that we employ without results. From my experience, it's clear that we need separate specialised facilities for drug rehabilitation, mental health and youth offenders. The one-size-fits-all model is simply not working. I ask myself if it's really worth sending an eighteen-year-old shoplifter to prison for a few weeks, or even handing down a community service order, only to have them back again year after year. The real issue is their drug habit and/or mental health problem. A longer sentence that would give such an offender a qualification, or a trade skill, whilst dealing with the issue at the heart of her re-offending would be more productive. The cost of the current approach is too high for society.

I believe that we need to address an already failing system. The prison population has doubled in size since 1991. This trend seems set to grow further.

Repeat offenders account for almost half of prisoners bouncing in and out of prison with their underlying issues never being addressed.

On my first day of training as a new prison officer, I remember being told that prison was not a punishment. Having their freedom taken away by the courts was the punishment. Prison was there to rehabilitate. This was an ethos I held dear, but found frustrating as we did nothing to promote rehabilitation.

In 2002 when I started at HMP Holloway, Europe's largest female prison, it was common for prisoners to spend up to twenty-two hours a day in their cells with little to keep them occupied. Visitors would be shocked at the level of noise, which would sound as if the prisoners were going mad in their cells. In the years that followed, I saw some reform and investment that had an effect on conditions and the way the prison was run. All of the cells got TV sets and staff levels increased which allowed for activities such as art lessons or time spent in the gymnasium. But is this rehabilitation? I agree with prison governors who say that, due to the short sentences that many prisoners receive, it is not possible for the prison system to be as constructive as it would like.

At a cost of £38,000 a year for each prisoner, I believe that there are more effective ways this money could be spent, such as drug rehabilitation and training. These are long-term solutions that can make a difference.

Chapter 14

The Last Tribe (Tanzania)

17th October 2018

10.00 a.m. - Arusha (Tanzania)

I would have spent the day in the Maasai village, but I really need the day to myself. I've just had breakfast with a White South African man called Darren and an Irish American guy from Boston called Jason. They are both drivers on tour trucks. Jason was wearing a green baseball cap, which read IRISH across the front. Before long, he was telling us about what he did on St. Patrick's Day, the highlight of his calendar. Although he has never been to Ireland, he has been to Jamaica. I've never been to Jamaica, but I have been to Ireland several times. It's strange how we're both so patriotic about countries we've never been to.

    I leaned back in my chair and looked at the three of us: an Irish American, a Black Briton and a White African. It's amazing how migration has changed the world. I considered for a moment these three very different relationships. Jason has the happiest marriage. He can rest assured that *Irish & American* will be deeply in love forever. As for Darren, after a history of violence and abuse, *White & African* are starting the long process of reconciliation. *Black & British* are developing their relationship. Some might say that multi-cultural Britain has failed. Unlike real marriages, divorce is not an option, although many would like to turn back the hands of time. Like any unhappy marriage, it's always the children that suffer most.

18th October

10.30 a.m.- Arusha (Tanzania)

I'm a little sad my time here in Africa is ending. However, I *hate* camping with a passion. I'm now sleeping with four mattresses and I can still feel the ground. The showers, where available, are communal and are either dirty, cold, or crawling with insects.

I noticed yesterday on the sides of most of the mini-vans that they have pictures of Bob Marley or Tupac Shakur, the Black American rapper. There are also many people wearing Bob Marley T-shirts and carrying bags. Every time I saw one, I wanted to say "I'm Jamaican". I felt so proud that these Black Africans felt a connection with Caribbeans and Black Americans.

3.00 p.m.

The Massai people walk with such pride wearing their red cloaks and covered in colourful jewellery. With their bold colours, they stand out from any tribe I have seen. They seem to have taken what they want from western and Middle Eastern cultures. A Maasai warrior can be spotted walking down the streets of Arusha with a staff in one hand and a smart phone in the other. I have learnt that the Africans didn't lose their culture when the Arabs and the Europeans came; it just added another layer to theirs in this deep and diverse continent.

I've just come back from the Maasai village. They build their huts in the traditional rounded fashion, with a straw roof and the outer walls made from mud and cow dung. When finished, they are a light grey colour. I was surprised at how small the village was; only about forty people including children. But that was just one man's family. A man may have up to eight wives, and is the chief of the family. When the sons are ready to marry, they choose a woman from another village and daughters leave their village to go to their husbands. So each village is a family unit. My guide, a twenty-two-year-old called Olestony, told me that there is one chief over the whole clan—which may consist of a number of family units spaced out. He said the women get married at about fourteen to fifteen years and the men at around eighteen to twenty years. He tried to reassure me that female circumcision doesn't happen anymore since the government banned it in 1998. I didn't get to speak to any of the women in the village, but when I asked one of the Maasai guides back at the campsite, he replied with, "Of course it happens still. It's our culture." I have learned just how diverse African culture is on this journey. There are over 3,000 different tribes with their own customs, language and history. Yet, I cannot understand how such an abusive practice can be justified in the name of culture.

We walked through the village. I went into a hut, and behind a partition, they had made beds from cow leather. On the other side, there was a small living area. They used a separate hut as a kitchen. The structure and set up of the village differed totally from the other villages that I've seen. All the men were out with the cattle, and the women (about ten), were collecting water from a hosepipe nearby to build a new hut. It was the women who smeared the mud on the outer walls of the hut and the women who also work on the craft market outside the campsite. Olestony said that there was a school two kilometers away that the children attended that was why there were no children of school age around at that moment. At the end of my visit, I exchanged email addresses with Olestony.

It's been great to forget about all my troubles at home, but tomorrow's my last day. After six weeks, I feel no closer to deciding on whether to leave my husband or to quit my job. Tomorrow, I leave for Nairobi where I can't put off the decision any longer.

Chapter 15

Day Forty-Seven (Kenya)

19th October 2018 7.00 a.m. - Nairobi (Kenya)

I crossed the border yesterday evening into Kenya. I am excited about being here, and even more excited when I saw my single room has its own shower. I even have my own toilet. I hitched a ride with Jason, the Irish American man that I met the other day. In the van, I couldn't take my eyes off the golden plains that stretched out for miles. For an hour, there was nothing, but tall, yellow grass that turned a dazzling gold when caught by the light. Then I'd spot a Maasai herding his cattle, or a small village in the distance. It's another picture of Africa in my mind that I'll take home with me. We came across a family of giraffes, but when they saw the truck they moved on—which was unlike the giraffes in the game parks that have become used to the cars. There was a good atmosphere in the van. We were all singing along to cheesy eighties pop songs like Kylie Minogue's "I Should Be So Lucky."

24th May 2006

7.30 a.m.

Standing in line to get my keys, a thrilled Level 5 officer told me they had released Ms Johnson from prison yesterday afternoon. I didn't get to say goodbye to her. I stood for a while, a little saddened. I then smiled to myself, as I wondered how long it would take for her to come back to Holloway and what outrageous crimes she would commit in her wheelchair to get back here.

"Ms Campbell, do you want your keys or not?" I was holding up the line.

It was Mr Smith's last day today. He's leaving the prison service for good. "So, you off then?" I said, as I walked past his office.

"Yes, I'm out of here at five and I won't look back," Mr Smith said, rubbing his hands together in excitement.

I noticed that he had a European holidays magazine open on the desk in front of him, but I didn't want to prolong the conversation by asking him what his plans were. He raised an eyebrow as if I was keeping him from something more important. A few seconds of awkward silence passed between us, as I stood in the doorway of his office desperate not to ask the obvious question.

"Ok then. Good luck," I said, backing away from the door.

"Okay," he replied, returning to his magazine.

Walking up to the landing, there was a buzz in the air of officers chattering. The list of prison officer moves was now out. I remember when there was a time when the thought of moving units was devastating for me, let alone moving Levels. Although

I've enjoyed working with remanded prisoners on Level 3, I think I'm more than ready to move on to a new challenge.

Today, there was quite a big shake up of prison officers. Walking around the prison, I saw that some were excited, and some officers were relieved because they're safe for another year and some officers were in tears. I let out a sigh of disappointment when I saw 'LEVEL 3' next to my name on the A4 sheet pinned to the wall. I'm not moving – yet another year on the same Level for me.

8.00 a.m.

"Ms Hall, where's the Observation Book?" Maria asked, holding out her hand. Maria turned to Ms Gillard, a new officer on her first day.

"First thing you do in the morning, or whenever you start your shift is read what officers have written in the Observation Book from the last shift. A prisoner died on the wing last night so, it's vital you read up to find out what happened," Maria said. Maria then turned to Ms Hall like a magician would turn to their assistant when they had failed to pass the necessary prop.

"We haven't got the Observation Book. Mr Smith said we should start a new one," Ms Hall said.

"Mr Smith?" Ms Gillard asked.

"He's a senior officer. He doesn't work on the landings anymore, but was put in charge yesterday evening, because the prison was short of staff. Maybe they took the Observation Book, because of the inspection," Maria said.

"Inspection?" Ms Gillard asked.

"Home Office prison inspectors have been in all week, today's the last day, thank God. Management have been so jumpy," I said.

Maria, who was no stranger to prison procedures, frowned with suspicion and rubbed her forehead. "Governor Rose told me this morning that the woman took her own life. So, as long as they followed the procedures, the prison has nothing to hide from the inspectors."

"That's odd, Mr Smith told me she died in her sleep and that she had a history of drug abuse," Ms Hall said.

"When I left work yesterday afternoon 'Crack Head' Ms Phipps was in the same cell with the woman who died, maybe we should ask her if she saw anything?" I said. "When I started my shift this morning, Ms Phipps had already been transferred to another prison. I didn't question it. You know she has a bit of a reputation for being a loud mouth, so I thought the Governor moved her because they didn't want her around during the inspection," Ms Hall said.

The unit felt unsettled. The women huddled together in the back of their cells and spoke to each other with hushed voices. An atmosphere of fear was left after whatever happened the night before. At the side of the dormitory opposite of where the prisoner had died, Ms Hall stood with her back to the wall and strained to listen in on the prisoners' conversation. She overheard one prisoner discuss with another how the officers dragged Ms Phipps off the unit screaming 'murder'. Maria went down to the segregation unit and saw that there were only two prisoners that were transferred to other prisons in the morning, a prisoner called Ms Marshall and Ms Phipps. The only note by Ms Marshall's name was that she had been convicted of Grievous Bodily Harm. On the report filed against Ms Phipps, it stated

'Ms Phipps has made defamatory and unfounded allegations intending to incite a riot' signed by Mr Smith.

We knew very little about what had happened last night. From the rubbed-out marks on the white board we could only make out the dead prisoner's number: 2000. We knew that someone had taken the Observation Book from the unit and that the other prisoners, Ms Marshall and Ms Phipps, who had both shared the dorm with prisoner 2000 had been transferred to another prison first thing in the morning.

"This is big. Why would they want to cover it up if it wasn't big? Whatever happened last night, Mr Smith doesn't want Governor Rose and inspectors to find out."

We nodded our heads in agreement as Maria went on.

"We have to find out what happened and let Governor Rose know," Maria said "Well I can speak to the officer who was on yesterday evening, I've got her phone number," Ms Hall volunteered.

"Okay, and I can speak to a member of the night staff. I've got her phone number," I said.

9.30 a.m.

Ms Rot called Ms Hook into the SO Office. "You're moving to Level 5 next week."

"I saw that, but you know we never get moved. Can't you sort it for me, Roty?" Ms Hook asked.

"Don't worry, I've already put in a special word for you," Ms Rot said with a smile.

"Thanks. I knew I could rely on you."

"You're going to Level 5, today," Ms Rot said. "Stay away from me, stay away from Sherry and if you need to pass through, take the long way around, because you're not welcome on the 3's anymore, is that clear? If I see you on this Level again, I'll have you in the car park. Close the door on your way out."

Ms Hook left Level 3 without saying a word to anyone. Ms Rot sat for a while, contemplating her next actions. "Sod it," she said to herself, rising from her chair.

Ms Rot entered the control room on the other side of the prison. The room was unfamiliar to her and the staff strangers.

"I'm looking for Sherry," Ms Rot asked.

"I'm covering for her for a few hours. I think she just wanted to stretch her legs. Sitting here all day can be a bit much," said an OSG sitting at the radio control station. "I can call her over the prison radio, if it's urgent."

"Yes, it's urgent. Do you mind if I make the call?" Ms Rot asked.

"No problem." The OSG got up.

Ms Rot sat at the radio station in the seat Sherry normally occupied.

"Can OSG Sherry contact the control room?" Ms Rot's voice beamed out on every officer, OSG, Governor and staff radio throughout the prison.

Ms Rot went on, "Sherry, this is Senior Officer Rot. Ms Rot. Roty. I'm no good at all this mushy stuff, so I'll keep it brief. I want you to know that I'm sorry and that I love you." She paused "I love you. Please forgive me."

There was silence over the airwaves.

"That's received. I love you too," Sherry responded over the radio.

10.00 a.m.

I was working with Ms Hall on B3 Unit. After we had escorted all the women to education, we returned to the unit and collapsed into the office chairs relieved that we now had time to ourselves. Maria came bouncing round from C3.

"Is the kettle on?" Maria said, shining. "You're chipper all of a sudden," I said.

"I've got a new job," Maria stated.

I sat up in my chair, straining to contain my excitement.

"Did you get on to the Prison Fast Track Scheme?" I asked.

"Forget about the Prison service, I'm handing in my notice today. I just got the call. I've been offered a job as a manager of a mental health unit in the NHS. Fifty thousand a year starting and '9 to 5'."

"Thank you, Jesus," Ms Hall said.

"Wow," I said.

"I mean what am I doing? I have a Master's degree in Finance, I can speak four languages. If the prison service won't recognise my skills, then it's time to leave."

"That's right," Ms Hall said, pouring the tea.

"When your boss doesn't appreciate your skills, it's time to get a new boss," Maria went on.

"That's right," Ms Hall added.

"I'll work for them for two years and if I don't get promoted to corporate director, I'll start looking for a new job. That's the only thing I've learnt from this place. Don't waste years of your life praying that you'll get noticed for all your hard work. We've got the grades, we've got the experience and some, but we are invisible here," Maria said.

We sat in silence for a few seconds. The sound of sipped tea gave comfort as we mulled over Maria's harsh words of truth.

"I don't mean you, Ms Hall," Maria realising that Ms Hall has worked at Holloway for many years.

"Don't worry, the Lord has answered my prayers. Sisters, I'm moving up to Level 4 next week. But not as an officer." We knew what Ms Hall was going to say next.

Maria and I moved to the edge of our seats ready to jump to our feet. "I'm going to be a Level 4 SO. Halleluiah. And part time, early shifts only, so I can put my babies to bed every night."

We jumped to our feet in celebration. "Somebody says 'glory'," Ms Hall shouted.

"Glory," Maria and I responded. "Somebody says

'glory'."

Mr Adie then appeared in the doorway with his forehead wrinkled by a disapproving frown.

"What the hell's going on here? You're not in church," Mr Adie said.

"Relax, Adie," I said, sitting back down.

"That's Mr Adie to you. Get back to work," he said, annoyed

Maria left with Ms Hall to the mess to get herself an egg roll and stop by the post room while it was still quiet.

They left me in the unit office alone with Mr Adie. While I tided up the office desk, Mr Adie sat looking at me with a smile on his face. I knew that he wanted to start something. On the landing, there was only the background noise of women working in the gardens down below our window and the wing cleaners at the other end of the landing cleaning the unit kitchen. I carried on with what I was doing and ignored his presence.

"Ms Campbell, what do you think of Governor Rose?" he asked. His question puzzled me. "Not much, Why?"

"Didn't you think it was strange that Governor Rose always has leave at the same time as Mr King?"

I knew what he was implying and believed it to be a ridiculous assertion.

"Ms Campbell, everybody knows apart from you. Don't you know that he's been screwing her for months in the Governor's office," Mr Adie said.

"And why are you telling me this, Mr Adie? What is it to you and what is it to me if he is? I don't care."

"Mr King doesn't care for you," he said.

I turned my back on him.

"You're so naïve," Mr Adie said.

"Whatever. Why do you believe that everyone's dodgy or screwing somebody over?" I asked.

"That's the way the world works and you're an idiot if you can't see it," Mr Adie said. "I might be a naïveidiot, but I saw that you were happy to screw over Maria when she was your tenant and I thought you were more than just a greedy landlord," I said.

"I have no idea what you're talking about. I'm only trying to protect you," Mr Adie said.

"I don't need protecting. I'm so sick of your negativity. Okay, so you got passed over for promotion for ten years, get over it. Just because that happened to you, it doesn't mean that that will happen to me. I think I'll be just fine. I choose to see the good in people," I said.

"It's a shame you can't see the good in me," Mr Adie said.

The prison alarm bell rang.

"Immediate assistance required on level 5," Sherry stated over the radio. Mr Adie looked down at his radio strapped to his waist and frowned. I felt that there was more that he wanted to say, but I was done.

"You'd better go," I said. He then ran from the unit.

I sat still behind the office desk looking down the corridor of prison cells. At the other end of the unit, an officer turned the corner with a prisoner and approached the office. It wasn't a long distance away, but it still took me a few seconds to recognize who it was. It was an officer from Level 4 approaching the office with Ms Brown. I had wondered what had become of Ms Brown and I longed to tell her how sorry I was. However, I went to great lengths to avoid walking through Level 4, where I knew that they had placed her since leaving hospital. It had been so long since I saw her up close. Her half dead face that had turned grey still burned in my mind. Yet here she was, approaching me, her face now full of life. I looked for somewhere to hide, but the prison that so often feels impossibly large became impossibly small. I could not hide from Ms Brown forever.

"It's all kicking off on Level 5. I have a feeling they're going to put the prison on lockdown soon," the officer said.

While the officer logged on to the office computer to check a prisoner's details, I went into the association room where Ms Brown was waiting.

"Ms Brown, how are you?"

"Oh, hello Ms Campbell. I'm okay thanks. How are

you?" Ms Brown replied.

"I wanted you to know how sorry I am. The last time we spoke, I said some things that were not appropriate," I said.

"I can't remember what you said. But I was not in a good space. I got a letter from Jamaica that day. My children said that they wanted nothing to do with me. I had a good little job on D3 and I messed it up. I always mess up and make bad decisions, that's why I'm here. It wasn't your fault. Ms Campbell, have you been carrying that weight around your neck all this time?" Ms Brown asked.

"What I said wasn't right."

"Okay. Even though I don't remember what you said, I accept your apology," Ms Brown said.

"Thank you."

"You know, Ms Campbell, after all this time, you should have forgiven yourself. I've messed up and hurt the people I love, but I've learnt to forgive myself. I had to.

That's the only way to move forward. I've also noticed that you try too hard to win the approval of others. Why?" Ms Brown asked me.

"I just what to be the best prison officer I can be."

"I don't know what or to whom you are trying to prove so much to. Maybe you don't need to be the best to be happy," Ms Brown said.

Ms Brown and the officer left me alone on the unit once again. She had a few months left in Holloway before she would be sent to a semi-open prison. Ms Brown had started over from nothing many times in her life and this time was no different. She was full of plans and hopes for her future. This time, she was even more determined than the last not to mess up.

10.30 a.m.

When Ms Hall returned from the canteen, we got hold of the officer that had worked on the wing yesterday evening, Ms Hassen. She had been delighted when SO Smith told her this morning unexpectedly, that she could take a week's leave.

"You know how short of staff the prison is. I thought I'd never be able to take leave," Ms Hassen said.

The line appeared to go dead when Ms Hall told her that a prisoner died on the unit last night.

"Hello, Ms Hassen you still there?"

Ms Hassen was still on the line, her focus switched from planning a few days on the beach in Margate to a razor-sharp recollection of yesterday evening.

"I don't know who prisoner 2000 is but a prisoner with a different number called Ms Marshall came in around 7.00 p.m. On her notes, I saw that she had been convicted of Grievous Bodily Harm after she had knocked a person's teeth out with the butt of the knife. She was still only classed as a medium risk prisoner so I put her in a dorm with Ms Phipps. Within five minutes of putting her into the dorm the cell bell rung.

Ms Phipps stood at the hatch and said that Ms Marshall had called her the N word. I moved Ms Marshall straight away into a single cell, made notes on her record and in the Observation Book. I went around to the SO's office to find SO Smith with his feet on the desk flicking through a gardening magazine." Ms Hassen recalled what Mr Smith had said to her.

"Why have you put her in a single cell? Put her back in the dorm. We might need that cell later." Mr Smith said to me as he returned to his magazine Ms Hassen said.

I wrote up the conversation in the Observation Book. I didn't sleep easy last night knowing that I'd put a violent racist in a dorm with a Black prisoner." Ms Hassen's voice cracked with regret. "Maybe I should have refused to move Ms Marshall back into the dorm. Maybe I should have demanded that Governor Rose come up to review the situation."

"We have to let Governor Rose know," Ms Hall said.

However, we still didn't know who prisoner 2000 was and what happened to her.

11.00 a.m.

During our conversation with Ms Hassen, three other alarms went off on Level 5, I knew whatever was happening up there on Level 5 was serious.

"I'd better go upstairs," I said to Ms Hall.

I bumped into Governor Rose in the stairwell.

"Sorry," I said, as we continued to walk up the stairs together.

"No, Ms Campbell, it's my fault, not looking where I was going as usual. I'm still half asleep. Jetlag, I only got back from Hong Kong yesterday."

At 10.45 this morning a group of prisoners, led by Ms Aziz, had taken over the whole of B5 and A5 unit. The prisoners were protesting about what they claimed was a coverup of a murder that took place on Level 3 last night. I arrived on C5 unit where the operation to retake the units was being managed by Ms Freeman.

There were officers putting on their riot uniforms and running around everywhere. "Amber, Where the hell have you been?" said Maria marching up to me.

"Here, you better get dressed," she pushed a riot uniform in my hand.

"All hell's broken loose up here, you're riot trained. There's a briefing in two minutes," Maria said.

In the small office, Ms Freeman seemed flustered with maps of the unit, she was with Mr King.

"Are you okay? I can take over," Mr King asked putting on his navy riot overalls.

"Don't you dare take this off me. I can handle it," Ms Freeman said.

"I know you can, but this isn't four prisoners on C1 Unit. Two units have been taken over. I think we need backup," Mr King said.

"I'll be able to make that call," Ms Freeman said, determined. She then left the room to conduct the briefing for officers in the association room.

Governor Rose walked into the office to find Mr King putting on his riot uniform. "What are you doing?" she asked

"I'm going in. Ms Freeman will manage the operation. If needed she'll call for outside reinforcements."

"You are joking," Governor Rose said.

"Why? Are you worried about me?" Mr King said.

"We can't call in Tornado, the media will be all over it. If Ms Freeman is not capable of deescalating this situation, then you need to manage it. That's a direct order,"

Governor Rose insisted

"Sorry, ma'am, I need to get to the briefing," Mr King said, as he walked out.

He opened the door and stepped onto the landing. Governor Rose called out after him "Mr King".

From where I was sitting in the association room listening to Ms Freemen's briefing I saw Mr King turn around to face Governor Rose in the doorway. I watched their every move from behind the wired glass of the association room. I blocked out the sound of Ms Freemen's voice and the distraction of Maria sitting next to me biting her figure nails. Governor Rose lent in close as though to kiss him on the cheek.

11.15 a.m.

In the briefing room, Mr King stood next to Ms Freemen as she read out the list of teams. She started with those who were going to be "Number One's" who were riot trained and would lead a team.

"Mr King, Mr Smith, Mr Peterson…" Officers were congratulated with a pat on the back by fellow officers as Ms Freeman called their name. I wasn't on that list. She then moved on to the team members

"Mr Adie, arm officer, Ms Rot, arm officer, Mr Potter, leg officer…" she went on. I was not on that list.

She then read the list of those officers assigned as 'debris runners'. These officers would assist the teams by helping to remove any debris. Maria, Mr Jamu and Ms Hall's name were called but my name was not.

"Why are you not a Number One?" Maria whispered.

I shrugged my shoulders. I expected my name to be on the list of Number Ones. After all, I was riot trained.

"I'm sure it's just a mistake," Ms Hall said.

Ms Freeman then read out the short reserve list. My name was at the top. My devastation was edged on the face of Maria and Ms Hall. My anger burned in the eyes of Mr Adie.

When the meeting dispersed, Mr Adie stood up shaking his head.

"This is not right, Ms Campbell, and you know Mr King is behind this. I told you, but you wouldn't listen to me," Mr Adie said.

Ms Rot came up to me. Mr Adie, Mr Jamu, Maria and Ms Hall stood in defence by my side.

"I just wanted to say, I think this is really crap. I don't know how they can justify putting only men as team leaders when some of them are not riot trained and you are. If you were a man, we all know you'd be a Number One," Ms Rot said.

"So, you think if she was a Black man, she would have a better chance?" Mr Adie asked.

"I don't know, I'm just saying this is not right," Ms Rot said.

"And if you were the PO, I'm sure that your teams would be led by Black women."

"I'd like to think I would put people in positions based on merit," Ms Rot said.

That led to a round of laughter from Mr Adie, Ms Hall, Mr Jamu and Maria.

"Listen, I don't want to argue with you guys. I just wanted to say that I don't think it's right. It's not been easy for me either. I know what it's like to be stereotyped and looked over," Ms Rot said.

"You said nothing when you were promoted over me, even though I had passed the

SO exams. Why don't you go and tell Mr King that you don't think it's right?" Mr Adie said.

"Okay," I said to Mr Adie putting my hand on his shoulder to stop him. Ms Rot who normally stands square on with arrogance was now stood sideways, unsure of herself.

"I'm sorry," Ms Rot said.

"Thanks." I appreciated the fact that she had come up to me.

Mr Adie grabbed his helmet and stormed out of the association room. Ms Rot left us and the room emptied, as officers took up their positions by the B5 unit doors. I tried to put a brave face on it. I turned to Maria and Ms Hall.

"Don't worry, I'll sort this out, go on ahead," I tried to reassure them.

I then marched up to Ms Freeman to ask why I was not a Number One. "I know, I know, you need to speak to Mr King," Ms Freeman said.

I could see Mr King going into the unit office so I stormed up to him. He slammed the office door shut in my face. Standing with my nose to the door, I could hear the laughter of Ms Hook behind me, she was watching my shame from a distance. I closed my eyes and took a deep breath. But this did nothing to quell my anger. I knocked on the door firmly. There was no response. I banged on the door.

"Mr King, I need to speak to you."

Without invitation, I then swung open the office door.

"Mr King, I'm riot trained, why am I on the reserve list?" I demanded.

"Just do what you're told for once," he said. "They'll be plenty of other riots for you to get involved in. I need you to sit this one out."

"You're right. There's a lot I need to learn. Maybe I could just cover for you for a bit? I mean you must be shattered after just getting in to London this morning from your holiday in Spain."

"I came back yesterday from Hong Kong and I'm fine. You'll be a team leader next time, I promise." He got his helmet and walked out, leaving me alone in the office.

I followed him on to the landing. "You liar," I said.

He stopped and turned around.

I continued. "You liar. This is all a game to you. String me along for months, years, making me think that I had a chance when all along you had no intention what so ever of giving me a chance. You know what I thought? You were something. I thought you were different. I thought you were going to change everything, this prison, me, the whole world, but no, you're just a liar."

He marched back up to me.

"Now get this into your thick head, I don't know what idiot passed you as a riot officer, but I don't want you anywhere near my men. Understand?"

He walked away leaving me speechless. I stood still for a while and waited for him to disappear out of sight as he walked down to the other end of the landing to the entrance of B5 Unit. I looked for somewhere where I could be alone, somewhere where I could hide away. There was an empty prison cell nearby, I went in and closed the door behind me. The noise of the army of officers marching towards the B5 unit and the batons beating the riot shields seeped through the closed cell door.

Mr King readied his troops, firing them up for what danger lay on the other side of the door. He banged on his shield with his baton. A thunderous sound of 100 riot officers returned his war cry by banging on their shields. A line of riot officers stood by the door with their shields locked together and their helmet visors down. The wooded batons banged on the high clear plastic shields in united chorus, harder and harder, louder and louder, faster and faster. The unit door was opened. As a deafening roar ripped through the prison from the officers determined to fight to the death and the women on the other side screaming back in defiance, I cried out in despair. When I dropped to my knees in tears, it fell quiet once again.

The Promise 1997

20th September 1997

Getting a Home Carer for two hours in the morning for my mum means that I can go off to college without worrying about how my mum's going to get up and get ready for her day centre. After going through about fifteen carers, we've now had the same carer, Bola, for over a year. Bola, from Nigeria, has become the big sister I never had. The years of slaving away in a factory and the stress of raising me and my brothers on her own has left their mark on my mum. Bola helps her slowly to the bathroom and back again. That's the most mum will walk today.

At work this morning, I started day-dreaming whilst cleaning the office computers, I dreamt about having a house with a garden, traveling the world and making a difference. Dreams that seemed so far out of my reach.

"Make sure you don't waste your life. Make a difference. Promise me," Mum said.

11.30 a.m.

I thought I was alone in the dark on the floor of a prison cell, but when I looked up, I saw my two best friends Ms Hall and Maria. I stood to my feet.

"It's okay, it's going to be okay," Maria said.

I pushed Maria and Ms Hall away. I wiped my running nose with my forearm.

"No, it's not okay, not for me. And it's not going to get

any better. You're both leaving. Leaving me here on Level 3, while you both go on to better things. At least after all your hard work, you've got something to show for it. What have I got? What have I done after all these years? I wasted time studying for the SO exam that I failed, wasted time getting riot trained. Everybody knows it, I'm a rubbish prison officer and I should have quit a long time ago."

I headed for the door that was slightly open. Ms Hall slammed the cell door shut and stood in front of it. She handed me two letters.

"This letter is from Ms Bennett who started college. The other letter is from the prison service HQ saying that because of your success, they will review support for disabled prisoners and staff in the whole country. Everybody knows that the only reason we have any Black managers is because you made a fuss. After eleven years of working here, I never dreamed that I could be an SO, until I met you. You didn't just pave the way. You cut down the forest, laid the foundations, paved the way put up the signs and then stood to one side while we all marched on through," Ms Hall said.

"We will always be here for you," Maria said.

"You've already proven that you're a great prison officer. Now you need to prove that you're a great riot officer and you're not going to do that in here," said Ms Hall.

"That's right," I said.

12.00 p.m.

"Staying awake was torture," said the night staff, Ms Nasser, over the office phone on load speaker "Sunday nights are always is torture. You know I don't have keys to the cells. If there's a problem with a prisoner in the cell, all I can do is press the alarm and wait for the five or so officers on night duty to arrive." She went on

"it was about 10.00 p.m. and I was just about to watch a film, when Governor Rose came on to the unit with a prisoner called Tiara Stacey, prisoner number 2000. I stood up from my seat and watched Governor Rose from the office doorway as she put the girl into a dorm with Ms Phipps and Ms Marshall. I noticed that the prisoner was only seventeen and on suicide watch.

"Sorry Ms Rose, but tonight I'm covering both B and C unit. With sixty-four prisoners, it will be impossible for me to watch this prisoner who's on suicide watch every fifteen minutes. Normally a seventeen-year-old would be put in a single cell on constant watch. Can an extra member of staff be assigned to watch her?" Ms Nasser asked.

"We don't have the staff for a constant watch. She'll be okay for one night in a dorm," Governor Rose replied, without even looking at me. the night staff said.

I mentioned that there had been concerns raised about Ms Marshall in the Observation Book.

"I read that. Ms Marshall is still only a medium risk prisoner and we don't have the staff for a constant watch on Tiara," Governor Rose said.

I watched my film on B3 wing and then I must have dozed off. When I woke it was 7.05 in the morning I jumped to my feet and walked around to C3. Before I got to the unit, I could hear the thunderous noise of panic from the women banging on their cell doors. I was shaking like a child's rattle when I looked through the hatch. I saw Tiara Stacey lying on the floor unconscious covered in blood in the arms of Ms Phipps. Ms Marshall paced the cell violently with a metal water flask in her hand, Ms Phipps's eyes followed her every step frozen in fear. Thank God, Mr Smith was there. He had just come in to work. He entered the cell slowly, but within two steps Ms Marshall lunged at him with the metal flask raised high. Mr Smith grabbed her arm, three other officers restrained her and took her to the segregation unit.

When I entered the cell, I knew Tiara was dead. I looked down at her body limp, her young face was stiff and a single line of blood dribbled from the corner of her mouth. Ms Phipps cradled Tiara in her arms, I stood watching unable to move. Governor Rose ran in and did chest compression and 'mouth to mouth'. She continued until the paramedics arrived while Ms Phipps and I watched on mute. I don't remember much after that. There was a lot of rushing around but I couldn't move. Ms Phipps suddenly found her voice and started screaming 'murder', she was quickly dragged off the unit. Ms Aziz was in one of the prison cells opposite and saw everything. They moved her to Level 5 first thing this morning.

I told Governor Rose that I fell asleep. I'll never forgive myself. Although my hands were unsteady, I wrote everything down in the Observation Book and gave it to Governor Rose," Ms Nasser said over the phone.

"Take a few days off sick," Governor Rose told Ms Nasser.

Governor Rose had introduced hot water metal flasks a few weeks ago to allow prisoners to make warm drinks overnight. Prison inspectors were normally impressed with such initiatives. Trouble had flared up on the Youth Offending Unit the day before and risked all the hard work that had gone into making a good impression. So, Governor Rose made the fatal decision to moved Tiara Stacey, prisoner 2000, for the night hoping to avoid any further disorder that could embarrass her on the last day of the prison inspection. Now she had a dead prisoner and a riot. Ms Nasser noticed the grey face of Governor Rose when she handed over the Observation Book. Holding the book open with two hands Governor Rose knew that a full investigation would question the wisdom of her new hot water flask policy and would condemn the decisions that led to the teenager being put into a dorm with a racist as unacceptable. Governor Rose was left in no doubt that her career in the prison service was over.

12.20 p.m.

The three of us walked through the ghostly prison that was on lockdown. The riot on Level 5 had sucked the life out of the prison itself.

"I hope Mr Potter's going to be okay," said Maria.

"So are things getting serious between you and Mr Potter?" I asked.

"He completes me," Maria said.

"Have you been watching *Jerry Maguire* again," I asked.

"This is the real thing. Real love. I thought I would never find true love. But I've realised that there are some men out there that are just simply amazing. I'm lucky I've found one, and when you find an amazing man Amber never let him go," Maria said

"I hope Mr Adie's going to be okay," said Ms Hall.

"I'm sure his poor tenants won't mind him being out of action for a few weeks," I said.

"What's your problem with Mr Adie? He's a good guy." I rolled my eyes as Maria went on. "How do you think I paid off my debts? Mr Adie let me stay in the flat he owns rent-free for years. I can never repay him and he's clear that I owe him nothing. He just wanted me to get back on my feet. He made me swear not to tell anyone," Maria said.

"It was Mr Adie that got you your own computer through 'Access to Work'," Ms Hall said.

"What do you mean, it was Mr King that sorted that out for me," I said.

"Mr King was happy to take the credit for all the research that Mr Adie did. Don't you remember? You were about to quit the job? Mr Adie went and spoke to Mr King to get you a computer. He's been looking out for you for a while," Maria said.

As we got closer to the control room that was based on the segregation unit, tension and fear met us on the stairwell. The frantic noise from the radios, officers yelling the whereabouts of different teams inside the riot zone overwhelmed the room. The smell of fumes from the backed-up empty vans left with their engines running waiting to take the rioters immediately to different prisons around the country. I'm not sure what I was expecting, yet I knew instinctively that something had gone wrong.

"What's happening?" I asked OSG Sherry.

"We've lost contact with a team," she responded, biting her lip.

"Whose team?" I asked.

"Mr King's team," she replied with tears in her eyes. "Ms Rot is on that team…"

I put one hand on her shoulder. "Don't worry, Ms Rot knows how to take care of herself."

Ten teams had gone in, but only nine had come back out again.

Ms Freemen stood talking to Governor Rose. The level of noise in the control room seemed to be rising to an unbearable state. Sherry covered her ears and sunk her head into her chin.

"Quiet!" an officer shouted.

Ms Freemen and Governor Rose rushed over. The room froze. It was Ms Rot over the radio.

"They've got Mr King. Mr King has been taken hostage," Ms Rot's crackling voice was chilling.

"I said Mr King has been taken hostage. Over," Ms Rot repeated.

Ms Freeman grabbed the radio. "Received."

"Two members of the team are injured. We had to leave Mr King behind. We had no choice," Ms Rot yelled into her radio.

Ms Freeman turned to Governor Rose. "I'll have to call in back up." "They'll take hours to get here. What about Mr King?" said Governor Rose.

There was a helplessness in Governor Rose's voice that made me warm to her for the first time. The way she clutched her notebook told me that she cared for Mr King in a way that I once did. I grabbed a helmet and picked up a riot shield.

"What was his last known location?" I said.

Ms Freemen dashed to give me a radio "A5 unit. Let me know as soon as you get in. But you need a team, I can't order anyone to go back in with you."

"I'll go in with you," Maria said.

"I'll go in as well," Ms Hall said.

"Me too," Mr Potter said.

"I'll go in too," Mr Jamu said.

"Can we have one more volunteer please?" Governor Rose asked.

She looked around the room full of battered and weary officers.

Mr Adie stood up.

"Okay, I'll go back in," he said.

We raced back through the prison, up the stairs past Level 3 and 4, towards A5 unit.

13.10

In single file, we tiptoed onto A5 unit. It was quiet, only the faint sound of prisoners making merry in the distance. The landing was littered with broken glass, picks of wood from smashed furniture and toilet roll like confetti, which lay on the lime green floor. Crouched down low behind our shields and against the wall, I signalled to the team to hide in the cells. I poked my head around the cell door to see if the coast was clear. It was. Only a riot officer's helmet lay on the floor, alone and vulnerable.

"Mr Adie, do you read me?" I said over my radio

"Yes," he said.

"I can't see anything. I suggest that we go down the landing cell by cell," I said.

"I agree," Mr Adie replied.

Out of the corner of my eye, I noticed a prisoner hiding under her bed. "It's okay," I said.

"No Entiendo. No English" the prisoner said.

I told the team over my radio that there was a prisoner hiding under her bed in the cell that could only speak Spanish.

"You can speak Spanish, ask her if she knows anything," Ms Hall asked.

"Hola, no te preocupes, estoy aquí para ayudarte. Puede decirme lo que ha pasado?" I asked the prisoner.

She barely took a breath when she responded to my question.

"She told me that there are around fifteen prisoners gathered in the kitchen. They've tied Mr King up in a chair. He's been beaten around the face and there's blood dripping from his leg. There's mattresses, wooden furniture and bedsheets all piled high in the middle of the other side of the landing," I said over the radio.

"That changes things. How are we going to get past all those prisoners?" Mr Jamu said.

"Can you cause a distraction at the unit doors, so we can get to the kitchen?" I asked Mr Jamu. "We just need to hold them off till Tornado get here."

We moved in as close as we could without being seen.

13.25

The sunlight shone through the window bars in the dining room, turning the room a golden yellow. The once structured room was a scene of disorder with overturned chairs and tables. Mr King sat tied down to a chair, his head hung low and his body slumped. Perhaps he had been struggling for a while and I had arrived at the moment of his surrender? A small pool of blood formed around his right foot. His navy riot overalls hid the red blood that had soaked his trouser leg. The prisoners mocked and laughed as one prisoner poked him repeatedly with his own baton. Another shredded HMP paper and sprinkled it down like confetti. The prisoners danced to music from a radio. Mr King sat silent as the prisoners roared in celebration. They knew that Mr King was no ordinary prison officer, he was a PO and head of the prison's riot team. I could see the excitement of their victory in the prisoner's eyes. I could not see Mr King's blue eyes; the weight of the humiliation had bowed his head. I had never thought of Mr King as a proud man until now.

"Overpowered by a group of girls," that's what they'll say, he must have thought.

How would he be able to walk tall in the prison again? Mr King had always been so in control. But here he was, weak from his injuries and needing help from me. It was an uncomfortable new position for both of us. His head jerked back upright and I saw a flash of defiance in his bright blue eyes. I knew then I was looking at the same old Mr King. He knew how to bounce back. He would shake off any questions about his abilities with confidence and say whatever needed to be said to get his own way.

Ms Aziz snatched the baton out of the hand of a woman, offended that he had raised his head; she beat it down again into submission. Her gold tooth became visible when Mr King yelled out in pain. She knew Mr King well. He had thwarted her plans to escape, riot and maim many times.

"We need to get ready for the next wave of officers," Ms Aziz said. "They'll come back with more officers, officers from every prison in the country and officers that are trained to take us down." Ripples of fear went through the women that had gathered.

"But we only need one. If we kill one of those screws, they'll know never to mess with us again," Ms Aziz said.

"What do you mean kill a screw? You're not serious are you?" Ms Locksmith laughed.

"Why Locksmith, do you like screws or something?" Ms Aziz said.

"No. I'm up for a laugh, let's say bollocks to the system and all that, but there's no way I'm going down for murder. I'm out in three months," Ms Locksmith said.

"I'm already in for murder, so I've got nothing to lose. Kill a screw, a snitch or officer's spy," she said while looking at Ms White, the wing cleaner. "It's all the same to me," said Ms Aziz.

"How do you know what's going to happen anyway?" Ms Locksmith asked

"I've started a riot in every female prison, I know how it works. A young girl was murdered in here last night, I saw everything and they're trying to cover it up. Are you going to stand by and let that happen? You think these officers care about you? They hate you; you're scum to them. They're all desperate to get back in here to beat the crap out of you. They love beating the crap out of you. Have you ever been beaten by a man who enjoys beating you?" The women nodded as if they remembered. "Well, that's what's coming, you going to let it happen to you again?" Ms Aziz asked the women. There was a roar of no's.

The prisoners then started making weapons out of wooden furniture and broom handles. They made masks from cotton bedsheets that they wrapped around their nose and mouth. Mr Jamu made a noise at the other end of the unit. The prisoners ran past the cells we were hiding in towards the B5 unit doors leaving Mr King alone. This was our opportunity. Maria, Ms Hall and I ran to the kitchen. I kneeled down to untie Mr King's feet. His head, which was bloodied hung low. He opened his eyes and was slow to gain focus. Helping him to his feet, I put his arm around my neck and had to carry his weight, while he dragged his leg behind him. Looking back, one of the prisoners saw Mr King and I limping out of the kitchen.

Ms Aziz screamed "NO!"

She charged at us with fifteen prisoners behind her. The prisoners tore round the bend.

"We're not going to make it," Mr Adie said as he turned around to face the mob.

I pushed Mr King into a near cell. Using my shield I pushed Ms Aziz to the floor. Ms Aziz bounced back up with a makeshift knife in her hand. She jumped on my back sending me to the floor. With one hand on my throat she lifted her other arm high to give me a final blow.

"No, not Ms Campbell!" Ms Locksmith screamed.

She kicked Ms Aziz in the side. As Ms Aziz culled on the floor in pain, I scrambled on to my hands and knees into the cell with Mr King and barricaded the door.

"Ms Campbell, are you okay?" Mr Adie asked over the radio, he and the others had barricaded themselves in a prison cell.

"I'm fine. Just stay put. Tornado are on their way," I

replied to Mr Adie over the radio.

Ms Aziz rose from the floor with the knife in her hand, determined to plunge it into Ms Locksmith. But stood by Ms Locksmith's side were two wing cleaners, Ms Black and Ms White, and behind them, the other women armed with makeshift spears and batons.

"You should be on the mental health unit. You need serious help," Ms Locksmith said to Ms Aziz.

The sound of boots and wooden battens against shields vibrated around the unit as Tornado drew near.

"They're here. What you gonna do? I'll tell you what I'm going to do, I'm gonna burn this place down and get out of here," Ms Aziz said.

15.20

Inside the single prison cell, Mr King was helpless as I dragged him across the floor away from the cell door and manhandled him into the corner. I took the green bedsheet off the bed and used my cutter to rip the sheet into a long strip. Sitting propped up between the foot of the bed and the sink, Mr King groaned in pain as I bound the bedsheet strips around his leg.

"So, what's the plan?" Mr King asked.

"Tornado will be here soon. That door will hold till they come and get us. We just have to sit tight."

"You know what I said to you wasn't true," Mr King said

"Don't worry about it," I said.

"I just didn't want you to get hurt."

"I don't want to talk about it. Let's just focus on getting out of here."

"You know I care about you so much," Mr King said.

"Governor Rose is worried about you. I think she cares about you a lot."

"Why are we talking about Governor Rose?" he asked.

"You know I really want to get out of here in one piece. My boyfriend would go mad if he saw what I was doing."

"You've got a boyfriend?"

"Oh yah, he doesn't work for HMP." Mr King must have known I was lying, but it made it easier for him to be honest. "So how long have you and Governor Rose been together?" I asked.

"About three years. We're getting married in the summer…"

I think as soon as the words left his mouth, he regretted telling me the truth. I slumped in the corner, as the reality of it all kicked me in the face.

"You're getting married?"

"Yes." He paused. "I'm sorry, I wanted to tell you about it earlier. We've got such a great relationship I didn't want anything to get in the way of that. I care about you so much. I didn't want to hurt you."

Mr King's voice sounded like a painful song to the music of crashing furniture, breaking bones and screams of resistance. I closed my eyes and took a deep breath. When I opened my eyes, I could see clearly. I could see what mattered to me. I didn't need to prove to anyone that I was good at my job. I didn't need the title of riot officer, senior officeer or any other titles. I loved what I was doing and if in fifteen years' time I was still just a prison officer, I'd be happy.

19.38

"Well, congratulations. Like I said, I think we should just focus on getting out of here. I don't know why Tornado are taking so long to put the riot down. Oh no…"

I froze in horror. Black smoke crept under the door. I knew immediately that the bonfire in the centre of the landing had been lit preventing Tornado from getting to our side of the unit. I kicked and swung objects out the way to dismantle the barricade not knowing who was on the other side waiting to do us harm. I could hear screams from terrified prisoners as they realised they were trapped. I turned around to see Mr King with his blooded hands raised to his face sitting in a pool of his own blood.

"Oh my God, I'm losing so much blood," he said, his voice trembling I rushed over to him

"It will be okay, we're getting out of here."

I lifted him up to his feet and dragged him to the cell door. I could only see an arm's length in front of me as smoke overcame the cell. I went to remove my shield, which was the only thing jamming the door shut.

Ms Aziz appeared at the hatch. Her eyes were blood shoot with rage and a crude implement was in her hand dripping with blood.

"Come on, come on, I'm waiting for you!" she screamed.

Her head then smashed forward on the cell door with a thump. She dropped to the floor out of sight. Ms Locksmith's warm face filled the hatch.

"Help us get out of here," Ms Locksmith said.

Stepping on to the landing I could barely see anything. I could hear cries of over thirty women coughing and fighting for breath on the smoked filled landing. My eyes streamed water, every step I took, hurt.

"Urgent assistance required on A5 fire stairs!" Mr Adie shouted into his radio.

We led the prisoners and Mr King to the A5 fire escape stairs. I could see the red door in front of me like a light house through the mist and fog of a storm. I looked back and saw Ms Aziz still lying on the floor unconscious.

"I have to go back."

"What do you mean. You can't, the smoke will kill you," Mr King said.

"I have to go back for Ms Aziz," I said.

I ran back in to the inferno on A5. Surrounded by black smoke by the flicking red and yellow flames Ms Aziz's lifeless body lay on the floor. I pulled her up to my shoulder and then saw Maria lifting her other arm.

"Let's get out of here," said Maria.

Ms Aziz started coughing and splattering, as we dragged her to A5. We were met on the stairs by two Tornado teams and a team of paramedics.

22.12

Leaving the prison with fire and ambulance crews surrounding the prison, I knew that I had played my part well. In a way, I could not believe what I had just been through. The fresh cool air as I walked through the prison gates hit me like a spring day at the end of a long winter. I was hopeful of better days to come. Days that I would make a difference, days where I would lead a Tornado team and days when I would see my friends do amazing things, I closed my eyes and took a deep breath thinking of those days to come.

"Ms Campbell."

It was Mr Adie.

"You still here, Mr Adie."

"I wanted to make sure you got out okay."

Stood in front of me was a man that I had not noticed before. He had shared the small amount of wealth and security that he had built for himself with Maria to help her get out of the hole that she was in. His generosity was overwhelming. He was a supportive friend when Mr Jamu needed him, a teacher when Maria and Ms Hall needed him. At my lowest point, he was there in the background fighting for me.

"You're okay. Praise the Lord," Ms Hall said as she came running up to me with Maria. Ms Hall wrapped her arms around me. Maria then joined in to make it a group hug.

Holloway didn't always value my skills, at times, I felt unsafe and there were so many obstacles, but wrapped in their arms, I felt unstoppable. We had kept our promise to each other.

Chapter 16

Day Forty-Seven (Kenya)

19th October 2018 10.00 p.m. - Nairobi (Kenya)

At 8.00 a.m. this morning, the campsite emptied as all the tour groups went to the Serengeti for three days. I'm no longer part of any tour group and I'm free to decide what I want to do. I departed about ten minutes after most of the travellers had left, so I could take the mini-van into town about forty-five minutes away. My hair appointment wasn't until 11.00 a.m., but I wanted to get there early so I could buy a cooked breakfast and have a look around the market, so I left the campsite early.

In the hairdresser's, I wanted just the first three rows of my hair to be re-plaited, but the assistant (who didn't have a clue what he was doing) cut off half of my extensions. So I had to get almost half of my hair re-plaited. I wasn't impressed, even though it cost me only 20,000 Tanzanian Shillings, £10, which included the hair. At home, it would have been about £40. I didn't get back until after 7.00 p.m.

When I got back to the camp, Adie stood at my bedroom door. "What are you doing here?" I asked.

"I missed you. And to be honest, I wasn't sure if you were coming back home to me," Adie said.

"Of course I was. I was always going to come home to you," I said.

The End